Exogenesis

"A journey from the prehistoric past,

through the present, and into the

distant future

...and back."

John Russell
Marshall

Brighton Publishing LLC
435 N. Harris Drive
Mesa, AZ 85203

Exogenesis

"A journey from the prehistoric past,
through the present, and into the distant future
...and back."

John Russell Marshall

Brighton Publishing LLC
435 N. Harris Drive
Mesa, AZ 85203
www.BrightonPublishing.com

ISBN 13: 978-1-62183-321-5
ISBN 10: 1-62183-322-4

Printed in the United States of America

First Edition

Cover Design: Tom Rodriguez

✒Genesis 1:1-2✑

"In the beginning GOD created the heavens and the earth...

...and the earth was without form, and void; and darkness was upon the face of the deep."

And therein begins our tale

Authors Note

THIS TALE IS PRESENTED AS PURE FANTASY AND IS MEANT TO BE TAKEN AS THAT AND NOTHING MORE. THERE IS NO INTENT ON THE PART OF THE WRITER TO ESPOUSE ANY PARTICULAR THEORY OR THEORIES REGARDING THE ALLEGED "GAP" BETWEEN GENESIS 1:1 AND 1:2. (I WILL ADMIT TO SOME RATHER STRONG INCLINATIONS TOWARD ONE PARTICULAR THEORY, BUT THAT'S ANOTHER STORY.)

ANY SIMILARITIES TO ANY MEMBERS OF THE GENUS "HOMO SAPIENS," LIVING, DEAD OR OTHERWISE, IS UNINTENTIONAL AND PURELY COINCIDENTAL AND IF I'VE OFFENDED ANY OF THEM I'M NOT TOO SURE THAT I REALLY CARE.

ANY SIMILARITIES TO THE LORD GOD ALMIGHTY ARE INTENTIONAL AND, AS I HAVE ALREADY MADE MY PEACE WITH HIM; SHOULD BE OF NO CONCERN TO THE READER.

~ JOHN RUSSELL MARSHALL

The Prophecy

The revelation of Jirash Kin, the first prophet of the one true god, Di'et, as it was given to him by the gods in a dream and as it has been faithfully recorded in the third book of Haan in the "Chronicles of Noor."

"It shall come to pass that a day will come when the world knows no peace. It shall be in that day that death and destruction will cover the land as locusts, and anguish and desolation choke men's hearts. Families will shear asunder, brothers will turn against brothers, and sons will smite their fathers. The gods themselves will strive with one another, and the foundations of the world will be overthrown. The mountains will tremble and break, and the oceans will walk across the land.

"Into that day shall come a deliverer: J'Osha, the 'Golden One.'

"He will be born a fair-skinned babe of royal blood who will, between one heartbeat and the next, become a man of great stature, speaking an unknown tongue.

"His name and his hair and his heart will be as pure gold.

"He will not know the ages or the seasons, but he will have the memory of things not yet come to pass. He will bring down kings and kingdoms as chaff before the whirlwind, and he will raise up a government of peasants and kings.

He shall not suffer death, but at his passing, the world will end."

Prologue

In the far distant past, before the passage of the great shining comet turned the world upside down, caused the shattering earthquakes that sent mighty Atlantis to the bottom of the sea, shook down the high mountains, and caused the seas to leave their beds and cover the mountains and the valleys; when the sun still rose in the west and the great hairy mammoth made the ground tremble with his passing; and long before man as we know him walked the earth, there were other men.

These were the first men.

They looked much as man does in this age, and they had many of the same strengths and weaknesses, but they did not know the depths of love and hate as men in the later ages, for man had not yet been given a soul. They worshipped strange gods, and the fear of magic dwelt in their hearts.

Before these first men, there were others who were more than men yet less than the gods. They walked not on the earth as men but moved with the gods among the stars and measured their lives as the lives of the galaxies.

These were the Daemoz.

Their number was more than ten hands of hands and their knowledge was almost as the gods. Their powers were awesome and far beyond the understanding of man.

In this time before time, when this universe still rested from the pains of birth, some of the Daemoz dreamed vain dreams in their hearts until their dreams began to eat them up.

They dreamed they would be gods.

While many suns were born, grew old, and died, the Daemoz waited and schemed evil schemes. When the time was right, some of them quietly moved against one of the lesser Daemoz, ate up his strength, and drank his knowledge, and then he was not.

For a time they rested and grew in their newfound powers, and then they quickly moved against others of the Daemoz, ate up their strength, and drank their knowledge. They became stronger until none of the other Daemoz could stand alone against them. The remaining good Daemoz gathered themselves together with the old gods to resist the attacks of the evil ones.

Before long, most of the good Daemoz had ceased to be and only a few of the vain ones remained and they thought themselves to be as mighty as the gods. For a time they were content to think of themselves as gods, and the old gods allowed them to rule the darkness and the things that dwell therein. They wallowed in their newfound powers and grew in strength and knowledge. They became evil.

The evil Daemoz were not content to rule only the darkness and to share the rule of the universe with the old gods for long. So the evil Daemoz came together and moved to do battle against the old gods and the good Daemoz to destroy them so that they might be the sole masters of the universe.

But the gods were almost as old as time and had long forgotten the ways of warfare, for many ages of time had passed since Chataan had been driven from this universe and banished into the outer darkness.

So the gods called upon the four great spirits of this universe and brought them together to do battle with the evil Daemoz.

From the burning heart of the mightiest sun in the center of the greatest galaxy in this universe came the spirit of fire. His strength was as the strength of the gods, and he did not know death.

He was called "The Arm" of the gods.

From the invisible mists of space that flow between the stars and carry the thoughts of the gods came the spirit of water. She had the memory of all that had been, the knowledge of all that was, and the sight of what was to be.

She was called "The Mind" of the gods.

From the cavernous maw of the impenetrable black hole in the center of this universe came the spirit of earth. He had the power to give life and to take life away, and he was the most faithful servant of the gods.

He was called "The Heart" of the gods.

From the quiet depths of the darkest, most remote corner of this universe came the spirit of air. It had fearsome powers over the living and the unliving, the dead and the undead.

It was called "The Soul" of the gods.

So the four great spirits of this universe gathered together with the old gods and the good Daemoz on the giant white star, which was the dwelling place of the gods, and planned to destroy the evil Daemoz.

Then the old gods and the four great spirits moved against the Daemoz and did battle with them.

Their warring moved across the face of this universe and lasted longer than man can dream.

Great galaxies were shattered into shining dust, and this universe was shaken to its foundations by their battles and many stars were born and died while they warred. The manner of their warfare was outside the comprehension of man, for their powers were unthinkable and beyond imagination.

They continued to do battle without ceasing and they did not tire, for they drew their strength from the primal forces, which are the very essence of this universe.

After a time, the gods and the four spirits began to prevail against the evil Daemoz; but they could not destroy them, for the evil Daemoz had powers almost as the gods. So the gods drove the evil Daemoz from this universe and banished them into the outer darkness until a way could be found to destroy the Daemoz, for they were evil and an abomination.

For a long time this universe rested and healed from the battle between the old gods and the evil Daemoz. And while this universe rested, the gods held council with the four spirits to find a way to destroy the evil Daemoz.

While they thought on their plans, many new stars were born and whole galaxies grew dark and cold and passed on into eternity.

Then the gods found a good place among the galaxies in this universe, and they called the good place "earth." They covered this earth with water and raised up places of dry land above the water. They put many kinds of plants on the earth, including grasses and grains; trees great and small, some of which bore fruits and other things to eat; bushes with thorns and with flowers and some with nuts and berries; and vines with gourds and melons. They put all these things and more on the dry land of the earth.

And the gods made living creatures. Fearsome gray dragons as long as a tree is tall, great cats with long teeth, snow-white unicorns with golden horns, giant flying lizards with talons like thorns, small horses, huge dogs, and birds. There were many birds, including some with feathers and some with scales. They placed these creatures on the dry land of the earth with many others they made and let them find their places in the forests and the jungles and the plains. They made all kinds of fishes and things that live in the seas. Some were smaller than a grain of sand and others large enough to swallow a man; some with fins, some with flippers, and some with long tentacles. The gods made a multitude of swimming things and put them all in the seas were the creatures flourished.

After a time, the gods made the first men and set them on the earth. Man and woman the gods made, and the men laid with the women and the women gave them children.

Part One

Ꮪ Chapter One ᏒᏗ

T he generations of man were many, and they moved about on the face of the earth and multiplied. Eventually there came to be four different peoples of the men of earth, and the four peoples went their separate ways and grew in number and wisdom. They built villages and cities in which to live on the earth.

So the gods sent the spirit of air to live with the people of the north where the steaming jungles were alive with magic, and the dark nights were filled with unnatural things that made brave men tremble and children cry in their sleep. These people had light hair and skin and pale eyes, but their minds were dark for their women had strange powers of magic and were feared by all men.

These were the Gwundi.

And the gods sent the spirit of earth to dwell with the people of the south in the forested hills where the cold crept in all year round. They were tall and thick of body, strong men who loved life and hated magic. They made many things from the wood and iron of the hills.

They were the Ghorn.

And the gods sent the spirit of water to dwell with the people of the west in the lands of mist among the high mountains. They were of fair skin and light hair and were not strong of body, but their minds were strong, for they studied all the mysteries of all the knowledge of the earth. They had strange powers of the mind and their wise men talked with the gods.

They were the Shanar.

And the gods sent the spirit of fire to dwell with the people in the plains of the east where the seasons are mild and the ways of life are pleasant. They were a proud people, tall and lean with dark hair and dark eyes.

They prized their strength and made wars among themselves for the land; and when they were not warring, they made games of combat and greatly honored the winners of the games.

They were the Yaq.

This earth on which the gods put man was a place of grayness, eternally shrouded in mists. The sun never shone through to the surface of the land, except on the highest peaks. Only the daily brightening of the hazy skies marked the sun's passing as it made its way across the roof of the world. At times the passing of the full moon lightened the dreary night sky, but no man ever saw its face.

Most of the few who dared to venture forth in the dark and notice the lighter skies, turned their faces away and trembled in fear as they wondered what awesome god walked the night skies. There were no harsh winters as in the later ages, and the summers of this land were mild, for the earth had not yet turned over and tilted sharply on its axis. In the midst of summer when the mists were thinnest, the midday sun stood straight overhead and the days were warm.

The winters were marked not by ice and snow, but merely by cooler nights and foggy days, for the sun passed only slightly lower in the north as it journeyed from west to east across the sky.

Most men did not number the passing years and took no notice of the time or seasons. Only the elders of the Shanar, who lived among the high western mountains and the chieftains of the Yaq on the open plains, recorded the changes between summer and winter by the angle of the suns passage through the mists.

The priests and scholars of the Shanar also recorded the time of the lightening of the night sky and, in futile wonder, recorded these things in their chronicles.

The Yaq chieftains kept tribal histories by carving rings and markings on long poles which were kept in the lodge houses. Each summer the Yaq carved a new ring on the pole. Between the rings they recorded simple symbols for births and deaths, victories in battle, and other memorable events.

Of all the peoples, only the men and women of the Shanar and the Yaq took permanent companions and celebrated this joining with rituals, although the rituals were very different.

A Shanar man respectfully courted the woman of his choice, and if she was willing, their union was made official by a ceremony overseen by a high priest if they were of the priestly class or by the village elder if of more humble means.

The Yaq, however, celebrated the union of a man and woman with festivals and games and much drinking; and eventually, most often, an orgy. This union was usually preceded by a time of living together as sort of a trial period.

As often as not, this trial period ended in a friendly separation. The village community usually raised children born during this trial period.

Most Ghorn men kept several women, the number varied according to their status or wealth or physical strength. Most men often had one who was the favorite but there was no ceremony involved. The men just took the women they wanted. This often resulted in bloodshed if there was another man also interested in the same woman. The women naturally had no say in the matter.

The Gwundi lived in village communes with no established family groups. In that the women—who were the heads of the communes by nature of their magical powers—to a large extent outnumbered the men, they picked and chose of them as they saw fit. The men didn't complain simply because there was an ample supply of women to go around. The wiser men strove to make themselves as physically attractive as possible to get chosen more often by the women in power. This also contributed to a stronger crop of warriors.

Naturally, the birthrate among the Gwundi was higher than the other peoples and all too often resulted in strange mutations due to constant inbreeding. These unfortunates were usually just eliminated at birth, which also served to keep the population under control.

No rain fell from the skies to water the earth, but heavy morning mists left the land covered with dew. Springs flowed from the earth among the forested slopes, and the jungles were continually wet with fog. These, with the melting frosts of the high stone mountains, grew into rivulets and streams, which in turn flowed together to become the rivers that watered the great prairie.

In the middle of the land of man, a prairie spanned ten days journey from the northern jungles to the forested foothills of the southern mountains, and spread across a full twenty-day's journey from the high western mountains of rock to the swampy eastern sea.

The western part of this prairie was a great arid waste of low rolling hills, unwatered by the rivers, which flowed to the east and made the central plains lush and green. Only nameless bands of wandering nomads who camped around the rare springs inhabited these wastelands as they struggled for a meager existence.

The central plains were scattered with groves of trees along the rivers and near the springs. To the east, the trees gave way to reeds and rushes, and the fertile plains turned into a great swampy marsh where the two large rivers became almost totally lost before reaching the sea.

North of the vast prairie and the steaming eastern marshes was a thick jungle of closely packed trees and giant ferns, interlaced with bushes and creeping vines.

In the northern jungle, fearsome beasts, fugitives from the distant past, roamed the high plateau and were kept from invading the lower sweeps of jungle by a high cliff which bisected the jungle like a wall.

On occasion, men heard the beasts' terrible roars in the distance. Once in the memory of man, a massive gray dragon—as long as the height of twenty men—came crashing down the cliff and shattered tall trees like straw in its death throes.

A wide river roared through a defile in the cliff and crashed to the rocks below. The river wound southward through the jungle and swept to the east, skirting the northern plains; then it spread into the wide swampy marsh before flowing sluggishly into the muddy eastern sea.

Another wide river crossed the prairie and made its way slowly from the forested slopes of the green southern hills through the heart of the prairie to where it also flowed into the eastern marshes.

South of the plains, the land sloped gently upward to the wooded foothills of the southern mountains. Among these hills were almost countless small lakes and springs and creeks that fed the southern river and made these hills a pleasant place where the Ghorn lived in comfort.

Far to the southwest, beyond the wooded mountains and across a vast, barren range of mountains, there was rumored to be an endless sea that was continually ravaged by violent storms. But no adventurer who had dared this perilous journey had ever returned to tell of his travels.

To the northwest, beyond the arid plains, the mighty Granite Mountain range rose like a wall above the floor of the prairie. The bare stone peaks of these mountains were continually blanketed with frost and freezing mists and nothing grew there.

Few men attempted to cross these mountains and fewer still survived the long journey. But just beyond those forbidding peaks were fertile valleys and pleasant meadows where the people of the Shanar lived.

Man had not yet mastered the craft of boat building because there simply was no need. When necessary, the people crossed the rivers, which were not fordable, by means of crude log rafts pulled across the rivers by woven ropes stretched from shore to shore. The only other navigable waters were beyond the swampy marshes far to the east.

In truth, the gods had made this earth a comfortable place for man, and man grew and prospered well in the land.

ᑫᑫᑭChapter Twoᕤᕤᕤ

Now all this time, the evil Daemoz dwelt in the outer darkness, and they grew restless and began to strive among themselves.

Finally, their petty strivings disturbed Chataan; and to their eternal damnation, the Daemoz discovered the true nature of evil, for they were as children playing in the dirt against the unspeakable foulness that was Chataan.

At first Chataan thought to annihilate the Daemoz for intruding on its solitude and began inflicting such unthinkable horrors on them as would make even the gods pale and would shatter the minds of men to think on even the smallest part of the agonies the Daemoz suffered.

Then Chataan paused in its play for it thought it may have found a way to avenge itself against the old gods who had driven it into the outer darkness. So Chataan spared the Daemoz and made vassals of them to do its will.

It would have been better for the Daemoz had they been destroyed than to live in servitude to Chataan, for Chataan was evil and an adversary to all that was good.

While this universe slowly turned and man spread upon the earth, Chataan pondered and finally began to spawn an evil scheme against the old gods; to use man against his creators.

So Chataan set up the Daemoz as false gods over man and seduced man into worshipping the false gods. It deluded man into making obscene sacrifices to the false gods. And so Chataan caused man to commit murder and fornication and to make slaves of his fellow man and to do all manner of other vile things.

And Chataan was pleased with the plan, for it was an evil plan. And Chataan gained much in power through its evil servants, the Daemoz, and by the foolishness and greed of man.

And the world knew no peace.

So Chataan was content, for a time.

In the northern jungle, life for the Gwundi was much harsher than for most of the other people since they were forced to wage a continuing battle with the jungle for living space. As soon as they'd finished clearing one area of the thick undergrowth to make room for a new dwelling, they had to go back to areas they'd cleared before to hack away the encroaching jungle. All too often when the Gwundi sent warriors into the jungle to hunt for meat, the hunters became meals for the jungle beasts instead of the other way around.

The Gwundi lived in small villages in clearings carved from the jungle in thatch houses built on stilts that were out of the reach of the hungry predators that roamed the jungles day and night. The Gwundi numbered about fifty thousand people in all, not counting the slaves whose number might vary from day to day. The life expectancy of a slave was rather short, due mostly to the harsh treatment they received. The slaves were usually taken in battle from one of the other jungle tribes, and their principle role was as living sacrifices to the awesome Gwundi gods. Those who were sacrificed may have had the better lot. The younger witches used the remaining slaves to practice their craft. Some of the gruesome results of these experiments were kept caged in the villages as a reminder to the people not to trifle with the witches.

Any other survivors were turned out into the jungle to fare for themselves and usually wound up in the belly of one of the great cats.

The Gwundi had short-handled axes of iron that they used to clear the jungle foliage. When necessary they used the axes as weapons to fend off attacks by warriors of other villages. They also had short bows and arrows made from the hard woods of the jungle trees, which were used primarily for hunting and also as weapons when needed.

By some peculiar trick of heredity, or possibly just a cruel practical joke of the gods, the Gwundi males had no magical powers at all, whereas most women possessed at least a little ability. Into each generation there were born a few women who had mystical powers far beyond the others, and occasionally one was born who could shake the very earth with her magic. This inequity continually irritated the male population. But there was simply nothing they could do about it except kill off all the women, which was altogether impossible considering their talents. Besides, most of the men were not really that unhappy with the situation as it was.

Since the earliest days of their civilization, the Gwundi were co-ruled by a king, who was their military and political leader, and a witch, the high priestess of their fearsome gods, who was their moral and spiritual advisor and the true ruler of the people. The Gwundi accepted this joint rule of witch and king for many generations until King M'lidni the Fourth tired of the alleged interference of the high priestess, Janga, in his military endeavors and made a nearly successful attempt to end the joint rule by assassination.

Janga barely escaped the assassin's knife, being awakened from sleep by the ancient yellow cat that was never far from her side, and she fled deep into the jungle to a cave that was avoided by even the wildest of the jungle animals.

The animals could not have explained, even if they had been able to communicate, just why none of them used this warm dry cave for a den.

They only knew that every time they wandered near the cave, they experienced stirrings of uncontrollable fear and fled trembling back into the jungle.

Even though it was Janga's cave, she was not completely immune to the feelings of terror emanating from it. The spells she'd cast about the cave were the strongest she was able to make, for hidden in that cave were all the implements she used in her magic. She wanted neither man nor animal disturbing her possessions.

Of all the creatures of the earth, only Janga's ancient yellow cat seemed undisturbed by the spells about the cave.

Janga gritted her teeth and pushed her way past the spells to the deepest recesses of the cave where for three days she sat cross-legged in the dirt before a guttering fire, burning sticks of old incense and the bloody red entrails of jungle animals.

She mumbled ancient incantations into the oily gray smoke of the fire in a language not known to mankind and performed many other old rituals that were indescribable in human terms.

Travelers who unknowingly wandered near the area of the cave during this time told of hearing terrible screeches and moans, as if something not of this earth was in great agony, and described foul, nauseating odors of dead things that permeated the entire jungle area.

On the fourth day, King M'lidni was holding court in his palace when he suddenly screamed in terrible agony and fell thrashing to the floor. For several minutes his body wracked with violent convulsions as he involuntarily emptied his bladder and bowels and vomited up all the contents of his stomach. His servants and guards stood by in fearful awe as the once proud king rolled on the floor in his own filth, reduced to a pitiful, groveling thing.

Finally he was still and, except for the shallowest of slow raspy breathing and a slight flickering of the eyelids, appeared to be dead.

Several days later, Janga reappeared in the village and went directly to the room where the king lay. She carried with her a small bag of odd-looking old leather, which she emptied on the floor at the foot of the king's bed. She began to sort through the contents of the bag, which appeared to be several small bones, some pieces of dried skin with stiff gray hair, a few curiously shaped stones of varied colors, some pieces of old dried meat, and a few other things best not identified.

As she arranged these things in a pattern in the dirt, it soon became apparent to the few who dared stay and watch that the bones were tiny human bones and the pieces of dried meat shrunken human organs.

When the pattern took the shape of a tiny human body, the remaining watchers suddenly remembered they had things to do elsewhere, and soon Janga was alone with the stricken king.

Janga began a guttural chant that gradually increased in volume until it seemed to fill the entire palace compound and eventually reverberated throughout the village and the surrounding jungle, drowning out the natural sounds and filling with mortal terror the hearts of all who heard, man or beast.

After several minutes, King M'lidni slowly opened his eyes and appeared to waken.

He then stood up awkwardly, nearly pitching forward onto his face. He took a few tentative stiff-legged steps, and then walked clumsily around the room for several minutes until he appeared to regain his balance and coordination.

But it was only the appearance of wakening, for it was just his body that moved. The spirit of M'lidni was gone, taken away by Janga's magic spells. What was left was merely the empty shell of a body that Janga manipulated like a stringless puppet.

For a time, Janga ruled the Gwundi through the king's now lifeless body; and although some suspected the awful truth, none had the courage to question M'lidni's odd, almost trance-like condition.

When she finally grew weary of the gruesome game, Janga allowed the king's body the appearance of a natural death and even gave him a royal funeral. The king's brother, Ilibli, made a claim to the throne but was quickly rebuffed by Janga, who had grown quite accustomed to her more or less solitary rule. When Ilibli became insistent and threatened to take his brother's throne from the queen by force, Janga raised an eyebrow, waved her hand, and muttered a curse under her breath.

There was a small explosion of foul, greenish smoke, and in the place of her would-be challenger stood a fat, squawking chicken.

M'lidni's son, M'gori, who was actually the rightful heir to the throne by right of succession, was about to contest Ilibli's claim to the throne. Instead he kept his silence and slipped quietly from the palace compound into the darkness of the village.

That night, Janga and her priestesses had chicken for dinner.

After that simple but extremely graphic demonstration of her power, no one ever again questioned Janga's right to rule in whatever manner she chose.

Chapter Three

M'gori had long resented the authority of the witch queen and inwardly agonized over the unbearable inequity of birth that reserved all magical talents for the Gwundi women. From his early youth, M'gori had been frustrated by a gnawing desire to be a witch with magical powers. He dreamed of someday being able to overthrow the queen with his magic and laugh in her face as he threw her, powerless, into the jungle to face the savage beasts.

Now he was forced into the intolerable position of having to serve the queen rather than rule beside her, which would have been hard enough to bear.

His frustrations as a youth had driven him to the brink of insanity, and now, as he brooded on the fate of his uncle and pondered his own bleak future, he stepped over the edge into the abyss of madness. Not raving lunatic madness, but scheming craftiness driven by his insatiable lust for power.

Outwardly, M'gori appeared to be only a little more moody than his normal sullen aloofness. Inwardly, however, there was a radical change in the young prince.

Where before there had been only a desire for magical talents, there now existed an uncontrollable passion that would have frightened even Janga had she known of it.

For some time, M'gori had been secretly watching the witches as they practiced their arts. While they had been engrossed in their magic, he'd been mimicking their rituals and memorizing their incantations, hoping to somehow overcome the natural barriers put in the way of his being able to use the secrets he learned.

He slowly accumulated a small horde of the witches' implements and potions, which he stole from the witches' rooms while they were asleep or away, uncaringly risking his life in the process. M'gori could see no purpose in continuing to live if it was to be only as a servant to a witch. Secretly he began to acquire a following of other young men who felt as he did about being ruled by a woman, and before long he had a band of about thirty sympathizers.

He realized that his group wouldn't be able to escape the notice of the queen much longer and made plans to leave the village. Slowly and carefully they gathered the tools and supplies they needed to start their own settlement.

When the time was right and they felt they had all they needed and could reasonably carry, the group slipped away in the predawn mists and headed for the cliffs in the north.

The Gwundi waged a never-ending battle with the jungle to keep it from reclaiming the clearings they tediously carved from the heavy undergrowth for their living space. So Janga and her people picked up all their possessions and moved.

They chose a spot where the great river cascaded down the steep cliffs and began to build a new city against the high wall where their backs would be protected from attack by the jungle animals or marauding warriors of other tribes.

On one side of the river was a relatively flat area of good size. The people cleared away the jungle and here grew the new buildings of the city clustered in family groups around central clearings. The people erected a stout wall of sharpened pilings about the perimeter of the city, partly to protect the inhabitants from the beasts of the jungle, and partly to keep the lush jungle growth away from the huts. Outside the wall, they cleared the jungle growth away from the city wall for about two hundred paces to provide room for crops and additional protection from sneak attacks by either man or animal.

On the other side of the river, piled high against the sheer face of the cliff, rose the multistoried temple palace of the witch queen and her priestesses. Next to the cliff, the rooms of the palace were constructed of wooden beams made from the jungle trees and stone gathered from the detritus at the base of the falls. Inside were dark windowless rooms where the witch queen and her priestesses performed their rites of worship to their god.

These stone rooms covered the entrances to several caves in the cliff face where some said their terrible god actually lived.

The outer portion of the palace, which was visible to the city dwellers, was built of wood from the trees of the jungle. Occupying the uppermost of these stone rooms were the dwellings of the queen and her priestesses, while the lower floors were taken up by the main temple room where the people could come to worship, and the great hall where the witch queen held infrequent audiences with her people.

In the river just below the falls, a system of dams and gates was constructed to channel water to the city and the fields. A complex system of woven ropes and hand carved pulleys provided the motive power for an elevator platform that lifted men and supplies to an outpost at the top of the cliff. From there, sentries could easily spot oncoming danger and warn the city below by blowing on a curved ivory horn carved from the tusk of a long dead mammoth.

Janga ruled peacefully for many years without challenge, except for one aspirant to the throne who tried to slip into the palace one dark night to assassinate the witch queen. The next morning, early risers found the would-be assassin's unmarked and unoccupied skin hanging on the outer wall of the temple.

No trace of the rest of him was ever found, and although many wondered, no one ever bothered to ask Janga just how she had removed the assassin from his skin without leaving a mark on it.

Never again was an attempt made on the life of a witch queen of the Gwundi.

On rare occasions, a young warrior would rise up in the middle of the night, in what appeared to be a trance-like state, and make his way to the dwellings of the queen. In the morning he would awake in his own bed exhausted, but with no recollection of what had transpired, or even that he'd ever left his bed. But for several days thereafter, the queen would seem in unusually good spirits and petitioners quite often found their requests granted with very little opposition or debate.

Once a year in the early spring, a young maiden would be selected by lot from among the priestesses to accompany the queen to the deep caves in the cliff at the rear of the temple. The brave ones who dared venture near the palace on that night whispered in terror of the terrible inhuman groaning and unearthly cries that came from the temple.

The next morning, the priestesses would carry the exhausted queen back to her rooms where she would lie for several days recovering from the ghastly ordeal. The maidens would never be seen again on earth, but it was said that they were blessed of the gods, accorded special favor, and lived forever in the god places.

One winter day, Janga gave birth to a daughter, who she named Gridri.

As the girl grew into womanhood, she displayed all the magical powers of her awesome mother, as well as the natural abilities of leadership.

Over the years she was trained in the rites of worship of the Gwundi gods, and soon she was ready to take her place on the royal throne of Gwundi.

So, after many years of productive leadership, Janga finally grew tired of the rigors of rule and gave way to her daughter. She then retired to the caves deep in the jungle where, it is rumored, she lived forever by her fearsome powers.

≈

M'gori cried out in frustration and swept the scrolls from the table, upsetting the incense burner and starting a small fire among the scrolls. This only added to his anger; and as he stamped out the flames, he screamed his wrath to the gods for the cruel trick they had played on him and all the other Gwundi males by giving magical powers only to the women.

For two full years he and his few followers had tried, in vain, every possible spell and incantation they could find, but always with the same result: nothing happened. M'gori had carefully transcribed the spells onto scrolls and taught them to his followers. While they all could recite them from memory, none could make them work.

Many of his original followers had left him and returned to the lower jungles and the safety of the Gwundi city. The few who remained were as frustrated as they were fanatical in their desire to master the magical arts. No amount of incense burning or animal sacrifice could add to the nothing they accomplished.

Finally they turned to human sacrifice in an attempt to gain the favor of the gods.

The men ventured down the cliffs, and during the dark of night, slipped into an isolated Gwundi village where they snatched a young girl of twelve from her bed and left the rest of her family in great pools of blood with their throats cut.

Quietly as ghosts they carried the terror-stricken girl back to their caves and the high plateau where M'gori bound her and placed her on a crude stone altar. The men danced naked around a great bonfire for hours while chanting the old incantations to call upon the gods. When the men's emotional fervor had reached an almost insane pitch, M'gori carved out the girl's heart with an iron knife and held it aloft for the gods to see.

Contrary to his beliefs, M'gori had long ago attracted something's attention. It was not the gods he'd called for, but one of the Daemoz who had been watching over the Gwundi for many long generations and waiting for someone to bend to its service.

This evil one had been watching and waiting to see just how desperate M'gori was and how far he would go in his quest for power, and now it knew. As M'gori held the still pulsing heart high in the air and felt the warm blood ooze through his fingers and trickle down his bare arm, he cried out in mortal anguish for acknowledgment of his request.

And it was granted.

M'gori couldn't know just what had answered his pleas. All he knew was that as he held the girl's heart in the air, suddenly it began to beat with an inhuman pulse as if it had a life of its own and seemed to struggle to escape his grasp. He dropped the heart in an almost uncontrollable impulse of fear, and then gasped in absolute terror as the dead girl reached out a small hand and deftly caught her disemboweled heart out of the air then placed it neatly back into her butchered breast.

Most of the cavorting men had missed this spectacle, but when the girl sat up and spoke to M'gori, all stopped in their tracks and some fainted from the shock of what they saw and heard.

"Your prayers have been heard, M'gori," she said in a sweetly innocent child's voice that somehow sounded to the listening men like the most fearsome and evil thing they had ever heard. "We have heard your call and have come to your aid."

The girl continued talking as she sat erect, and the men watched in awe as the ghastly wound in her chest healed before their eyes. "We will make you the most high priest of our worship, and this girl will be your high priestess in our service. You will have powers that you have never dreamed of in your wildest dreams; and if you serve us well, we can make you master of the world!"

M'gori staggered back from the shock of the words, and then fell to his knees and buried his face in his hands and cried openly in joy that at long last his prayers had been answered.

If he knew what the future held for him and just what type of service his new deity would require, he would have taken the knife from the altar and willingly cut his own throat on the spot. But those things would remain hidden from him until it was much too late to do anything to alter his fate. Now he wept happily while some of his followers wondered whether they'd been wise in following M'gori and what the fates had in store for them.

But even M'gori was stunned and revolted by the young girl's next surprising words. "Come, make love to me," she said as she lay back down on the altar and stretched her slim arms toward M'gori. "Come. Seal our pact with our love."

M'gori's stomach turned in disgust at the thought of making love to the grotesque thing that the girl he'd just murdered in a sacrificial rite had become. As he turned his face away from her, she laughed in a manner that sent chills of terror through the hearts of all the men there.

What they heard was not the innocent laughter of a young girl, but the arcane braying of a fiend from the netherworlds and M'gori began to get a glimpse of what he had gotten himself into.

M'gori and his men retreated to the caves and cowered in fear until daylight, while the fiend of a girl sat upon the altar and chanted in unintelligible gibberish to the lightening skies.

Soon, however, M'gori's revulsion was replaced by a feeling of elation as he discovered the abilities he was being given. As the girl had stated, he received powers beyond any he had ever dreamed of. As he practiced those powers with her guidance, he forgot his earlier fears.

He found he was literally able to read the thoughts of his followers, control their minds, and erase any thoughts or ideas that didn't exactly suit his purposes. M'gori was able to impress his will into their minds to get them to do his bidding, as if they were an extension of his very own mind and body. They were under his total control. He had merely to think a command and it would be carried out without question.

True, the men lacked initiative and desire, but they also lacked any thought but to serve M'gori in all ways possible. M'gori was the absolute ruler of his followers, and he reveled in the idea.

It never occurred to him that the one thing that drove him from the Gwundi was still with him: he was still under the direction and control of a female, and a mere child at that.

Over the years, M'gori sent his followers out into the jungles to recruit more men from the tribes of the Gwundi to increase the size of his flock. Some of the new recruits even brought along their women, who were unhappy with their lot in life and wanted more power than the queen was willing to give them.

With the guidance and assistance of his small priestess, M'gori soon built his empire into a vast city of more than three thousand men, women, and, as nature took its course, many children.

Every one of them was completely devoted to their lord, not out of choice, but because of the supernatural power M'gori exercised over them.

As his powers and his following increased in scope over the passing years, M'gori began to realize that one thing still escaped him. He watched his young priestess stay the same age as when he first took her those many years ago. At the same time, he watched his hair turn white and his skin begin to wrinkle with age. He knew he would one day lose his entire realm to the one enemy he couldn't defeat: death.

Finally one night, in deep desperation, he went to the priestess and complained bitterly of the seeming injustice of having to surrender all that he had worked so long for. Now when his people were becoming a powerful nation and beginning to make great progress, he was growing old and would soon die.

For hours he pleaded with her to entreat her gods to give him the one thing that would make him all-powerful: immortality.

Only if he lived forever could he really enjoy the fruits of his labor, and only then could he properly serve the unknown gods who had become his benefactors.

The Daemoz that occupied the body of the girl, while in full agreement with M'gori, was still unable to grant that request on its own and was reluctant to approach its master with a request from such an insignificant mortal. This Daemoz well remembered the wrath of Chataan and had no desire to disturb the master unless some gain against the old gods could be realized from this situation.

The priestess temporarily pacified M'gori with the promise that she would do whatever was possible, and he went back to his home satisfied but still depressed.

The priestess went far into her cave temple, and while the body went into a deep trance, the Daemoz conferred with the other Daemoz.

They agreed that this mortal might be able to further advance their master's campaign against the old gods by drawing more mortals away from their worship and into the trap of serving Chataan.

Fortunately for the Daemoz, their master agreed with them and gave them the authority to grant this one request under the condition that M'gori be required to do more than just worship. Total commitment to full-time service was required of him.

Had he realized then exactly what it was that was granting his request and the price he was going to be required to pay for immortality, M'gori would have gladly forgotten the whole idea and returned to follow the Gwundi queens in humble servitude.

The Daemoz returned to the sleeping girl, and the priestess went to M'gori with the news that his request would be granted after certain ceremonies were observed.

That night, as many years before, a silent group of men stole down the cliffs and raided a small Gwundi village for prisoners. This time they killed only the old and infirm then took all the younger people with them back to the cave city and herded them together into the darkest recesses of a large cave. Guards were set to prevent escape and the rituals began. At the darkest hour of the night, great fires were again burning around the stone altar where the young girl had been sacrificed and turned into the awful thing that ruled with M'gori.

This time they tied a young boy to the altar, and as M'gori ripped the bleeding heart from his chest and held it aloft, the revelers shouts reached a level heard for many miles through the jungle and struck fear into the hearts of all who heard.

M'gori then began to eat the still warm heart, and as the sticky blood squirted from his lips and ran down his chin, his followers gasped in awe as before their eyes his graying hair turned black and his skin turned from a pale gray to a vibrant healthy pink.

He seemed to grow as they watched his old back straighten, and M'gori once again stood tall and proud before his stunned followers.

Instead of a tired old man of some eighty years, now they saw a young man in the prime of life, who reveled in the prospect of reigning forever.

ᴄ◯Chapter Four◯ᴐ

S outh of the great prairie in the heavily forested rolling foothills of the southern mountains lived the people known as the Ghorn.

They were tall and heavy; muscular men with red hair and fair skin that usually displayed a generous amount of freckles. They possessed great physical strength from a lifetime of labor and, if they had been so disposed, would have made good soldiers.

The Ghorn, as did the Gwundi, made slaves of their own people as well as others they captured in battle or bought from traders. Most families owned at least one bond slave of the Ghorn as a house servant and a few slaves of the other peoples to do the more menial tasks.

The slaves, whether Ghorn or of some other people, were not mistreated and after many years of faithful service were able to work their way out of bondage.

The Ghorn had no powers of magic or sorcery as the Gwundi and Shanar did, except for an occasional mutant who possessed some rudimentary form of magic abilities. These were driven out of their communities as soon as their peculiar talents were discovered and either died of starvation or joined one of the wandering bands of plains nomads.

The Ghorn numbered fully fifty thousand men plus women, children, and slaves, and lived in villages of strong log houses with sod roofs and dirt floors. Each house had a single room that served as living room, kitchen, and bedroom with a large central fire pit for cooking, light, and heating.

Most of the villages, consisting of a few thousand people each, were loosely governed, if at all, by a benevolent father type who was more advisor and protector than ruler, and who was more or less agreed to by all the villagers.

Many of the men supervised the slaves who worked the mines in the hills that produced the ore from which the raw iron they smelted was made into tools and, on occasion, weapons that were traded to the merchants of the other peoples for meat and skins. Other men worked slaves at clearing land for expansion of the villages or for crops tended by the women and children. Even with the use of slaves, everyone man, woman, and child had an assigned task, and they worked at those tasks without thought of days off or vacations. The idea of not working simply never occurred to them.

They used the iron to make heavy axes that were used both for cutting down trees and for dispatching enemy warriors on the rare occasion of a disagreement between villages. The Ghorn also had long swords that they kept handy for just such an occasion.

The largest of the Ghorn villages was so by virtue of having been located next to a large tributary of the great river, as well as being in close proximity to a rich ore deposit that provided much metal for tools and trade.

A wise overseer named Morl managed this village. In light of his approaching middle age, Morl chose to be called "The Old Man." His favorite mate, Llona, about half his age, preferred to call him "King" and quite naturally desired to be called "Queen."

This affectation rather amused Morl, who most often and with irreverent glee, addressed Llona as "Babe." Morl's continued lack of apparent personal ambition and complete disregard for all of Llona's attempts to elevate them to a position of royalty, coupled with their vast difference in age, led to the usual conclusion: Llona looked elsewhere for someone who would be more likely to treat her like a queen.

Morl, being a wise man, was well aware that something was amiss in his relationship with Llona, and even harbored some doubts as to whether he was in fact the true father of their daughter, Valona, who was almost an exact copy of her mother in appearance and temperament and seemed to have none of his traits.

Nor did he take Llona's philandering too seriously, for there were several red-haired, freckle-faced children and young adults in the village who bore more than just a coincidental resemblance to Morl. He knew well that if he complained too loudly, it would sharply curtail his own dallying, and he would probably have to give up most of his attractive young concubines.

Morl and Llona lived together in comparative harmony for several years until Llona found a likely candidate to take Morl's place and establish a royal line. The fact that this worthy individual, Horth by name, was probably one of Morl's older illegitimate sons didn't deter Llona even a little bit.

She led him on and inflated his ego until he not only believed he could rule as king, but that he was the rightful heir to the as-yet-nonexistent throne.

Morl was disposed of by the ridiculously simple method of sticking a foot long knife into his sleeping body and throwing the still warm body out the back door to be disposed of by the always-hungry village dogs.

Horth was already known as one of the wealthiest men in the village, which made him all the more attractive to Llona. He also had a reputation as the strongest man in the area, as well as somewhat of a brawler, so he had little difficulty convincing the local citizenry of the rightness of his claim to leadership. There were a few grumbles when he proclaimed himself king, but when the people found that he intended to let everything run about the same as before, they quietly went about their business.

Horth's only affectation as king was to build himself a much larger house with several specialized rooms instead of the single room hut common among the Ghorn. This suited Llona fine until many other multi-roomed houses showed up in the village and she really had nothing but a title, which almost everyone ignored, to set her apart from any other wealthy matron. Llona quickly found she was just as frustrated with Horth as she had been with Morl. She not only began to berate him herself, but also turned her now maturing daughter against Horth.

Horth was becoming uneasy about the succession of the crown, for he had as yet no male heirs, except by his slave concubines, who would not be accepted as heirs to the royal line. The mere thought of leaving the leadership of his people in the hands of Llona and Valona sent chills through him. His irritation became all the more pronounced when his brother's mate gave birth to a lusty pair of twin sons.

He put up with the two females nagging, harassment, and the resultant frustrations for much longer than most men would have endured them in hopes that his mate would give him a son to inherit the throne. However, he had a well-justified suspicion that Llona had been avoiding the royal bed just so that her daughter would be the only heir to the throne and Horth's fortune.

Unknown to Llona and her daughter, Horth had been accumulating a private hoard of the soft yellow metal that the nomads had discovered in the creeks of the plains. While totally useless for tools or weapons, this metal was almost compulsive in its attraction and was coming to be in great demand by the women for ornamental jewelry.

After Horth's favorite concubine, Alora, presented him with a good-looking and very healthy baby boy, Horth resorted to the simple old-fashioned method of dragging the loudly complaining queen off to the bedroom and exercising his husbandly rights.

Soon thereafter, Llona gave birth to a handsome, strapping son who Horth named Jhor.

And just a short time later, Horth sold Valona, now grown quite attractive in spite of her acid tongue, to Rhon, the leader of the plains nomads, who had come to trade skins and meat for iron tools. Llona acted quite predictably to this outrageous treatment of her only daughter and screamed herself into a royal fit.

Horth then displayed either his very bad temper, or very good judgment, and removed Llona's head with one powerful swipe of his long sword. He gave her the same treatment as had been accorded his predecessor, and then moved Alora and her young son, Lon, into his royal house as his mate and queen, in spite of the raised eyebrows of the villagers.

Lon was just one summer older than Jhor, and Horth rightly felt the boy would make the young prince a fine companion as they grew up together. Also, Lon's mother, Alora, had all the intelligence and abilities necessary to raise his young son as prince and heir, as well as the physical attributes and cuddly disposition to keep the king's feet warm on those chilly winter nights.

In that there had never been an actual king of the Ghorn before, Horth had no idea just how one went about this business of being king. His short tenure during the ill-fated mating with Llona was, he knew, not really the way a king should rule his people. Llona had been more interested in the title and really didn't care if the people knew what or who the king was, as long as they called her the queen and she had more slaves and a grander house than anyone else in the village.

So Horth began to experiment with kingship.

His infrequent contacts with the Yaq and Gwundi, mostly through the nomad traders, and the stories he'd heard of the mysterious Shanar far beyond the mountains, had given him some slight idea of how those people were governed.

He couldn't begin to consider himself a war chief like the Yaq leaders, and he had no magical powers as the queens of the Gwundi. The mere thought of those awesome females sent chills of fear through him as nothing had done in his life.

The Ghorn had no magic and shunned even the mention of it for fear some witch or sorcerer might hear their thoughts and use some unthinkable form of witchcraft against them. Horth was intelligent enough to know that if he made the people of his village unhappy, he could expect much the same treatment his predecessor had received; so before he started to do anything, he solicited the assistance of several of the wiser and more honest men of the village as advisors.

At first he had some difficulty convincing them to leave their jobs and join him in what they considered to be unprofitable idleness. But he finally swayed them to his side by proposing something that never heard of before in all the land of man. He offered to pay each of them a salary in metal for serving on his advisory council.

When they thought about this radical new idea, they all accepted readily; and a new way of life was born in the land.

After several lengthy council meetings, during which Horth was required to thump a few stubborn heads to establish his authority and maintain order, he began to introduce some new ideas to the people.

He started by organizing all the workers into regular crews and figured out ways to set up work shifts so that everyone, except the foreign slaves, had regular rest days. At first the people grumbled some, as most people will when confronted with the necessity to think about some new idea. But they soon ceased their complaints as they found new and entertaining things to do with their free time, and they saw that more work was actually being accomplished in what seemed to be less time.

The Ghorn built a large timber fort and stockade to guard the entrance to their valley, and they erected a smaller outpost fort near the iron mines in the hills. A new profession, soldier, was created to man the forts; and Horth saw to it that they were not only well trained for the duty, but also well paid. He even allowed some of the indentured slaves to become soldiers and thus work their way to freedom.

The real clincher to Horth's popularity came when he started a system of wages for the common workers and paid them for their labors in the precious metal that, unknown to the majority of the people, was more plentiful than had been thought. The people soon discovered that the only thing better than a wise, rich king was a wise, rich, generous king. So they worked their collective tails off for him and, of course, for the iron.

Word of Horth's wisdom and generosity inevitably spread to other nearby Ghorn communities, and soon flocks of people began deserting their ancestral homes to migrate to his rapidly growing realm to try to get their share of the wealth.

Rather than attempt the futile task of driving them all away, Horth and his council picked the more intelligent from among the newcomers, instructed them in the new ways, and sent them back to their communities with a few of Horth's aides as overseers to teach their own people. The overseers soon became governors in the king's name, and Horth's span of authority increased until he ruled more than a third of all the Ghorn.

Horth's home village had grown to be a large city and occupied nearly the entire valley, crowding out crops and leaving little room for expansion. So he began to expand the mining and smelting operations until they took up most of the work force. He then started selling the crude iron to the other villages for food and trade goods. Soon his capitol was the merchant center of the land and very little labor was done by anyone except the slaves.

All this was fine and good for the people and made Horth a very rich and powerful man, but he was no longer enjoying himself. He found he didn't have the time to do any of the things he'd imagined he would be doing at this point in his life, and he wanted a break.

Each man, woman, and child in his realm slept every night in a warm dry bed with a full stomach and had plenty of time for leisure activities.

Some said that even a slave in Horth's city lived a better life than the average person in the other villages.

Everyone was happy. Everyone, that is, except the king. The king was so busy with the details of governing his rapidly expanding kingdom that he rarely had time even for a leisurely meal, and he couldn't remember the last time he'd gone drinking or hunting with his friends.

Prince Jhor was reaching maturity, and Horth thought it about time the lad began to shoulder some of the load. Indeed, the prince was fully as tall as the king was, although not yet as heavy, and showed promise of soon outgrowing even his huge father. Jhor had spent nearly all his life being prepared for the throne of Ghorn by a succession of tutors and teachers and had learned at least a part of every trade in the kingdom.

Young Jhor had been raised with his half-brother, Lon, and his twin cousins, Hath and Thon and the foursome had become virtually inseparable companions. The lads were constantly playing at soldiering and had seemingly forgotten that Lon was really the son of a slave. The twins and Lon completely ignored the fact that Jhor was the heir to the throne and gleefully took advantage of him being the youngest and smallest of the quartet. They regularly made him the object of their practical jokes and all too often the recipient of a not too royal, but still friendly thumping.

Finally, Horth called his advisors together and told them to prepare the prince in earnest to assume the throne of Ghorn.

In the ensuing years, Jhor absorbed all the intricacies of politics the royal advisors could cram into him. He showed an amazing aptitude for leadership, as well as the desire to take on as much of the responsibilities as he could. He still set aside plenty of time for activities with his cousins and Lon, so quite often his father's advisors had to hunt him down to continue his lessons.

At the beginning of Jhor's twentieth summer, Horth looked about him and saw that the management of the land had been completely taken out of his hands, which was just fine with him.

He had finally achieved the goal he'd set for himself when he took the throne; he had become obsolete.

So the king quit.

ᚲ᠎᠎Chapter Five᠎᠎

In the rugged mountains of the far west lived the Shanar. They were a small wiry people who herded goats and sheep in the high valleys. Where they could find and suitably clear a reasonably flat plot of earth, they planted crops of grain and vegetables to support the population of about sixty thousand.

They had no slaves, for the mere idea of one man depriving another of his liberty or forcing his will on another was totally abhorrent to them.

They were a peaceful race ruled by a caste of scholars and wizards who lived and studied in the white stone buildings of the "Valley in the Sky," which was nestled high among the frosty peaks and was reached through a narrow pass from the valleys below.

Each spring as the frost cleared from the pass, the villagers made the trip to the Valley in the Sky to consult the seers and find what the coming year had in store for them.

That the seer's predictions were amazingly accurate was not at all a mystery, for the scholars and wizards possessed supernatural powers of the mind, and on many occasions they caught glimpses of the future in their dreams and meditations.

Dominating the Valley in the Sky was the "Palace of Light," perched high on a rocky crag at the southern end of the valley where there were no passes to the outside world, but merely a steep, twisting path to an ancient temple of gray weathered stone. In this temple, a few old priests studied the writings of their predecessors and recorded the history of mankind while they waited patiently for the coming of J'Osha, the "Golden One."

The Palace of Light was the temple and private residence of the emperor of Shanar. He was chosen from among wizards and scholars by a sharing of the minds of the elders in a telepathic union to determine the wisest and most qualified to rule. No man selected in this manner had ever ruled poorly, nor had an emperor ever been challenged. For when someone more fit to be the emperor matured among the scholars and wizards, he was acclaimed emperor and the rest acknowledged him as leader of the people.

The most outstanding, and least seen, feature of the Palace of Light was the emperor's private upper room. It stretched the height of six men from its red-tiled floor to the domed ceiling and was four arm spans from wall to wall. The room was a perfect cylinder with blue-titled walls unbroken, except for the single arch of a narrow door, and lighted by three candlesticks against the walls.

In this room, the emperor burned musty old incense in an ancient brazier; and in its smoke, he often read the past or glimpsed the future.

Now the emperor, clad only in a simple white tunic, sat cross-legged on the floor, staring into the gray-green smoke curling upward from the brazier to the darkened heights of the room.

Shallim, beloved and benevolent emperor of the Shanar, was again burning the rare old incense and speaking ancient incantations, hoping the gods would favor him with another glimpse into the netherworld where the gods dwelt. At times he was allowed to see the past, and this information was passed on to the old priests and prophets to be recorded in their history of mankind.

Once in the far distant past, the old gods had blessed the fabled prophet Jirash Kin above all other men with a wonderful, though very confusing, prophecy of a coming deliverer of mankind.

This enigmatic prophecy had been carefully transcribed and was passed on from generation to generation. It was the object of great discussion and debate among the scholars.

On several occasions, Shallim himself had been privileged to view strange scenes that were not included in the histories, nor were they in the memories of the old ones. The scenes could only be interpreted as future happenings. On those rare occasions, Shallim and the other scholars spent long hours debating the visions to determine if they were relevant to the Shanar and should be passed on to the people.

Some of the visions were so strange as to be completely beyond understanding, but the scholars dutifully recorded them and stored them away in the crypts for future generations of scholars to ponder. On this day, Shallim was surprised and delighted to see a familiar figure in the wavering smoke; the very lifelike image of his beloved wife, Mihar, cradling a tiny baby girl tenderly in her arms.

Although he was of middle age and rapidly passing those years of being able to father a child, Shallim never ceased to pray for another child. Now it appeared that the gracious gods were about to answer his prayers. He and Mihar had been blessed with a fine son, Hirash; and while both loved him deeply, Shallim knew that Mihar fervently wished for a daughter. For many years he'd prayed that his wife's wish would be granted.

Shallim jumped up from the tile floor as quickly as his creaking knees would allow and, almost upsetting the brazier, ran to tell his wife the happy tidings.

Only the gods know how history would have been written or if Shallim would have been so joyous if he'd stayed to see what further transpired in the smoky vision. For if he'd stayed, he would have seen his as yet unborn daughter dead at an early age, but not before she had borne a son who would bathe the land with the blood of many savage wars and set in motion the events that would lead to the end of all mankind.

But the fleeting joys of life, however delightful they may be, ofttimes cloud the reason of even the wisest of men. So Shallim ran happily to tell Mihar the news.

Mihar, however, already had more than just a strong suspicion that she was with child and was merely waiting for the right moment to break the wonderful news to her husband. So when he burst into her chambers, swept her off her feet, and waltzed her around the room in a very unemperor-like manner then exclaimed happily, "We're going to have a daughter," Mihar pulled away from him and plopped on a cushioned bench in a not too well feigned pout.

"Beloved husband," she said, trying to sound angry, "you are the light of my life, the very master of my existence, and the most revered emperor of our people; but sometimes, trying to live with you is an imperial pain in the neck because it's impossible to keep even a little secret in a house full of mind readers and wizards. And there are some things a woman likes to be able to announce for herself, such as expecting a child; and it's not fair, because you already know it's going to be a girl, and I'm just really beginning to be sure I'm going to have a baby and…"

As she paused to take a much-needed breath, she saw the look of awe on her husband's face and giggled in spite of herself.

Then both began to laugh; and as Shallim tried to embrace Mihar, they slipped off the cushions and onto the floor where they rolled helplessly in laughter.

To the servants running in to investigate the peculiar noises coming from the royal chambers, the sight of the imperial couple rolling on the floor convulsed in happy laughter was indeed an odd one. They could only stand in the doorway and shake their heads in disbelief and wonder if the strain of ruling the realm had finally gotten to their emperor.

Young Hirash, being only seven, thought it looked like a fun game and pulled away from his governess to join the festivities on the floor. Soon all three were sitting on the floor, weak from laughter, with tears of joy streaming down their cheeks.

Before long the entire palace was abuzz with good news of the forthcoming blessed event, for most of the household had been aware of the frequent prayers sent to the gods from the royal chambers. For several days, an almost party like atmosphere pervaded the Palace of Light. And as the word spread to the valleys below, the people sensed that this was a sign of favor from the gods and foretold of good fortune for all Shanar.

Southwest of the swamp on the open prairie where the rivers flowed toward the eastern sea lived a proud race of warriors known as the Yaq. They were tall muscular men with straight black hair and laughing dark eyes that usually disguised their emotions.

They rarely settled in one place for more than one summer and lived in the open air in tents of animal hides stretched over long straight poles.

They were expert horsemen and hunted with long, slender lances fashioned from the straight branches of the trees that grew by the river. The Yaq lived well off the land wherever their wanderings took them. A select few of each clan's greatest warriors carried short swords of iron that they treasured above all their other possessions. Many of the warriors carried short-handled iron axes that easily cut through the light shields carried by most of the Yaq.

The people greatly honored strength and athletic prowess. When the hunting was done and the meat dried and salted for storage, they often held games based on all forms of physical combat. Their games, both on horse and on foot, took on an almost carnival atmosphere, and the winners were accorded honor and respect by their people.

They also brewed a strong drink from the juice of the prairie cactus. When the hunting and games were over, they feasted and drank for many days. Many were the children that were sired on the nights of these feasts.

The Yaq worshipped strong gods of the elements like the thunder gods who sometimes walked noisily across the sky and lit up the clouds with their sky fire, or the water gods who brought life to the land.

They kept no slaves as the Ghorn and Gwundi did, simply because they didn't want to be bothered watching them. If an enemy was taken in battle, he was sent on without his head to wander forever without rest between the earth and the god places. On rare occasion, a chief was taken alive and was kept by the clan as a pet. That life was not a pleasant one, for the captured chief would be frequently beaten and starved and usually died a slow and painful death, crippled and reduced to little more than a cowering animal.

The Yaq numbered close to a hundred thousand men, women, and children and lived in tribes or clans ranging in size from just a few families up to gatherings of more than a hundred family groups, who lived together in relative harmony.

The largest of these clans was the Bear clan, which was led by the mighty war chief, Yokagi, who ruled not only by the strength of his arms and the agility of his feet, but by the might of his mind and the nimbleness of his wit.

Yokagi's size alone was impressive, for he was among the tallest of all the Yaq. His heavily muscled body was in sharp contrast to the other strong, but lean, Yaq warriors.

But by far, the most striking thing about him was the cloak and headdress he wore, which were fashioned from the skull and furred skin of a giant black bear that he'd slain single-handedly with only his father's long knife when he was little more than a boy.

Even though Yokagi had won the battle and wore the bear's skin as a trophy, the battle had not been altogether one-sided; for Yokagi still wore the deep scars of the bear's talons on his back and chest, and he'd lain in his father's tent for many days while he recovered from the wounds inflicted by the dying bear.

The tale of that feat was told and retold at many lodge fires and was reaching the proportions of a legend among all the clans of the Yaq.

Yokagi had somehow grown faster than the other boys his age and had excelled at all the hunting and sports activities, usually besting youths who'd seen several more summers. Quite often the friendly combats became real fights, as older boys grew frustrated over Yokagi beating them at running or wrestling or javelin throwing. Yokagi seemed to be unaware of their jealousies and continued to put his all into every match, for losing at anything was unthinkable to him.

While most of the older youths in the clan were jealous of his abilities and avoided him whenever possible, the younger boys looked up to him as a hero and idolized him, even to the point of mimicking the way he walked and talked. This only made the older youths more jealous and created greater problems for Yokagi.

Before he could grow a beard, Yokagi had grown as large as many of the men of the clan. The chiefs saw him as a great warrior prospect, if not a potential chief. He found that extraordinary things were expected of him, and the ordinary was never enough to satisfy the men of the clan. He finally realized the reason for the other boys' animosity, and, although he couldn't understand it, he learned to live with their jealousies. He avoided contact with them and spent more and more time alone running in the foothills.

It was on one of those days that Yokagi earned the bearskin trophy that began the legend and eventually made him war chief of all the Yaq.

He was running alone in the hills above the camp, naked, except for a loincloth and headband, and carrying his father's long knife strapped between his shoulder blades. Running almost blindly, he followed a small creek that flowed at the bottom of a steep-sided wash. As he rounded a turn in the gully, Yokagi ran headlong into the side of a great black bear drinking from the creek, and thus began the legend of Yokagi and his bear headdress.

Yokagi did not dare turn his back on the startled bear to flee, and the banks of the gully were too steep to climb. So his only choice was to stand and fight. He swept the long iron knife from its harness and held it at arm's length in front of him to keep as much distance between the bear and his own body as possible.

The bear started lumbering toward him, and then reared up to its full height, towering above Yokagi. It roared it's fury at the puny human, who had startled it out of a peaceful drink.

Yokagi staggered backward, as much from the bear's foul breath as from the mighty roar, and then the bear lunged at him with its massive arms outstretched to engulf him in what was definitely not a fond embrace. Yokagi took a quick step back then dove to the sandy creek bed at the very feet of the bear and rolled quickly to a squatting position under the bear's belly. The startled bear leaned down to see where the pest had gone, and Yokagi stabbed upward with all his might into the exposed throat of the bear. The bear reared to its full height, nearly tearing the knife from Yokagi's grip, and tried to roar in pain.

But the sound that came from the bear's throat was merely a gurgling hiss, for Yokagi's blow had struck both the bear's jugular vein and windpipe, and blood was coursing into the already dying bear's lungs.

Yokagi jumped up and drove the knife farther into the bleeding throat and, grasping the bear's hairy chest, struck again and again as the mortally wounded bear staggered backward in panic, trying to avoid the frightening thing that was clinging to its hair with one hand, while driving the knife repeatedly into its wounded body.

The bear frantically clawed at its attacker, tearing great gashes across Yokagi's bare back before flinging him into the creek.

The dying bear started to rear up for a final attack, and then cried out one last time in what sounded much like a whimper. Then it fell with a crash to the sandy creek bed and was still.

Yokagi lay on his back in the cold water, cleansing his wounds in the only way he could and stared at the dead bear. He hardly believed that he'd single-handedly killed the great beast that was the namesake of their clan. When he tried to move, Yokagi discovered three deep puncture wounds in his left shoulder and several long slashes across his chest that he'd apparently been too busy to notice during the fight.

When the wounds stopped bleeding, he rose stiffly from the water and carefully cut off the bear's head, then started the long walk back to the village.

Several times he had to stop and rest and he knew he was rapidly weakening from the loss of blood, but he would rather die than leave his prize behind. He was determined to carry that trophy in his own hands back to his people. Surely this feat would satisfy the old men who demanded so much of him.

When Yokagi staggered into the village carrying the great bear's head, the sight had the desired effect on the clansmen. The first to reach him was his father, who swept the youth up in his arms and ran with the limp body to the tent of the healer. Though almost unconscious, Yokagi retained an iron grip on the head until his father promised that he would personally care for the prize until the boy awakened. Yokagi, no longer a boy but a man who was simply younger than the rest, slipped mercifully into a deep restful sleep while the healer attended to his wounds.

Several warriors backtracked his trail and found the great carcass in the creek bed. They skinned and butchered it, and carried the hide and meat back to the camp. Before leaving, they buried the carcass and erected a large pile of stones to mark the place where Yokagi had killed the bear. There was so much meat that it took six warriors to carry all of it and much was left to the wild animals.

By the time Yokagi regained consciousness several days later, the hide had been lovingly cleaned and dressed by his mother and sisters. They'd fashioned a headpiece of the skull and padded it with soft leather, and then made the rest of the skin into a great cloak, lining the shoulders with soft doeskin so the cloak wouldn't chafe Yokagi's skin. The great paws were fastened spread out over the shoulders with the long claws hanging down like pendants.

The effect was stunning. And from that day, no man ever again questioned Yokagi's right to be called a man or challenged his eventual right to the exalted position of war chief of the Bear clan.

The people of the Bear clan were not merely named after the bear, they worshipped the great black bear as a near god, and Yokagi's feat of slaying so mighty a bear was talked of around council fires for many generations.

Chapter Six

In the unsettled areas of the vast arid western plain that separated the races of man, lived nameless nomads, outcasts of all the races.

They were a mixed group of misfits.

Many were merely wanderers who couldn't adjust to communal life and chose the more solitary but much harsher life of the nomads. Some were grotesque mutants, whose physical deformities had driven them from their ancestral homes. Others appeared normal but lacked minds and had to be cared for as little children.

There were a few who had peculiar mental powers but lacked the intelligence or the initiative to control them. They sometimes wreaked havoc among the nomads with their uncontrolled outbursts of magic.

Some were petty criminals who'd fled their peoples to avoid punishment for their wrongdoings, and others were simply mixed breeds who'd left their communities rather than face the scorn and ridicule they faced at the hands of their people.

Whatever it was that set them apart from their native peoples seemed to draw them together as a close-knit group.

Not outcasts or criminals or mutants, but a separate people unto themselves, free to wander wherever they would, except to return to their ancestral homes.

They were not a happy people; for they were, in spite of their false front of fierce pride, outcasts and wanderers forever doomed to be alone and different despite their numbers.

These people had long since ceased being solitary wanderers and had banded together into a large group, which made it more difficult to move quickly or to hide from the scouts of the "civilized" people. But loneliness often forces men into otherwise untenable situations, and the company of other humans was more valuable to them than marginal safety.

Occasionally, inbreeding caused an even stranger child to be born into the settlement to inherit the everlasting curse of being different. Some of them had unnatural powers of the mind, which were beyond mortal comprehension and which they more often did not understand themselves.

No one remembered who the first of the nomads were, for there had been many generations of wanderers and very little of their history had been passed on to successive generations. What they did have was highly colored by many retellings from generation to generation.

The nomads struggled for existence and roamed the plains trying to avoid contact with the other peoples. For such contact invariably meant death if they were captured by the Yaq or slavery at the hands of the Ghorn. A much worse fate was in store for those who fell into the clutches of the Gwundi, for the young witches would use them to practice their magical crafts. The lucky ones died quickly, but a few who were not so fortunate lived on as grotesque caricatures of humanity.

They couldn't settle long in one place or chose a more pleasant spot to camp because of the likelihood of being spotted. As a result, most had lived their entire lives with never more than a tree over their heads for a roof. Rarely did they have the luxury of pitching tents and staying in one place for a time. Even then they slept with guards posted to warn of approaching travelers or wild animals.

Occasionally a leader would emerge from their ranks and for a time their lot would improve slightly. But for the most part, they lived on the brink of barbarism.

One such leader was Rhon, grandson of a Ghorn woman branded a witch, and driven from her land by fearful narrow-minded people, who couldn't tolerate anyone who did not fit their mold.

Rhon was born in a nomad camp and knew no other life, save for the stories told to him at his grandmother's knee. He did not long to return to her ancestral home, except at the head of an army to avenge the terrible wrong done to his beloved grandmother. He did yearn to improve the lot of the nomads and worked day and night to that end.

His dream to help his people seemed a futile one for many years until the fateful day when one of the men was fishing in a stream near a new campsite and found a small lump of soft yellow metal in the creek bed. His first impulse was to throw it back into the creek, but as he held it in his hand, it seemed to have a warmth of its own and held a strange fascination. So he kept it. When he found more of the shiny pebbles in the creek, he kept them too.

When he returned to the camp, the man had several good-size fish and a pouch full of the yellow pebbles. When he showed the pebbles to his woman, she scolded him for his foolishness and threw the pouch into the corner of their tent.

But shortly thereafter when he returned to his tent, the fisherman found the woman sitting on the floor almost lovingly fondling the lumps of metal.

A few days later, he discovered that the yellow metal was soft and that he could work a small hole in it or shape it with iron tools. So he took the pebbles and strung them together on a leather thong and presented it to his woman as a necklace. Soon his woman was the envy of the camp. When questioned, the man readily showed the other men where he had found the pebbles. Not long after, most of the women, and quite a few of the men, of Rhon's group sported golden necklaces and other ornaments.

Morale among the band of nomads greatly improved for a time, and it did not take long for word of the soft yellow metal to spread to other nomad camps. It seemed the people equated their good fortune with Rhon's attempts to improve their lives, and they credited him for the fortuitous accident.

Before much longer, small groups began to wander into Rhon's camp to join his band and look to him as their leader.

Indeed he looked the part of a leader. Rhon was a physical enigma among the mutants and half-breeds of the nomads. He stood tall and straight and had a heavy chest and shoulders, and limbs like those of a great tree. A lifetime of hardship on the plains had not altered his handsome features, but it had hardened his character and left him with a humorless sober outlook on life.

Rhon inherited much of the talents of his grandmother, who as a girl exhibited abilities that branded her as a witch and, in the minds of the Ghorn, an undesirable person. Her family showed unusual compassion. Rather than simply kill her, they banished her from their land to the life of a nomad.

Rhon had the uncanny ability to read the emotions of those he came in contact with and instantly assess a person's character. No one could ever lie to Rhon without his knowing it, and he could not be cheated or bluffed.

He also had another trait that served him well as leader of so many who could not control their own powers. No spell or curse could be cast on him without his expressed conscious agreement. It actually took intense cooperative concentration on his part for magic to be used against him.

Rhon had risked his life many times as leader of the nomads. He often fought challengers from within the group, as well as outsiders, who tried to take the leadership from him. Not that being the leader of such an ill-begotten gang of misfits was such a desirable task. Rather, it was probably one of the most thankless jobs of any among the races of man. But Rhon felt a kind of responsibility to the hapless people, and some strange inner feeling he could not pin down seemed to tell him he must lead.

Now after years of running away every time they saw dust on the horizon and living in a state of almost constant fear of anything that moved, the nomads may have begun the long difficult road to acceptance by the peoples. And that was only because of a chance meeting with a lone traveler from Ghorn who had become ill while charting the plains one spring day.

Rhon found the man wandering, out of his head with fever, near a river where the nomads had camped for a few days. Rhon's first impulse was to strip the man of his clothes and any other valuables and leave him to die, but the man awakened from his fever long enough to plead to the gods for help in a pitiful voice wracked with pain and suffering.

Rhon was not as dependent on the gods as many of his people claimed to be, but he was reluctant to chance their wrath by such open defiance as the killing of a man who cried out to them so plaintively. And he sensed something good about the man that made him pause. So he reluctantly dragged the man back to the camp and nursed him back to health.

Also, Rhon was slightly more kindly disposed toward the Ghorn than the fierce Yaq or the eerie Gwundi, for his grandmother had been of the Ghorn. Although she'd been declared a witch and driven from the place of her birth, she'd always loved her native land and people and had imparted that feeling to her young grandson many times during his youth.

What the ill traveler needed most was simply food and water and several days' rest. So when he awakened from his deep slumber a few days after Rhon found him the traveler was almost completely well, though still weak.

At first he was full of thanks to his hosts for saving him from almost certain death, but when he discovered he was in a camp of the plains nomads, he instinctively reached for his long sword. The sword, naturally, was nowhere within his reach, having been safely hidden away by Rhon.

When the traveler, who said his name was Hathor, remembered that the nomads had saved his life in spite of who they were and who he was, he apologized for his hasty actions and again thanked Rhon but with much greater sincerity, tempered by shameful humility.

In the next few days, Hathor and Rhon talked much and became as close friends as men could under the circumstances. Hathor, it seemed, was the elder brother of a man named Horth, who had just become king of the largest community in Ghorn. His council was often sought by the new king.

During their long talks while Hathor rested and regained his strength, he and Rhon discussed steps to establish trade between the nomads and the people of the new king. Hathor promised to speak to his brother and open trade with the nomads for much-needed meat and skins that were so rare to the Ghorn for grain and metal tools to make life much easier for the nomads.

When Hathor left to return to his home, he took with him a few furs and skins and some dried meats to show the king, as well as the best wishes of all the nomads.

Rhon and his people prayed fervently to all the gods they could think of, and a few more just in case, that Hathor wouldn't betray them and return with warriors to wipe them off the face of the earth.

Some of the nomads were so concerned for their safety, in spite of Rhon's assurances of Hathor's good will, that they fled the camp and hid in the wastes for many days until at last Hathor returned leading a horse laden with metal tools and utensils. He had to explain many of the utensils to the nomads, for they had never seen an iron cooking pot or a knife that could cut meat with a single slice or heavy iron axes that could fell any tree on the plains.

They rejoiced in their newfound treasures and loaded Hathor's horse with such a quantity of furs and skins and dried meats that the poor beast had to be unloaded of half the trade goods before it could walk without stumbling. Hathor promised to return with more tools, and even told Rhon he would bring him a sword to replace the one that Rhon had taken from him at their first meeting and that Rhon had returned as a gesture of his trust and goodwill.

Rhon then gave Hathor a small leather pouch containing several small lumps of the yellow metal as a gift for Hathor's mate, not knowing the consequences that a small act of friendship would bring.

During the summer, the nomads taught the Ghorn traders the secrets of salting and drying meat so that it would keep instead of spoiling in just a few days and how to capture and tame the wild horses that roamed the vast prairie. The Ghorn in turn brought grains and vegetables the likes of which the nomads had never seen and instructed them in the ways of planting and cultivating the crops.

The nomads soon found that the yellow metal became the most sought after trade material they possessed and wisely kept the source a well-guarded secret.

For several years, trade continued between the Ghorn and the nomads who were no longer outcasts and wanderers. They'd actually begun to build a permanent settlement at the river crossing on the western plains under the protection of the Ghorn.

They were becoming a "people."

ᢗᔍᔍ Chapter Seven ᔍᔍᢗ

If the nomads had been in the habit of keeping track of their birthdays, Rhon would have been just a few days short of his thirty-third year when he made a trade with the Ghorn king for something that was to change his life and contribute to the fulfillment of the ancient prophecy, which he knew nothing about.

On this particular spring day, Rhon and two of his men had made their way to Horth's city with three horses loaded with trade goods: meat and cheeses, as well as skins, furs, and pelts of many small animals found only on the fertile plains.

They were looking forward to a day of friendly haggling, and then a night of drinking and storytelling around Horth's warm fireplace. Rhon had no way of being even slightly prepared for the offer Horth was to make him that night.

By nightfall, all the trade goods had been disposed of, and Rhon's tools and other provisions had been prepared for loading on the horses in the morning. Rhon and his companions settled down with Horth and Hathor for an evening of roast meat and vegetables washed down with strong dark ale.

Horth had spent as much of the day bragging about his newborn son as he had bargaining with Rhon, and it was apparent to all that the new prince would be the evening's main topic of conversation, at least on Horth's part. During the meal, Horth's daughter, Valona, had been wandering in and out of the room and interjecting barbed comments at her stepfather and his guests.

Horth was obviously trying to avoid any more embarrassment to his guests and ignored the remarks as much as he could until he asked Valona to bring in the baby so the visitors could see his son. She replied with a murmured comment to the effect that he probably wasn't the father anyway, so what difference did it make who saw the child.

She then made the foolish mistake of passing within arm's reach of her stepfather and he reached out with a speed that surprised everyone in the room, especially Valona. He grabbed her slender neck in one huge hand, pulled her face close to his, and bellowed into her suddenly ashen face, "One more peep out of you, and I'll feed you to the dogs like I did your father before you!"

Valona was petrified for a moment, then took a deep breath and screeched at the top of her lungs, "You won't dare hurt me. My mother is the queen, and you're only a brawling lout that couldn't even...aaawwk!" The rest of that statement was cut off rather abruptly as Horth clamped his other massive hand over her mouth and nose, effectively stopping not only her tirade, but also her breathing.

Rhon, in his slightly drunken state, wasn't terribly upset at the rough treatment of the girl, but he was slightly disappointed not to hear just what it was the girl thought Horth couldn't do. But when she started to turn blue from lack of air, he politely pointed out to the king that even a disrespectful snot of a girl was better than a dead one, for, after all, she showed promise of being rather pretty some day and might be worth something.

Horth took his hand away from her unconscious face, held her limp form at arm's length as if she were no heavier than a twig, and stared intently at her for a minute. "Worth something, huh?" he snorted. "What's she worth to you? One of those horses?"

Rhon was so surprised that he was unable to answer for some time. He knew that many people, including the Ghorn, owned slaves, but he'd never thought of owning one himself; rather, he'd tried hard all his life to keep from becoming one. The more he thought about it, the more ironic and humorous the idea seemed to his drink-fogged brain.

Rhon the outcast owning a slave. He loved it! "Right," he shouted. "I'll trade you a horse for the girl if you're really serious."

"Done," roared Horth with a laugh. "You've got yourself a slave girl, and I wish you luck in trying to tame her. She's going to nag you to death just like she and her shrew of a mother have been trying to do to me for years. Take her and be off before her mother finds about it. For then you'll have both of them to reckon with, and that's more than any man should be cursed with. Believe me, I know!"

So Rhon took the still dazed girl, popped a large cloth sack over her head before she could even begin to regain consciousness, and tied her across the back of one of the remaining horses. Horth gave him a large skin of ale, commenting that he would probably need all of it and more before the trip was done, and then they were off.

Slowly the girl regained her senses. Valona had never been as frightened in her young life as she was then. As a matter of fact, she had rarely been afraid of anything. After all, she was the daughter of the queen and nothing was ever allowed to frighten her.

What did frighten her now though was that for the first time in her life that she could remember, she had absolutely no control over what was happening to her. And to make matters worse, she had absolutely no idea what was happening to her. She vaguely recalled her stepfather manhandling her like a slave; then everything got fuzzy. The next thing Valona knew, she was tied up in a sack and apparently hung over the back of a horse with a monster of an insensitive brute riding the horse.

She regained consciousness, found herself in this unladylike position, and promptly screamed out at her unseen captors her resentment at the manner in which she was being treated, and at any and all who were responsible for this treatment.

The only response that outburst elicited was a resounding smack on that portion of her anatomy that was uppermost at the time and a growl of anger from the unseen rider of the horse.

She involuntarily cried out again, this time in pain, but with the same result. She started to respond to the latest violation of the royal derriere, but checked herself just in time to avoid another whack.

After what seemed like an eternity in her uncomfortable position, they stopped. Someone unceremoniously dragged Valona was from the horse then set her roughly upright on her feet.

As rough hands started to untie her bonds, her mouth got the better of her brain again and she started to blurt out, "Well! It's about time, you—" She never finished that statement, for an unseen fist struck her on top of the head, knocking her senseless to the ground.

When she awakened again, she could no longer feel the rough cloth around her, but it was as black as if she was still inside the bag. As her eyes became accustomed to the dark, Valona realized she was on the plains in a grove of trees and it was the darkest night.

She found herself seated on the hard ground with her back against the course bark of a tree. Her hands and feet were tied firmly, and a rough rope around her waist bound her firmly to the tree. Again she found herself in a very uncomfortable position and was totally helpless to do anything about it.

A strange deep roaring sound, like a savage beast growling deep in its throat, frightened her out of her momentary self-pity and half out of her wits. She screamed out in terror, fearful of being eaten alive by some hideous beast, and the noise stopped.

"What's the matter with you?" a man's deep voice snarled at her out of the darkness. "You want to get smacked again?" Go back to sleep and let me do the same."

She then realized that the fearsome noise that had so frightened her was nothing more than one of her captors snoring, and she broke down completely and cried as she'd never done before from the combined effects of the fright, utter frustration, and the total hopelessness of her situation.

A different male voice grumbled out of the darkness. "Hit her again, Rhon, or we'll never get any sleep."

"Ah, the poor kid's just scared," the voice identified as Rhon said. "Let her cry it out, and she'll be all right in the morning."

"I won't last till morning if I have to listen to that all night," complained another voice. "You bought her, you keep her quiet!"

Suddenly the importance of that last statement sunk into her confused brain, and she stopped her hysterical sobbing and gasped, "Bought? You bought me? How could you buy me? I'm not a slave to be bought and sold! My father's the king. And when he hears about this, he'll have your heads on pikes outside his door."

"Hah! Who do you think we bought you from, sweetheart? Your own dear father traded you to us for a workhorse, and I'm starting to think I got a raw deal. You may be kind of pretty, but if all you can do is bawl, I might as well give you to the Yaq for a plaything and take the loss of the horse."

"Don't give her to the Yaq," laughed one of the other men. "If you don't want her, I can think of a couple of things I could do with her to make standing night watch a lot more interesting."

All the men broke into raucous laughter, and Valona shuddered at the thought of what they obviously had in mind. She swallowed her pride and fought back her tears. "Please tell me what's going on. Did my father really sell me? And what's going to happen to me?"

"Yes, he really sold you. Like I said, he traded you for a horse." The one called Rhon stood up and came close enough that she could see his face in the dim light. She recognized him as the leader of the nomad traders, who had been bartering with her father.

"As for what's going to happen to you, girl, I really don't know," Rhon said. "We were all half drunk when we made the trade, and I never really thought much about it." Rhon sat down in front of her, and in the growing light of early dawn she could see a puzzled look on his face as he stared at her. "I really don't know what to do with you now that I've got you. The thought of owning a slave seemed kind of funny when I was drunk, but now it doesn't sit well with me."

"You could let me go. I promise that if you let me go I won't let my father hurt you," Valona pleaded. "My mother will be so glad to see me that she'll probably reward you."

"I'm not worried about your father," Rhon told Valona as he untied her. "He was glad enough to get rid of you. And if the talk we heard while we were leaving the city is true, your mother can't even help herself, much less you. I'm afraid you're as good as an orphan, kid. Your father doesn't want you, and your mother is dead and gone."

Valona stared at Rhon for several minutes without a sound, then buried her face in her hands and sobbed weakly.

She was just too tired and stunned by the recent events to react violently to anything. Rhon finished untying her and took her in his arms. He cradled her like a baby against his chest, trying in his rough way to soothe her. He sat rocking her gently in his massive arms when finally exhaustion caught up with her, and she dropped into a fitful sleep.

Soon it was light enough to travel. While Rhon tenderly cradled the sleeping girl, the other men loaded the horses. Then the small party set off for the nomad camp.

Rhon easily stood up with the small figure and set off on foot, not wishing to disturb her any more than necessary, while the others led the horses.

The trip was strangely silent, for Rhon's companions sensed a change in their leader. Indeed, a change was taking place. As Rhon walked along with the heartbroken girl in his arms, he raised his eyes toward the morning skies and swore a solemn oath to every god there was that as long as he was leader of the nomad people, there would be no slaves among them. And that no man of the plains people would oppress any other man as long as Rhon could hold a sword in his hands.

The men spent the remaining three days of the trip back to their camp in an atmosphere of unusual quiet.

Rhon walked in what appeared to be sullen silence, leading the horse that Valona rode in silence, and responded to questions with only a grunt or nod instead of his usual friendly manner. After a few attempts at conversation, the men too kept their silence, partly out of respect for their leader's feelings but mostly because they'd never seen him act in this manner and were a little afraid to disturb him. They knew that while Rhon was a fair and just leader, he also had a short temper and often reacted without thinking of all the consequences.

Valona rode like a person in a trance and offered no comment or argument when told to mount or dismount, nor did she participate in the nightly conversations around the campfire.

The only sound she made was an occasional muffled sob as she reflected on her seemingly hopeless condition. Rhon didn't spend those few days engrossed in happy thoughts. The more he considered his actions, the more he had to admit to himself that he'd been, and still was, a colossal fool. He couldn't pass off his stupidity in buying the girl by blaming the alcoholic fog he'd been in at the time. Even so, he was sure he would have never even thought of doing such a thing if he'd been completely sober and in command of his senses. Now he was faced with the problem of what to do with her.

Rhon was reluctant to send her back to her stepfather to face an uncertain future with him, what with her mother long since reduced to dog food, and he had grave doubts about his people's reaction to him bringing home a slave, even though he didn't intend to keep her as a slave.

By the time the group reached the more or less permanent camp of the plains people, Rhon was almost convinced that soon he would be an outcast among the outcasts, shunned by his own people.

He instructed his men to take the trade goods and distribute them among the people, and then he took Valona to the tent of a kindly old widow named Zhorf, who had the motherly qualities he thought Valona needed at that time. Zhorf also possessed the ability, valuable in this instance, to influence the emotions of other people merely by touching them.

Rhon quickly explained a little of the girl's situation to Zhorf, and the second she took the frightened child in her arms, Rhon could see Valona begin to relax as her fears and sorrow were washed away by the subtle magic of the widow.

Leaving the girl in her able hands, he then put his fate, and possibly his life, in the hands of his people. He sent word to the ten elders of the people and called them together in the council tent at midday.

He sat cross-legged on the dirt floor, pondering what course of action to take when he presented his folly to the elders. As the dimly seen sun reached the zenith and the elders were finally gathered, he told them how, in his drunkenness, he'd squandered a valuable horse and some of their trade goods on a mere girl who had been spoiled by soft living and could contribute little to the fragile economy of the nomads colony.

The elders listened in silence while Rhon explained all that he'd done, bringing shame and dishonor on all of them all by bringing a slave into the camp.

He concluded by stating that he'd lost the right to lead and would step down to make room for a new leader of the people.

For several minutes all was still. No one spoke or moved, and a few of the older men actually appeared to have fallen asleep. Finally, the elder Ahurn, generally conceded to be the oldest and wisest man in the colony, broke the silence.

"I have seen six generations of my children suffer and sometimes die at the hands of the other peoples. We were chased from our tents and slaughtered like animals by the Yaq or were captured and enslaved by the Ghorn. Many of our people starved and died while the other peoples slept in their beds with full bellies every night. Things were like this for countless summers, and it looked as if it would only get worse.

"Then Rhon came of age and became our leader. Since that time, no man among us has suffered at the hands of another. No child has died from hunger or cold, and the Ghorn no longer enslave us but trade with us and share their wealth. The Yaq now avoid us because of the weapons we have and the way Rhon has trained us to use them. Now we eat well of all kinds of food and we have warm clothes to keep away the chill of night. We are no longer enslaved and driven from our homes, and we are a free people. All of this happened because of Rhon.

"I am an old man and I talk too much. All I will say more is that Rhon has made a mistake. He came to us with an open heart and admitted the mistake. This does not make him unfit to lead our people. He has gained wisdom and compassion from this and will be a better leader. So be it!"

The rest of the elders nodded their agreement and rose to leave the council tent.

"Wait," Rhon called out to Ahurn's retreating back. "What am I to do with the girl?"

The elder Ahurn turned and, with the slightest trace of a smile on his wrinkled face, told Rhon, "That's your problem. Use some of the wisdom and compassion I gave you credit for and solve it yourself."

With that, he turned and followed the other elders out of the tent, leaving behind a much relieved, but very confused, young leader.

Rhon sat in bewildered silence until the dim sun began to sink toward the eastern horizon, and the hazy skies started to darken. He then rose, no closer to a solution than he'd been on the first night after leaving Horth's city. He went to the tent of the widow and found Valona sleeping soundly on a pile of furs near the fire. The old lady refused to let him wake the girl, so he wandered the camp for most of the night before dragging himself into his tent for a few fitful hours of sleep.

Long after dawn, the clamor of the morning's activities awakened Rhon, and he staggered red-eyed from his tent to face his problem. He found his problem where he'd left her, in the tent of old Zhorf, but she was now wide awake and full of questions as to her future.

Zhorf had finally convinced her that the nomad people were not cannibals and had no intention of eating her for breakfast, as she'd heard from her mother on many occasions. She was now more curious than afraid. But when Rhon told her that she wasn't a slave and was free to stay or go as she wished, she broke into tears and buried her face in her hands.

"Leave," she sobbed. "Where would I go? My mother is dead, my father doesn't want me. There's nothing left for me. Oh, I wish I was dead!"

It took all of Zhorf's magical abilities to calm the girl and assure her that life was really worth living after all. "It's all right, honey," she crooned in Valona's ear. "You can stay right here with us. We've never had royalty among the nomads before. You will be the first princess of the nomad people and someday maybe your child will rule as Rhon does now."

Valona didn't seem too impressed by Zhorf's play on her ego, but eventually calmed under the old widow's powerful influence and sat with her head pillowed on Zhorf's ample breast, sniffling unhappily to herself.

Rhon, who was now completely bewildered by the female mind and its workings, left them to themselves and went in search of breakfast.

It took Valona but a few days to realize that the nomads were humans after all and they actually were rather nice people, if you overlooked those with the peculiar mutations and abnormalities.

She soon accepted the nomad way of life and decided that she would stay among them and try to become one of them. But this was not at all as easy as it sounded at first.

The royal treatment she had become accustomed to among the Ghorn was completely foreign to the nomads, and it took a great deal of tears and tantrums before she realized she was no longer a princess and was not going to be treated like one, in spite of Zhorf's statement.

The major problem she faced after the initial adjustment was simply that she didn't know anyone other than Rhon and Zhorf. The few girls close to her age were busy with chores and had no time for her. Zhorf was friendly but old and slightly infirm, so she was not a good companion for a high-spirited young girl.

So Valona usually tagged along with Rhon, sometimes just watching and asking questions about the nomad people and their way of life. Quite often, however, she got in the way and had to be gently but firmly removed from underfoot by Rhon or one of his friends.

Eventually, Rhon more or less unofficially adopted her, more to get her out of the way than anything else. He would have been greatly surprised if he'd thought to use his abilities to read Valona's feelings toward him. For, after the first few months of her stay with the nomads, her attitude toward Rhon had changed from one of somewhat fearful respect to one of borderline adoration.

Indeed, by the end of the mild summer on the plains, Valona had fallen head over heels in love with Rhon, a condition that was becoming readily apparent to everyone but Rhon. Not that Valona spent all her time with Rhon. She had discovered that, contrary to her first impression, there was something she could do to help the people, at least the young females. The girls, most of whom were or could be very pretty if they only knew how, used no cosmetics of any kind and cut their hair only when it got in the way. They usually dressed for comfort with no thought of how they looked.

Valona recalled her royal upbringing and the way her mother's handmaidens had helped her dress and comb her hair and to use scents and colors to make her as attractive as possible. She started passing this information on to the girls of the colony, and the young men soon noticed the changes taking place in the girls' appearances.

Word got around quickly of the cause of these changes, and soon Valona had to set up a makeshift beauty shop in a small tent next to Zhorf's to handle the requests from the women of the camp.

Within a few weeks, most of the younger women in the colony, and quite a lot of the older ones, had patronized Valona's tent. Most gave her small gifts in appreciation. Before long, she'd erected a newer, larger tent and was well on the way to becoming a rich businesswoman. The men made their response to the new looks well known by the increased attention they paid to the women, and in the spring a flock of new babies were added to the colony.

Chapter Eight

On this particular dreary morning as the gray skies became fully lightened by the rising sun, Yokagi, Great War Chief of the mighty Bear clan, sat proudly erect on his giant brown stallion and surveyed the bedraggled remains of the once proud Fox clan gathered before him.

His warriors had just finished rounding up the survivors after overwhelming the Fox people in a surprise raid on their village just as the skies began to lighten in the west. Yokagi felt justifiable pride both in his warriors and in his own strategy.

The Fox warriors had only scant hours before returned from a highly successful raid against the Dog tribe down river, and the victorious people had been celebrating well into the night. When the Bear warriors rode out of the dark into their village, the few Fox who were sober enough to rise from their stupor and find their weapons were quickly dispatched to their ancestors.

The survivors were herded together like prairie sheep and now stood with their heads bowed before Yokagi, stripped of their clothing and their pride, with their hands lashed behind their naked backs. Yokagi's smirk of self-satisfaction only helped to lower their already glum spirits.

The captured women and children were gathered in a large group to the rear of their men, and while they retained what little clothes they had been wearing, their pride had suffered almost as much as the men's.

Yokagi's men stood guard with their long lances poised, ready to send what was left of the Fox to their ancestors. They knew that they would then be free to choose as they wished of the Fox women, either for more or less permanent concubines or merely for temporary pleasure. Most of the Bear warriors had their attention divided between guarding the prisoners and sizing up the prospects among the captured women.

Some of the women, obviously planning ahead with an eye to gaining favor with one or more of their conquerors, were openly flirting with them, which only added to the anticipation of the Bear warriors, and to the misery of the defeated Fox.

However, Yokagi had a surprise in store for both clans. It was a gamble that, if it paid off, would set in motion his plan to make him the greatest war chief in the long history of the Yaq and possibly even consolidate the tribes into one great nation.

Only his older half-brother and trusted aide, Kana, knew of the plan. For Kana was not only his brother, but also his closest friend. They fought side by side in battle and drank side by side in the feasting, and their closeness suggested they were joined by more than mere blood.

While Kana didn't have the natural flair, or ambition, for leadership that his younger brother possessed, he did have an uncanny talent for sizing up a military situation and developing strategies to deal with the situation. This talent alone would have kept him at Yokagi's side as advisor even if they weren't brothers.

Kana knew that what went well for Yokagi also went well for the Bear clan; and as the clan's fortunes improved, so did the lot of all the Yaq. And, quite naturally, Kana's status would rise along with his brother, the Great War Chief.

At Yokagi's gesture, Kana singled out Jiro, the defeated Fox chief, and brought him before Yokagi. Jiro well knew what little the future held for him, for he had done the same to the Dog clan just the evening before. His shame was great for when the Bear war party had attacked his village, Jiro was lying in a drunken stupor and had come staggering out of his tent to complain about the noise, which was aggravating his monumental headache. Now as he began to sober, his headache seemed to grow even worse, but he ruefully reflected, he would probably soon be relieved of both the headache and the head.

Jiro stood resigned at the side of Yokagi's horse, staring down at his bare feet in the dirt. He did not have to look at Yokagi to be aware of his captor's appearance, for although he'd seen only twenty-five summers, Yokagi was spoken of among the other clans as a great warrior chief.

Yokagi then broke the gloomy silence with an offer that brought Jiro's head up in surprise and began to lift his spirits from where they had sunken into a deep pit of despair.

"I, Yokagi, chief of the Bear people who rule all the plains and the rivers; I, who talk to the wind and to the mighty gods of thunder, have decided in my great wisdom and mercy to grant favor to my cousins, the Fox. If the Fox will swear on the bones of their fathers to follow me and be my people, I, Yokagi, who the gods of thunder would make chief of all the Yaq, will allow the Fox to keep their women and their children and their lodges and all their possessions, and will treat them as brothers."

He then paused and reflected momentarily on his pretty speech, then spoke again with a wave of his hand to Jiro. "Let Jiro speak for his people."

But Jiro was afraid to speak. He was almost afraid to breathe, for he felt he must be having a dream brought on by his drunkenness, and to breathe or move might awaken him and spoil this beautiful illusion. The massed Bear and Fox clans stood in stunned silence, looking from one chief to the other and waiting to see what was going to happen next.

A low murmur began to grow among the groups, and finally Yokagi broke the uneasy silence. "Does Jiro speak for his people?"

Jiro promptly threw himself on his face in the dirt almost under Yokagi's horse and cried out, "Oh great, Yokagi, blessed son of the gods of thunder and rain and wind."

At this even Yokagi raised his eyebrows and shifted uneasily on his saddle blanket, for he thought Jiro was pouring it on just a little heavy.

Jiro continued without lifting his face from the dirt. "Jiro, who was once the chief of the Fox, has lost the right to speak for his people, for he was not taken in battle as a true chief but was taken in his bed like an old woman. Jiro cannot speak for the Fox; but as for Jiro, he and his house will follow Yokagi and will serve him faithfully forever. Let the Fox warriors speak for themselves, for they were brave in battle and have won the right to stand and speak as men. They have no chief to speak for them, only an old woman."

Yokagi could not suppress the thought that while Jiro may not have been a great warrior, he certainly would make a good horse trader. He put on his best stern and benevolent expression and reached out his right hand to Jiro.

"Stand, Fox brother. Go to your lodge and put on the clothes of a man who is a chief. From this day forward, you shall ride at my left hand."

This brought a resounding cheer from the Fox warriors, who had just been given their lives by Yokagi and now owed him those lives. All the Fox, women and children included, began to chant their allegiance to Yokagi, except one old warrior who started to cry out that he would never stoop so low as to serve a sow of the Bear clan. However, the latter part of this brave declaration was heard only by the gods, for his head jumped from his shoulders and bounced in the dirt as Kana's long sword flashed though his neck.

"Are there any other fools who would go to meet their ancestors carrying their heads rather than join Yokagi?" roared Kana as he snatched up the dripping head and waved it above the crowd.

The sight of that grim spectacle and the thought of sharing the fate of their recently departed loudmouthed companion apparently helped convince the remaining Fox men of the wisdom of following Yokagi. Their shout of allegiance was unanimous.

Yokagi ordered his men to free the Fox warriors. Then he told the Fox men to go to their tents, put on their clothes, and gather their belongings. The men were cut loose, and all but one ran to their tents. This lone warrior stalked to the group of women and delivered a solid openhanded slap to a pretty young female who had been openly flirting with the Bear warriors. As she sprawled in the dirt, the warrior strode in naked majesty to his tent to the ringing cheers of the men of both clans.

Several days later, a new village had grown in the valley between the old villages of the Fox and Bear clans. Where a small creek joined the river stood a large grove of trees in the midst of what had been the most prized and most fought over area of the prairie. This now became the new home of the much larger Bear clan, which now included the Fox sub clan and the center of Yokagi's realm.

Over the next year, the combined forces, under the leadership of Yokagi with the advice of Kana and Jiro, added six more clans to the growing Bear clan. An ever-increasing number of conquered clans elected to follow Yokagi rather than go headless through eternity.

One day an emissary of an as yet unconquered clan approached the village wearing the white feathers of peace. He came somewhat reluctantly, being sent by his people as the loser of a lottery, and firmly convinced he would be returned missing some rather vital body parts.

He bore an unusual offer from his chief, Lica, of the Leopard clan, one of the larger and stronger clans of the plains. Lica's idea was that if he swore fealty to Yokagi before the Bear clan moved against his people, he could avoid the battle, which, with the current size of the Bear army, would be lost before it began.

Lica reasoned that if he offered peace and kept his word, he might be allowed to retain his head, position of leadership, and possibly even gain the respect of Yokagi and a position of favor.

It took very little discussion for the Bear leaders to accept Lica's peace offering, and, much to the delight of the emissary, Yokagi sent back some fine gifts to show his respect for the wisdom of the Leopard chieftain.

Yokagi then reversed the procedure and sent emissaries with gifts to all the remaining nearby clans, who were beginning to wonder who would fall next to Yokagi's armies, offering them the peace and protection of his leadership. Most readily accepted and joined what was rapidly becoming not just a larger Bear clan, but a nation of the Yaq.

Those few clans who tried to maintain their independence and individuality received little or no sympathy for their wishes and eventually joined with somewhat diminished ranks and new leaders.

One clan, whose chief loudly protested that his warriors would fight to the last man before swearing allegiance to the Bear chief, promptly chose themselves a new chief who was more interested in a long and healthy life than tribal pride. This clan sent Yokagi a gift of the former chief's head spitted on a pike.

Yokagi accepted the gift and their friendship.

By the time he had passed thirty summers, Yokagi ruled a loosely knit union of about forty tribes or about a third of all the Yaq.

Of his followers, there were over ten thousand warriors at his call, but Yokagi was not happy.

Much to his consternation and growing embarrassment, he had no male heir. His many wives and mistresses had borne him many fine, cuddly daughters, but no sons.

Young Hirash of Shanar was overjoyed at the prospect of acquiring a baby sister, for although he was only seven, he was intelligent enough to know that, as an only child, his mother treated him like a baby. Soon he would be able to do all the things the other boys his age were doing, because his mother would be totally absorbed in the new baby.

As the weeks and months passed, it became clear to everyone in Shanar that the blessed event would take place at about the same time as the annual spring pilgrimage and festivals.

The entire valley began to make preparations for what promised to be the happiest occurrence in the long history of Shanar.

As the anticipated birth grew close, tents and booths filled the floor of the valley near the imperial palace and soon they were overflowing with pilgrims hoping to be near when the child was born, possibly even to gain favor with the gods, or just out of curiosity. As might be expected, some enterprising persons began wagering as to the exact day and hour of the birth.

Soon almost everyone but the wizards were caught up in the excitement and had placed bets on what they hoped was the correct time of birth. However, as might also be expected, the child did not cooperate with the bettors and popped red faced and squalling into the world ten full days before the projected date.

This caused lighthearted dismay among all the bettors, except for an unmarried herdsman who had never learned to count past ten and had unhappily, until he was proven right, chosen what everyone else derided as entirely the wrong date.

Lisha, as she was named by her ecstatic parents, may have come into the world red faced and crying, but it soon became apparent to all observers that she would quickly grow to be the fairest of the fair.

By the third month of her young life, Lisha had grown to be a blue-eyed, golden-haired beauty whose rosy-cheeked smiles were already melting strong men's hearts. As she grew older, she seemed to grow more beautiful each passing day.

By the time of her thirteenth year, she had a firm grip on the heartstrings of every male in the valley between the ages of eight and eighty.

Her brother, Hirash, had long since taken upon himself the role of protector of the royal virtue, and he carefully screened all her would-be suitors. Much to her chagrin, he rejected all too many to suit her wishes, as he personally judged them unworthy of her affections.

Hirash made a vow that he would not marry until Lisha reached her eighteenth year when she should be, by his reckoning, mature enough to fend for herself socially. This outraged Lisha, but merely brought understanding smiles to the faces of her parents when she complained of her brother's restrictive overprotection.

While she fully enjoyed her role in life and the attention it brought her, Lisha was much too intelligent to be misled by that attention. She knew that as the daughter of the emperor she would be looked up to by all the people and her every move and word would be subject to much discussion. She realized that her good looks alone would not carry her through life and that a keen wit and educated mind were much more important.

So, being the daughter of the greatest sorcerer in all the land, she began following her father as he went about his business of sorcery whenever she could. She asked seemingly innumerable, and often unanswerable, questions about the various spells and incantations employed by the wizards and about all facets of their craft.

It was not too much longer before she began to understand the fundamental concepts of the wizard's spells and from there it was just a short step to trying some of the spells in the secrecy of her rooms. Most of these attempts at wizardry were total failures, but her first and most spectacular success necessitated calling out the royal guard and several powerful wizards to dispatch the frightening thing she had called into her boudoir from the netherworlds. After that unfortunate incident, her father made her promise to restrict her experiments to more controlled surroundings with expert supervision.

Hirash, true to his vow, remained unwed until after Lisha's eighteenth birthday. Though his actions when in the company of a certain young lady of the court named Irini made it clear to all that he somewhat resented the hastiness of his vow not to marry until Lisha was of age.

Very soon after Lisha celebrated her eighteenth birthday, Hirash and Irini were married in a ceremony that can simply be described as befitting the union of the first born of the beloved and benevolent emperor of Shanar and the eldest daughter of one of the most respected families in all the land.

The celebration lasted twelve days.

By this time Lisha had become quite adept at most of the spells and incantations and, though she hadn't told her father, had on several occasions glimpsed a sight of future happenings without the need to burn the old musty incense, but just by the awesome power of her young mind.

So, a few days after her brother's wedding to Irini, she crept up to the tower room and recited the incantations in a manner that would have greatly surprised her father by their speed and simplicity. She had developed the uncanny ability to sort out the mumbo jumbo and get right to the heart of the spells. Soon she seemed to go into a half-awake trance and stared at the walls as if she were looking right through them and far into space.

She'd hoped to get some insight into what the future held for Hirash and Irini, but what she saw in her meditation brought her to full alertness with a cry of dismay and sent her flying from the room in a state of near heartbreak. For she had seen the grim conclusion of her father's earlier vision of her birth and the subsequent terrible events.

She ran to her rooms and flung herself on her bed. As she lay there sobbing, she could not, try as she may, wash the image from her tortured mind of her still young body lying in state while the nation mourned, and the too clear image of the world washed in blood by her offspring.

She stayed locked in her rooms for several days, refusing to come out for meals and not answering questions put to her through the locked doors. At first her parents ascribed the unusual mood to the "loss" of her dear brother to "another woman" and patiently waited for the mood to blow away. Finally, when her parents were becoming concerned that she might be ill and her father was about to call on the palace guard to batter down the door, Lisha came out of her rooms, pale and drawn, but strangely calm and silent. For she had decided that if her child was to be the cause of so much death and destruction, she would do everything in her power to see that she had no child.

Thus it shocked her parents and utterly crushed the spirits of many young admirers when several days later she announced that she was going to the old temple in the mountains to live a solitary life of study and dedication to the gods.

No amount of pleading or argument could dissuade her from her proclaimed course, and within the week she and a few retainers made their way through the rocky pass to the ancient temple where a group of old scholars and prophets spent their days in solitude transcribing the bits and pieces they gleaned from the past into a history of mankind.

Once she had settled into a room in the temple, Lisha

sent her servants back to the palace and began her life of seclusion. It took hardly any time at all for the men to accept her, for even they fell under the spell of her charms. And when they discovered she had inherited much of her father's powers of the mind, she was totally absorbed into temple life.

Lisha studied diligently under the scholars in an attempt to gain some insight into her apparent dismal future, but nothing she could find changed the grim outlook. Her resolve to remain childless only strengthened with each passing month.

While Lisha had vowed to remain childless, others had not, and once again the Palace of Light was astir over an upcoming royal birth.

Hirash and Irini had wasted no time and again the royal halls echoed with the cries of a newborn babe.

This was Rakh, firstborn of the firstborn of Shallim. The imperial grandfather was often seen strutting about the palace with his grandson in his arms and loudly proclaiming to all within earshot that this was the most handsome babe ever born into the entire world of mankind.

The household servants soon learned to agree with his proclamation and to casually remark on the child's striking resemblance to his grandfather.

So while Rakh began his long journey to manhood, Lisha drew more and more to herself and even avoided contact with the friendly scholars with whom she lived.

On rare occasions, the men caught a glimpse of a darkly hooded figure silently gliding from Lisha's rooms to the kitchens, or to the high windy tower, which even the more solitary men avoided because of the eerie sounds made by the mountain winds whistling through cracks in the stone walls.

At these times, the men would merely shake their heads in wonder and sorrow for the beautiful young princess, so recently the favorite of all the land, now living so lonely an existence.

Chapter Nine

As the number of Yokagi's daughters increased, so did the whispered questions about his manhood and, therefore, his right to reign as war chief of the Yaq. One of the less cautious warriors laughingly questioned Yokagi's masculinity due to his apparent inability to father a son. Fortunately for that ill spoken loudmouth, Yokagi recognized the comment as a jest and merely broke his jaw, rather than plant his head on a pike outside the chief's lodge. Yokagi's temper and patience both grew shorter until one spring day his mate, Rilath, gave birth to a healthy baby boy. Yokagi promptly named the boy after himself to squelch any possible rumors that he was not the natural father of the child and that one of the other warriors had contributed to the cause.

As the years passed, much to Yokagi's relief, the boy grew to be the image of his father. By the time young Yokagi was twelve, he was almost as tall as his sire and showed promise of growing into a much larger copy of the original.

When Yokagi reached his eighteenth summer, his father, now fifty summers old, ruled fully two-thirds of the Yaq people. He held sway over an area that stretched from the great western desert across the plains almost to the eastern sea and reached from the edge of the northern marshes to the low foothills in the south.

Those clans that did not swear outright allegiance to Yokagi were mostly isolated in the hills and studiously avoided contact with his people. Several times in the past year, the Yaq warriors had clashed with Gwundi scouts from the north as the clan inched toward the fertile plains, exploring the edges of the great desert.

Though Yokagi had recently passed his fiftieth summer, he was still as much a warrior as he had been at half that age. However, his brother and his son, backed by many protesting wives and daughters, tried to persuade him that he no longer needed to lead the warriors into the now much less frequent battles.

Yokagi countered with the argument that if he stopped leading his men, the people would lose respect for him as chief.

After several such discussions, which invariably turned into heated arguments won by no one, and that often found Yokagi threatening whoever dared to bring up the subject again with great bodily harm, he grudgingly relented and agreed to step down as war chief in favor of his son.

This brought cries of protest from Rilath who did not want to see her son injured or lost in battle. Peace was finally restored in the household when it was agreed that young Yokagi would be trained by his father and uncle for one more summer, and in his twentieth summer he would take his father's place as war chief while his father ruled the Yaq nation from what was now the great capitol city of the Yaq people.

The young Yokagi had accompanied his father and uncle on many war sorties since he was thirteen and was no stranger to battle. So the training he received was more in the arts of strategy and leadership than the more physical aspects of combat.

His father grudgingly, but still with a great deal of pride, pointed out that his son was in every way a better warrior than he himself had been in his prime, and no man in the nation could teach the young brave anything about any form of combat.

In the spring, shortly before young Yokagi's much anticipated twentieth summer, a scouting party returned to the city with word that a large party of Gwundi had been seen building a settlement on the edge of the prairie near the great river.

They reported that this appeared to be a permanent settlement, as the Gwundi had brought women and children and many wagons of what looked like household goods.

Young Yokagi went to his father and pleaded that this was the ideal time for him to lead the war party without the presence of his father and uncle so that he could prove his leadership abilities to the men and, although he didn't mention it, to himself as well. Yokagi agreed but with one condition, that he and Kana would go along as observers without interfering in the youth's leadership. The youth argued without success that if the older men went along, the warriors would naturally look to them for their reactions to his orders and decisions. In the end, the senior Yokagi won out and the war party was assembled.

Yokagi's unspoken reason for wanting to go was that he thought that this may be his last battle, if one developed, and he wanted his warriors to remember him as a Great War Chief to the last.

Unknown to the Yaq, their scouting party had been seen by the Gwundi settlers. Not because the scouts were negligent in their surveillance of the Gwundi, but rather by means of the sorcery of the priestesses in the encampment. Those priestesses lacked the awesome powers of their queen, but they did have sufficient talent to enable them to detect the Yaq scouts and watch their activities as they in turn spied on the camp.

So when the Yaq war party roared down on the settlement, they were met, not by a rabble of confused and frightened villagers, but by well-prepared soldiers who were equipped with a new and frightening weapon as yet unheard of by the Yaq.

While the straight-grained woods of the plains were well adapted to lances, which the Yaq warriors carried, the Gwundi had fashioned the springy woods of the jungles into short strong bows that they used with deadly expertise.

Before the Yaq warriors advanced close enough to the settlement to even issue a challenge, men and horses began to fall to the deadly feathered shafts that flew to meet them. By the time young Yokagi could rally his shaken and confused warriors and fall back out of range, fully two dozen of his hundred-man party lay in the deep prairie grass.

Some staggered to their feet and tried to pull out the shafts that had knocked them from their horses, only to be feathered again with another well-aimed arrow from the Gwundi bows. They fell again and did not rise from the grass. A few of the horses also had been hit, and they ran about in panic adding to the confusion.

As the young chief tried to rally his men, thinking that his first war party as leader was probably going to be his last, he turned back to look over the scene of the short one-sided battle. He saw a giant figure rise from the grass and tear an arrow from his chest only to be hit by another. He fell and rose again; and with a cry of rage, he tried to pull the shaft from his body then was struck twice more.

This warrior stood for a few seconds then turned away from the Gwundi camp and, lifting his face to the skies, let forth a cry filled with such great mortal anguish that all the warriors of both sides stopped short in their tracks.

As this anguished warrior turned, young Yokagi recognized the figure as that of his own father without the familiar bearskin headdress and cloak. Without thought for his own safety, young Yokagi spurred his stallion forward toward the stricken chieftain, intent only on rescuing his father.

Then to his horror, he saw three more feathered shafts seemingly sprout from his father's body, and the gallant warrior tottered and fell on his face in the deep grass.

Before the full realization of what he was seeing had time to sink into his shocked brain, young Yokagi's horse stumbled as it was hit full in the chest by another shaft. He tried desperately to hang on and turn the horse, and then was thrown to the ground as the horse died and fell. He rolled to his hands and knees to keep low in the waist high grassland and not provide the Gwundi a good target for their arrows.

As young Yokagi shook his head to clear from it the shock of the fall, he heard his name being called from the direction of the milling Yaq warriors. He turned and rose high enough to see his uncle racing toward him, hanging low on the side of his horse. Yokagi leapt up and raced to him as fast as his mighty legs could carry him, and then caught Kana's arm and vaulted to the horses back behind him.

A few seconds later, they were safe among their own men out of range of the deadly arrows.

The young chief shouted the disheartened mob of Yaq warriors into some semblance of order and led them from the open prairie to a narrow vale in the nearby hills. Then he dismounted the troop and saw to it that the wounded were cared for.

Yokagi told Kana to set lookouts to guard against an attack by the Gwundi and walked downcast out of the camp. Kana knew better than to interfere in his nephew's grief, which was only slightly greater than his own, so he directed the placing of the lookouts and went behind a bush and silently wept for his fallen brother.

Yokagi climbed to the top of a rocky knoll, out of sight of the camp, stripped to his loincloth and stood at the base of a solitary tree growing on the peak of the knoll. He gathered wood and started a fire with flint from his pouch, and then sat cross-legged in the dirt at the base of the tree.

He sat rock still, without a sound, until the fire had burned down and the coals glowed in the gathering dark. He then took his knife the knife that his father had given him, the knife that had killed the great bear whose hide now lay in the grass next to the fallen body of his father—and made a shallow cut from the middle of his wide chest, over his heart, across his left shoulder and down the back of his arm to the back of his hand. Changing the knife to his left hand he made another cut starting from over the heart, down the back of his right arm to the back of his hand.

Thrusting his hands into the still warm embers, he grabbed handfuls of hot ashes, which he rubbed into the bleeding wounds. He rubbed the ashes and soot into his hair, on his face and his entire body, and then threw himself onto the remains of the fire.

While he lay in the ashes, dark clouds began to gather and darken the evening sky. Thunder rumbled distantly in the north, but no other sound was heard in the prairie. Even the dogs were silent. The thunder rolled closer and flashes of lightning lit the sky as the departing spirit of the great Yokagi, war chief of all the Yaq nations and favorite of the thunder gods joined his gods in the northern sky.

Finally, young Yokagi lifted his ashen face to the dark sky and for the first time lifted his voice in anguish:

"Great gods of thunder, hear my plea. Look down on your servant and grant me vengeance on the slayers of Yokagi. I who was once also called Yokagi shall from this time be called 'Yoki' which is 'Half of Yokagi' for there is only one Great War Chief Yokagi who is now with the gods and no other mortal is fit to wear that name. Grant me the wisdom of my father that I may serve you and your people as he did!"

He who was now called Yoki fell on his face in the still warm ashes. Suddenly, a mighty bolt of lightning tore the dark sky and the ground where Yoki lay shook with thunder. His hair stood on end, his skin tingled, and the smell of the lightning filled his head.

The tree in front of Yoki had been struck by the blast of lightning, and was spilt to the ground. It now stood blazing in the night.

Yoki felt great drops of water fall on his bare back and looked up into the sky in reverential wonder, for no man had ever before seen rain fall from the skies.

"The gods themselves are crying at the passing of Yokagi," he thought in wonder. *"Their tears are like a waterfall. Truly this is a great sign."*

Yoki looked back at the tree and even his brave heart shook with fear, for the tree still burned in the midst of the falling rain and the water did not quench the flames. The tree burned on as if it were the driest day of summer. The tree burned and was not consumed, and Yoki realized with a start that the rain was only falling in the small area surrounding him and the tree, and the rest of the hills were dry.

He sat in silent worship in the falling rain and let the tears of the gods wash away the dirt from his skin and the pain from his heart.

When the sky began to lighten in the west, the rain slackened then stopped altogether, and only then did the tree stop burning, but it was still not consumed. Yoki looked about him and made a silent vow to the gods that from that day until the end of time this place would be a holy place where the gods met men and here Yokagi would be buried.

He picked up his father's knife, rose, and walked down the hill to where his warriors sat huddled in their robes, silently grieving in the early morning mist.

Kana ran to meet him and stopped short as the questions that he started to voice died in a gasp when he saw his nephew. For the young man who had walked sadly out of his sight the afternoon before had returned half a day later a totally different person.

His already great stature seemed to have grown, and where his face had shone before with youthful vigor there now appeared the mature countenance of a man of great inner strength and resolve, and his once jet-black hair was now streaked with white and gray.

"Yokagi?" whispered Kana.

"I am Yoki," the young man answered. "Yokagi now lives with the gods of thunder. They have shown me their powerful signs and have granted me vengeance on the slayers of my father, Yokagi."

The amazed warriors, who had heard the thunder and seen the flash of the lightning, gathered about the pair and began to talk excitedly about the changes they saw in their young war chief.

"Send riders to all the villages," ordered Yoki. "Send the word that Yokagi has fallen. Gather all the warriors at this place and we will have vengeance on those who would dare to harm the favorite of the gods of thunder. I will not sleep in my lodge until the plains are washed red with the blood of the slayers of Yokagi."

Riders were hastily dispatched to the nearby villages and three days later fully two thousand heavily armed, mounted warriors were gathered in the valley.

These inspired warriors created their own thunder as they rode out of the hills to wash over the Gwundi settlement like a prairie fire.

The ensuing battle was as violent as it was brief. Within the hour, barely fifty adults and a like number of children remained of the original five hundred settlers.

Of these, the Yaq found to their surprise, almost thirty were brightly clad priestesses who were the apparent rulers of the Gwundi, for the rest of the survivors stood clustered in a group behind the priestesses as if seeking protection from the warrior horde.

Yoki's original quiet rage had been tempered somewhat by the heat of the brief battle. As he sat his horse before the captives, he now wondered what to do with them. He was reluctant to slaughter women and children, and the men that were left were too few and too old to bother with.

Also, when he found that the priestesses and their witch queen controlled the people mostly through fear of their witchcraft, he was moved by prudent reason to be lenient. And besides, he wasn't too sure how one went about killing a witch and really wasn't too confident about risking it.

Finally he decided. "You are free to return to your people," he said. "Go back to your lands and leave the plains to the Yaq who have lived here since the beginning of time. If your people are foolish enough to come this way again, the land will run red with your blood and my warriors will not spare even your holy people."

With this edict, Yoki spurred his horse around and turned his back on the remnant of the settlers. With his head high, he rode through his assembled army and their voices lifted as one in a mighty cheer, their lances lifting in the midday brightness in a salute of love and loyalty to their chief. The warriors gathered all the weapons of the Gwundi and collected all their religious artifacts, much to the dismay of the priestesses.

As the Yaq warriors rode away, the remaining Gwundi stood silent for some time, and then began to gather what was left of their possessions to return to the safety of the jungle.

Yoki and Kana recovered the body of Yokagi from the grass where he'd fallen and carried it tenderly to the knoll where the tree had burned in the rain. Yoki then did something that startled even the hardened warriors on the hill: he took Yokagi's large knife and carefully cut open his father's chest, removed his heart, and wrapped it in a leather pouch then tucked it tenderly in a fold of his cloak.

They laid Yokagi in regal splendor, wrapped in his bearskin cloak with spear and sword at his side, on a bier erected under the twisted branches of the tree. The elder warriors took Yokagi's bear headdress and presented it to Yoki, insisting that it rightfully was now his to wear.

Two thousand warriors in full battle dress gathered on the sides of the hill and stood in silent tribute to their fallen war chief. Suddenly, the silence was shattered as a tremendous blast of lightning ripped the sky and consumed the bier in a blinding flash of white flame.

Most of the warriors fell backward in fear and cowered on the ground as deafening thunder repeatedly rocked the earth and sky around them.

The lightning and thunder moved away to the north; and as the shaken warriors gathered their nerve, they looked in wonder on their new leader, Yoki. Silently, the army moved down the hill and broke into smaller groups that made their way to their own villages.

The events on that hill would be told around lodge fires for many generations and many of the warriors swore to their dying day that they heard the name "Yokagi" echoed in the rolling thunder on that now sacred hill.

Yoki and the warriors of the Bear clan returned to their village. While most tended to their wounds, Yoki rode out to the place in the creek bed where Yokagi had killed the great bear. He moved aside the pile of stones and lovingly buried his father's heart in the earth among the decaying remains of the great bear; then rebuilt the pile of stones so no wild animal would disturb the heart of Yokagi.

Chapter Ten

Just about everyone in the nomads camp, and especially Valona, was greatly surprised that it took Rhon more than a year to realize Valona's feelings toward him ran deeper than a desire for fatherly affection. He was easily old enough to be her father and the thought simply never occurred to Rhon that she might be in love with him.

Though it was obvious to each person who came in contact with them or who had ever watched the look on Valona's face when she was with Rhon, he went about his everyday duties blissfully ignorant of what was beginning to strongly influence her every action and thought.

Finally, old Ahurn took Rhon aside and, as tactfully as possible, asked if he'd thought about taking a mate and raising a family. Rhon admitted that it had crossed his mind on occasion but that he hadn't given it much thought because most of the younger women were already spoken for and there were few likely candidates among the older women.

"What are your feelings about Valona?" Ahurn asked. Shocked into total silence by the question, Rhon failed to reply immediately and Ahurn continued. "Everyone knows she loves you; and if you don't do something about it fairly soon, she is going to be a very sad young lady. Several of the younger men have begun to take notice of her, but all are afraid to say or do anything for fear of offending you."

"Valona what?" Rhon gasped. "She loves me? But she's just a girl. Why, I couldn't..." Words seemed to fail Rhon, and he stared at Ahurn with his mouth open.

"Yes, she loves you. Not as a father or just as a friend, but as a mate. If you took the time to look at her, you would see she is becoming a very beautiful woman. And if you don't take her for yourself, soon someone else will. Then you will be the loser and some young man will have a fine woman to give him many strong children."

This revelation was too much for Rhon to absorb in such a short time, and he just stared at Ahurn while his mind raced in circles. Suddenly he stood and shook his head.

"I need time to think about this," he said. "My head is all messed up inside. I can't think good right now."

"Don't take too much time or there won't be any time left," the old man chided Rhon as he turned to leave. "If I was your age, I'd take her myself," Ahurn laughingly said over his shoulder as he ducked through the tent flap. Rhon could hear the old man happily chuckling to himself as he walked away through the village.

Rhon paced his tent for some time, and then headed out into the open prairie to try to sort his thoughts in peace and solitude.

He walked until it was too dark to see his way, and then sat on the bank of the river tossing pebbles into the dark water, struggling with his feelings until daylight.

At midday he still sat on the bank of the river lost in thought. Only when his stomach's violent rumbling reminded him of its empty condition did he return to the camp. After a large meal, his stomach felt better but his mind was still unsettled.

The thought was beginning to work its way into his befuddled mind that his learning of Valona's feelings about him made him feel good inside and that he really did care for her.

Finally, he decided to ask old Zhorf for advice, as she'd been closest to Valona and probably knew more about her than anyone else.

Her reaction to his questions didn't help his confusion or his ego a bit. No one likes to be laughed at, especially one who is already suffering emotionally.

So when Zhorf broke into laughter when he asked if she thought he should ask Valona to be his mate, Rhon almost ran out of her tent. Only her apologetic call stopped him, and she explained that she was only laughing because just that morning Valona had cried on her shoulder in exasperation and fear that Rhon would never realize how much she loved him.

Later that morning, Rhon became even more confused when he asked Valona if she would come to live in his tent and be his mate. For instead of the happy response he'd expected, she broke down in tears and ran to her tent sobbing. He stood in front of the tent for a few minutes, trying to decide whether he should go after her or just go get drunk and forget the whole thing.

As he pondered the strangeness of the female mind, Valona pushed the flap of her tent aside and stepped out into the daylight with tears still brightening her eyes. "It would please me to come to your tent and be your mate," she said quietly. "I will be faithful to you and cook for you and give you many children."

And she did.

The next spring when the rivers were full, fish and game were plentiful, and the prairies were green and sprinkled with flowers, Valona gave birth to the first of several sons and daughters; a strapping, healthy son they named Rollo.

Jhor and his half-brother, Lon, were raised by a varied group of men selected for their individual expertise in their particular fields, and by a succession of their father's wives and concubines, none of whom lacked either beauty or brains.

Horth may not have had any idea what a king should act like when he took the throne, but he was bright enough to know what a man needed to be a good ruler. He saw to it that his son was educated in the best manner the Ghorn could provide.

So, while Jhor's education did not match that of a prince of Shanar, he probably was being prepared to rule his people far better than most royalty.

Horth rightly suspected that his concubines were preparing Jhor to meet the world in more ways than one, and that his education was not entirely unpleasant. And, naturally, Lon shared in all facets of that education.

Jhor had inherited all the best traits of both of his parents. He had his mother's personal charm and good looks, as well as her high intelligence and his father's strength and physical abilities. He learned to blend both sets of characteristics with his father's good common sense.

By the time he was twenty, Jhor was nearly as heavy as his father and a hand's width taller. His head was topped with an unruly mass of reddish-blond hair that fell to his heavy shoulders and was usually kept more or less in place with a leather headband.

With laughing blue eyes and a smile that melted all too many girlish hearts, whether young or old, Jhor was by far the most striking figure in the land of Ghorn. And he was ready to ascend the now well-established throne of Ghorn.

He had been carefully schooled for many years and was as prepared for the throne as all the kings' men could make him; so when his father abdicated in his favor, Jhor was ready and willing to assume both the title and responsibilities of king.

Jhor's ascendancy to the throne of Ghorn only slightly tempered the attitudes of Lon and his cousins, who still addressed him in private as "runt," even though the twins were a mere finger's width taller and no heavier. Lon though was even taller than the king and easily carried considerably more weight, as well as being a year older.

When in public, they addressed him in an almost reverential manner. When they were alone, however, he was the constant butt of their practical jokes and derisive humor.

Horth waited around until he saw young Jhor firmly established on the throne, and then retired happily to a well-stocked harem where he died peacefully in his sleep many years later.

It didn't take Jhor long to discover that his father had been doing entirely too much of the work. He found there were many extremely well qualified men who could supervise the jobs better if the tasks were organized and relegated to those men best suited in each field.

Jhor gave the king's councilors, who had stayed on after the old king retired, the job of organizing the laborers and appointing the men to head each division.

Before long, his only real duty was to receive and approve regular reports from his councilors.

Jhor attempted to install Lon, Hath, and Thon in his royal cabinet as advisors to the throne, but they all respectfully declined, stating the restrictions of those positions would stifle them.

So Jhor became a good king while his companions went about having a good time soldiering and wenching.

Jhor quickly grew restless with little to do and started to spend a lot of time wandering around the realm, making many suggestions, and occasionally lending a hand with the labor at the mines or in the fields and generally just getting in the way.

The workers soon began grumbling about the king's meddling in the work and slowing things down, and the overseers found themselves in the delicate position of having to tell the king, however politely, to mind his own business.

The king went home and sat on his throne and pouted, for it was not his nature to sit and do nothing, but no one would let him do anything. It seemed to Jhor that the people thought he should just sit on his throne, look important, issue infrequent proclamations, and stay out of the way.

Before too long, his councilors became hard pressed to find things for the king to do and began inventing tasks and duties for him.

Jhor easily saw through their schemes, as well as the reasons for them, and became even more depressed and moody.

Then one day someone suggested that the king send an expedition to explore the as yet uncharted lands to the south and west.

Jhor agreed that it sounded like a worthwhile enterprise and signed the royal decree, all the while wishing he could go along. The idea of exploring vast wildernesses sounded thrilling and adventurous to the king. The more he thought about the idea, the more it attracted him.

He decided that he could and would go exploring. He was, after all, the king. And who was there to tell him what he could or couldn't do? Besides giving him something to do, the expedition would get him out of the people's hair for a while.

So Jhor appointed his uncle, Hathor, as regent to rule in his absence. He gathered about him a dozen of his closest friends, and they began to make plans for their adventure.

Jhor first chose, to no one's surprise, his half-brother and best friend, Lon, and then picked his twin cousins, Hath and Thon, who were playing at soldiering with the new army. They were constantly getting into trouble for fighting. And if they could find no one else to fight with, they fought each other. When they did, their fights usually ended in a draw with both laughing in the dirt, exhausted and bloodied but unhurt. Often Lon and Jhor would unite against the twins, and the result was about the same.

Of all the men in Ghorn, only Lon could best either of the twins in single combat and Jhor was almost his equal.

But no one could wrong any one of them without the other three leaping to his defense, and it is very doubtful that any ten men in the land could defeat that quartet.

The rest of the party was made up of the same type of young man, all close friends of Jhor, Lon, and the twins, who felt stifled by the pressures of life in the growing capitol city of the Ghorn.

Winter was now approaching. It didn't seem the best time to start across the high mountains, so the men had a full winter for planning.

The long delay proved to be beneficial, as the original plan included an abundance of food and equipment that would have provided for half a hundred men and required twenty horses to carry. But at last common sense prevailed, and the provisions were trimmed to what could be carried on two horses and on the backs of the men themselves. They first thought to take along several slaves to carry the provisions but finally decided that they would be better off without them, for even a faithful slave is still a slave and needs to be watched. Also, Jhor felt that Lon would be less self-conscious, being the son of a slave, without having several slaves in close proximity.

The small band set out in the early spring filled with lighthearted anticipation of what lay ahead. They took with them the finest iron weapons the shops of Ghorn had ever produced, long heavy swords that could cut a small tree with a single blow were slung on their backs, and razor sharp short knives were carried at their belts.

Most of the men also carried straight thick lances tipped with heavy iron heads, which doubled as walking staffs. A few carried strong short bows, which they had taken in trade from the Gwundi people of the jungle.

They carried dried meats and fruits, nuts, flour, salt, and the other bare necessities for preparing meals and a goodly supply of golden chain with which to buy other supplies from the scattered villages along the first part of their journey.

The young men forsook their fine apparel and wore only rough woodsman's clothes with heavy leather boots and vests. They did not expect to be treated as royalty by the few people they might meet and indeed didn't intend to tell anyone that the leader of their party was the king. Many people of the outlying towns did not recognize the authority of the king, and a confrontation could be uncomfortable, if not dangerous.

They well realized that their journey, while possibly a great adventure, could be quite deadly.

Horses were rare among the Ghorn and much too valuable as pack animals to be ridden, so the small band packed their provisions on the backs of two strong horses and set out on foot.

They knew that a rugged mountain wilderness sat to the south, which earlier explorers had roughly charted. Further south, if one dared that journey, it was rumored that a great stormy sea existed from whose shores no man had ever returned. But no man of the Ghorn could say what adventures awaited in and beyond the high mountains to the west.

The group set forth on a bright, chilly spring morning with the best wishes of the entire city to cheer them on. All the tearful, passionate good-byes had been said the night before; for any group of young men like this always leaves behind their share of fair young women who are saddened by the departure.

The usual gang of small boys and dogs accompanied them noisily for a while, but soon fell far behind at the pace set by the strong legs of the travelers.

For three days the band followed the small river downstream to where it joined the great river that flowed to the plains.

At the junction of the two rivers they turned westward, intending to follow the larger river to its source in the mountains and then continuing through the mountains to see what mysteries lay beyond them.

Chapter Eleven

On the morning of the fifth day, one of the Ghorn men woke at dawn to find a young deer drinking from the nearby stream. He quietly picked up his bow and loosed an arrow, and then the men had fresh meat for a few days. Generally they lived off the land and didn't have to resort to the dried meat for sustenance, but there were a few wistful murmurs about the quality of the food at the city and many more murmurs concerning the current total lack of female companionship.

On the whole, the trip was a pleasant one. And even though the fare was simple and the companionship somewhat lacking in warmth and tenderness, all were genuinely happy that they had come, for the time being.

The going was relatively easy for about fifteen days, all uphill but not too difficult for healthy young legs and backs. They passed from thick woods of familiar tall straight trees into vast groves of dark twisted trees with heavy branches and rough bark, the likes of which they had never seen before. As they climbed, always keeping within sight or hearing of the river, the men passed through quiet meadows of deep grass and many colored flowers.

Here they found abundant game to augment their supplies, and all ate well for many days.

Soon the trees gave way to stunted growth, and the meadows were less grassy and covered more with thick, spongy moss. Then the trees began to thin and the ground became rockier. The men were required to climb around several waterfalls where the river cascaded down steeper hillsides.

It was on one of those rocky climbs that the first of their many misfortunes befell them. One of the men stepped on a loose rock, which moved under his foot, and he fell into the river, breaking his leg in the fall. Lon and Hath jumped into the river and dragged him to safety before he drowned, but the party was now burdened with a member who was crippled and unable to travel.

The problem of what to do with him was resolved when two of the men, who were growing weary of the increasingly difficult trek, volunteered to carry the injured man back to a village they'd had passed two days before and stay with him while word could be sent back to their home for someone to come after them.

After much discussion, the men decided that was the best plan short of simply abandoning the injured man, which was not in their nature anyway. So they made a crude litter, and the trio started back down the hill.

The remainder of the group spent the night at the top of the falls, sheltered by an overhanging rock face, and then started up river in the morning.

For several days, the overall mood of the band was somewhat less cheerful than when they started, but soon youthful enthusiasm prevailed and all was well for a time.

One dark night, they camped in a small depression in the midst of an outcropping of rock that protected them from the chill winds, which seemed to have become their almost constant companions.

The horses were unloaded and hobbled downwind of the encampment. All of the band of men were sleeping soundly in their bedrolls around the sputtering fire when the stillness was torn by an unearthly scream of terror from the horses.

As they rolled from their blankets and groped for their swords, the men heard another terrible sound that mingled with the horse's fear-stricken screams. A heart-chilling roar came from no beast known to any of them and the unmistakable sound of chewing and breaking bones, as if some gigantic animal was actually eating the horses.

Being closest to the horses, Lon jumped to his feet and ran, sword in hand, around a huge rock then froze in his tracks from the awful sight before him. A monstrous gray bear, which bore only a slight resemblance to the brown bears he knew, stood nearly twice the height of the horses and had its massive jaws clamped on the neck of one horse. The bear was tearing the horse's head from its body with its foot long talons.

Jhor and Thon ran into Lon, jolting him from his semi-trance, as they bolted to see what was after the horses. They too were stunned into inactivity by the sight of the monstrous, shaggy gray bear eating the horse alive.

They were all quickly roused to attention when the bear turned his gigantic head in their direction and roared, dropping the now dead horse from its bloody jaws. At the bear's first step in their direction, the men split apart and attacked from all sides. It was not youthful bravado that prompted the attack, but rather simply the desire to live. They knew without discussion that they all couldn't escape that awesome beast, so fight they must, and fight they did. The others soon joined the three; and in just a few more seconds, the men were busy trying to keep the bear confused with the many sided attack so that it wouldn't know which way to turn.

As soon as the beast turned toward one of the men, one of the others would strike a mighty blow at its backside, causing it to turn again toward the new attacker. The flickering light of the campfire cast an eerie, nightmarish hue on the gory scene as the men hewed at the beast from all sides, inflicting what should have been mortal blows. The bear didn't appear to be even slightly weakened by the wounds, but seemed to gain strength as the blood flowed freely from the many deep cuts on its body and splashed on the combatants as they tried to avoid the slashing claws. Unfortunately, all the brave warriors were not agile enough to dart outside the reach of those swinging claws. The bear caught poor Hodar full in the chest, and he died before he even knew he was hurt. His partly disemboweled body was hurled ten paces by the force of the blow, and the bear seemed to pause momentarily as if trying to decide whether to pursue the kill.

That short pause was all the time the others needed. Five swords swung as one at the heavy gray neck, cutting deep through muscle and bone to sever vital arteries. The bear roared with pain and reared to its full height, then fell directly onto one of the men who was trying to free his sword, which had become stuck in the massive body.

Jhor and Thon leapt on the bear and thrust their swords with all their might into the exposed back, penetrating the heart and completing the kill. Then the group strained with all the energy they had left to roll the great carcass off their fallen companion. When the dead bear rolled clear, they saw with pained hearts that young Jan was dead. For with its last effort, the bear had clamped its great jaws shut, crushing Jan's blond head like a sparrows egg.

As they were sitting breathless about the steaming carcass of the dead bear, one of the less weary went to see what had happened to the other horse, which had torn free from its tether and bolted into the night. He returned with the unhappy news that the horse had run full tilt off a steep cliff and dashed itself to death on the rocks below.

The four survivors recovered the bodies of their two comrades and wrapped them in blankets, then huddled around the fire in stunned silence with their swords at hand until dawn lightened the skies. They were too shocked to talk about the events of the night.

When it was full light, the men silently buried their two comrades, and then took stock of the remaining supplies to decide what to take and what to leave behind. The thought of turning back may have entered their minds but it was never voiced, for that would have been an open admission of defeat and completely unacceptable to their way of thinking.

Their first idea was to skin the bear and use the thick pelt for blankets against the increasing cold. But if they'd carried that bulk, they would have had to leave more valuable cargo behind. So they butchered it and took the more tender portions for meat, because fresh meat was getting harder to find in these high places.

The travelers loaded what they could carry in backpacks and tried to put as much distance as possible between them and the gory scene before night fell. It was not so much sentiment as good common sense that prompted this action, for the dead animals would surely attract more predators, and they didn't want to be anywhere in the vicinity if another bear or a pack of wolves showed up to feast on the carrion.

That night they built a larger fire and posted watches, but still no one slept soundly. Many times during the night one of the men awakened at some slight noise and grasped at his sword, only to be reassured by the watch that all was well.

In the morning they pressed on along the river, which was now no more than a creek that they could easily wade across. Late that afternoon, one of them spotted some fish in a pool at a bend in the creek, and they spent some time there fishing. For the next few days they added fresh fish to the meager menu and their spirits rose greatly.

Soon, however, the creek became too small to support fish big enough to eat, and one afternoon the men found themselves faced with a dilemma. The creek disappeared in the middle of a marshy meadow, and it was impossible to tell where to pick it up on the other side.

Indeed, they found at least a dozen rivulets flowing into the meadow and had no other course but to follow the valley uphill and hope to find a pass to the other side of the mountains.

Nights were now bitter cold and it was more difficult to find wood for a fire. Every day found them less far along than the day before. The icy air was becoming thinner, making climbing more difficult and the supplies were getting low.

Some were beginning to think that they should at least go back far enough to find fresh meat before going on.

The youthful enthusiasm with which they'd begun their journey almost a hundred days ago had turned into grim determination to finish, no matter what the cost.

Their spirits had sagged one frosty morning as they breakfasted on dried meat, hard biscuits, and water, when Lon looked up and saw a small mountain goat peering at him around a rock. As he was about to whisper to the others, an arrow whistled past his head and struck the goat in the flank causing it to bolt and run.

Jhor swore at his own bad aim as all six leapt up and ran in pursuit of the wounded animal.

They chased and tracked the hapless goat for an hour before they found it where it had dragged itself under a rock ledge, half dead from loss of blood and exhaustion. Lon finished the goat off with his knife and carried the carcass back to their camp for careful butchering. The meat was somewhat tough but edible and lasted ten days in the freezing air and added much-needed variety and nutrition to the meals.

Four days after the last of the goat meat was gone, the weary travelers topped a stony ridge and found themselves looking down at a series of lower peaks and hills fading into the mists of distance. To their left were high, barren peaks that still towered over them, but to their right, northwest, was a beautiful vista of gradually receding valleys and ridges that showed inviting spots of greenery.

They crossed the ridge and camped that night in a rocky cleft sheltered from the wind, which whistled around their backs from across the ridge. The exhausted travelers set up a hasty camp and immediately fell asleep, blissfully released from the anxieties of the previous weeks, and completely unconcerned about setting a guard.

Lon slept a troubled sleep that night and woke before dawn with a roaring headache and a deep pain in his chest. When he tried to sit up, he felt as if all the muscles of his back and shoulders had atrophied and would not respond. He felt cold and hot all over at the same time; and when he tried to move his head, his stomach churned violently.

He crawled to where Jhor was sleeping and awakened him with a shake. It didn't take long for Jhor to tell what was wrong with his half-brother.

He'd seen many people die from the effects of the damp foggy air of the forests, and he now saw the same symptoms in Lon.

He woke the others with a shout, and a fire was quickly built in the lee of the rock. They wrapped Lon in all the heavy blankets they had and brewed strong soup with the few provisions that remained. Jhor tenderly fed Lon the soup only to have him throw up everything as coughs and convulsions wracked his body.

As soon as it was light enough to move on, they made a litter of their lances and blankets. Hath and Thon picked up their heavily bundled friend, and the party set out down the slope hoping to find aid for their stricken companion.

For three days the men took turns carrying Lon while he appeared to grow weaker and soon even stopped protesting at being carried like a baby. They were all becoming gravely concerned about Lon who had slipped into a deep sleep and, except for an occasional moan, appeared almost dead.

On the fourth day, they topped a rocky rise and saw an old stone tower protruding from behind the next rise. They hurried on and soon came upon an ancient gray stone temple sitting on a rocky crag just ahead of them. Their hearts leapt as they realized that there were people around the temple.

They carefully lifted Lon's deathlike form, and the weary band started down the slope toward the temple.

For more than two years, Lisha had lived among the old priests and prophets in the bleak temple without a visitor to break her solitude. Not that her family hadn't tried to visit her to persuade her to give up this seemingly foolish activity. Her father had pleaded with the gods to give him some reason for her actions, but all he did was in vain.

For some unknown reason, the gods had, as it seemed, shut their ears to Shallim and his pleas. He'd turned over almost all of his duties to the other wizards. They too were frustrated in their attempts to discover what dark secret had driven Lisha from her home to the cold confines of the old temple.

She had refused to see any of her visitors, even though she loved her family and missed them very much. Lisha knew that, although the future held great trials for her, there was little she could really do to stop the plans of the gods, and she would be hard pressed to resist the pleadings of her loved ones. When her father did visit occasionally, she hid herself in the tower and refused to unlock the door for fear she would weaken in her resolve and return home to the beautiful palace of her birth.

During one of these visits, which were becoming harder to stay away from, Lisha had remained locked in the tower long after her downcast father had left the temple. Her young heart threatened to break within her as she lay sobbing on the cold wooden bench.

She turned to the narrow window and with tears pouring from her eyes she flung open the shutters to throw herself to the rocks below and end her misery in the only way she could think of to thwart the terrible fate that awaited her. As she stood in the open window trying to gather the nerve to jump to her death, she looked up toward the rocky pass high above her in the mountains and, to her amazement, saw what appeared to be a group of men struggling down the rocky slope toward the temple.

She stepped back, and rubbed the tears from her eyes and looked again with the same result.

There were four or five men and they appeared to be carrying something large, about the size of a man. She realized as they drew closer that they were in fact carrying another man wrapped in blankets on a crude litter.

Forgetting her former deadly purpose, she rushed from the tower and alerted the old men of the approaching group. A few of the men ran to assist the strangers, and soon all were inside what meager shelter the temple could offer.

Lisha was taken aback by the great size of these men, all of whom appeared to be little older than herself. The two who were carrying their companion, who appeared near death, refused to set him down until they were assured he would be well cared for. Soon they were warming themselves around a roaring fire while the priests ministered to the sick one, whom they called Lon.

Lisha went to the kitchen and dipped a large bowl from the ever-present pot of soup simmering on the fire, and took it to the room where Lon lay. Tenderly she raised his young head and carefully dripped the warm broth into his limp mouth. At first he seemed too weak even to swallow and gagged slightly on the soup, then swallowed a little, and then a little more.

One of the priests brought some herbs and a strong potion with great healing powers, which they made from the roots of a rare plant that grew only in the rocky crags. They managed to get Lon to take the potion and keep it down. Lisha continued to feed him the soup, and soon he started to regain some of his color and no longer appeared as if he was on death's doorstep.

For three days Lisha sat at Lon's bedside, patiently feeding him and tenderly wiping his fevered brow with cool cloths. The priests brought food to her several times a day to help her keep her own strength up. And when she dozed, it was always at the side of Lon's bed.

The priests hadn't seen Lisha this active in all the time she'd been with them, and they were more than happy to see her with some purpose in her young life.

Lon's companions were firmly shooed from the room whenever they tried to come near him and soon, with the assurance that their friend was receiving far better care than they could give him, they left him in the capable hands of his beautiful nurse.

While they waited and watched, they told their tale to the old priests and prophets who were amazed by the adventures the band had been through in so short a time.

The men of Shanar had heard tales of other peoples from beyond the mountains, but that was their first contact with anyone other than their own kind.

A messenger was sent to the palace to advise the emperor of the visitors, and soon a delegation arrived to welcome the men from over the mountains. During their conversations, Hath let slip that Jhor was the ruler of the Ghorn and the sick man was his brother. The priests hurriedly sent more messengers to the palace to prepare a welcome and feasts worthy of a royal guest.

At first Jhor refused to leave, for Lon was still too ill to be moved, and he would not leave his brother behind. Shallim himself assured Jhor that the best of the royal physicians couldn't give Lon better care than he was already receiving. When he found out that Lon's nurse was the daughter of the emperor, Jhor agreed to leave the temple on the condition that he be kept advised of his brother's condition.

Lisha was totally unaware of the activities in the temple hall, for she'd become absorbed in the care of the beautiful young man that had been dropped into her life from nowhere. The dire prophecy was pushed completely out of her mind by the ever-increasing attachment she felt for Lon as he lay helpless on the crude cot.

After many days of constant care, it became apparent that Lon would recover. Soon he was sitting up in bed long enough to eat without being fed by someone else. Only then did Lisha leave his side during the night, returning in the morning to sit with him and minister to him.

During those nights, however, the memory of the prophecy came back to her, and she became sadder and more miserable than before, for now she realized she was falling in love with Lon and the hated prophecy loomed ever closer to reality.

As Lon recovered, he too realized that his feelings for his nurse were more than gratitude, and this helped his will to live grow stronger with each passing day. The moments when they were apart seemed an eternity to Lon, and he couldn't wait for the tender touch of her hand on his cheek each morning.

The old priests became aware of Lon and Lisha's feelings for each other, and they welcomed the change in their young ward's disposition. But they saw only a young girl in love during the day and did not see the heartbroken tears as she cried herself to sleep each night.

For she knew she was completely in love with Lon and, having loved him, could never bear to live without him. She also knew that such a love was doomed to end too soon, and the knowledge tore her apart.

Reason and logic have no power against love and eventually love wins. In spite of all else, love conquers.

Her fear of the prophecy and the resolve never to wed had almost won out over her love. But one morning Lon took a sudden turn for the worse, and she laid by his feverish body crying for two days while praying to the gods as she cared for him as well as she possibly could.

Then the fever broke and Lon awoke to find her lying asleep at his side with her hand against his cheek. He turned his head and kissed that hand and she awoke with a start, then threw her arms around his neck and proclaimed her eternal love for him. They lay side by side, just barely touching, for several minutes without saying a word.

Fortunately for them, no one interrupted the scene, for the priests might have misunderstood what they would have seen. They couldn't have comprehended a love so deep that the merest touch was all that was necessary for pure ecstasy.

Soon Jhor and the rest of their band returned to find Lon well along the road to recovery. He was able to get up and feed and dress himself, but he was still far too weak to make the trip back to Ghorn. Jhor felt it was time for him to return to his duties, but he was reluctant to leave Lon behind, even in such good hands.

Shallim suggested sending along a well-stocked caravan so there would be no shortage of supplies and Hath and Thon agreed to stay with Lon while Jhor and the others went back to Ghorn. One of the wise men suggested sending a large work party as well to clearly mark the trail and improve the route to make it easier for future travelers, as it appeared there would be many more trips over the pass in the near future.

There was still much good weather before the frosts set in, so a party was quickly assembled. They set forth from Shanar to Ghorn to complete the job of clearing the trail while the weather was on their side.

Chapter Twelve

When Lon was well enough, he and Lisha were escorted back to the Palace of Light, and Lon was given a royal suite near Lisha's rooms.

Lon and Lisha spent virtually every waking hour together, and it was apparent to everyone that there would soon be another royal wedding, this time uniting much more than just two families. Mihar and Irini gloried in the preparations for the wedding long before either Lon or Lisha said anything about it.

The women knew that no power on earth could stop the natural course of love, after all, they were women, and women know such things.

By the time the frosts had cleared from the mountain pass, Lon had fully recovered and preparations were complete for his wedding to Lisha, except for the return of the party from Ghorn. Everyone in Shanar was happily abuzz with the excitement of the forthcoming wedding.

Everyone, that is, except for a beautiful young princess who still occasionally cried herself to sleep in the privacy of her rooms, and an old recluse of a wizard who lived in the dreary basement rooms of the old temple.

Lisha had confided her fears to him in the earliest days of her stay in the temple and had elicited a promise from him to never tell anyone of the prophecy. While he had not broken his promise, he'd looked into the future for himself and, already knowing in part what he was looking for, was able to see the whole picture. He used methods frowned upon by the younger wizards and went deeper into the future to see other things that confused and frightened him.

What he saw was a great conflict between good and evil that could result in nothing else but the end of the world.

For years this old man had been recording all the old spells and incantations on plates of the purest gold, which would last through countless years of time. Now he increased the pace of his efforts, because he felt there may not be much time left, for him or for the world as he knew it.

With tools of the hardest metals, he inscribed onto those golden plates the wisdom of the ages. As each plate was completed, he carefully wrapped it in thick leather and placed it in an old crypt deep in a cave behind the temple once intended as the last resting place of some long forgotten priest or wizard. When the last of the plates was complete, the old man placed it in the crypt, crawled in with it, and died.

Meanwhile in the Palace of Light, all was in readiness for the great wedding. Jhor and his family had arrived from Ghorn with an even larger caravan than the one that had departed before the frosts. The two families exchanged many wondrous gifts.

Jhor and his cousins had agreed never to tell the Shanar that Lon was actually the son of a slave, and Jhor had declared to his people that Lon was in fact his full brother and joint heir to the throne. None dared question him and, as Lon was as beloved by the people as was Jhor, no one wanted to.

There was some slight disagreement as to where the wedding would take place, but the women won their way and treated the people of Shanar to a wedding and feast that put all others before it to shame.

Lon and Lisha spent a strangely quiet time together after the wedding. Lon decided it was simply due to a young girl's shyness and waited patiently for the mood to pass. He had only once asked what she'd been doing in the lonely temple, and her response was evasive enough to let Lon know that it was not a matter to bring up again for some time.

After the feasting had died down, the new royal family set out for their new home in Ghorn amid motherly tears and fervent good wishes. Naturally, upon their arrival in Jhor's capital city of Ghorn, the party started all over again and lasted many gloriously happy days.

Those who could not accompany the wedding party to Shanar had decided to present their king's brother with a worthy gift, and as soon as word came that he was leaving Shanar for home, construction began on a new home for Lon and his bride on a hill at the edge of the city overlooking the entire realm.

It was truly a royal residence. All the skills of the best artisans had gone into the magnificent palace, which was the first and finest of its kind in Ghorn.

As an additional wedding present, Jhor appointed Lon his second in command and made him leader of the army with complete control of the forts and stockades. Hath and Thon, still resisting any form of responsibility, were given their choice of jobs and chose simply to serve under Lon as he saw fit. He gave them important sounding duties with little or no work involved and everyone was happy, or so it seemed.

While Lon and Lisha were deeply in love, their relationship was clouded by her refusal to have children. Lon was as understanding as a husband could be, but he still couldn't accept her refusal to give him a reason.

Three years passed and trade grew between the Ghorn and the Shanar, as well as with the Yaq and Gwundi through the now prosperous plains where people were no longer nomads, but settled in a growing city by the southern river.

Meanwhile, Jhor had taken a beautiful girl as mate and soon they had two lovely daughters who were the pride of all Ghorn.

Finally, Lon's pleadings broke down Lisha's resistance and, in spite of her worst fears of doom, she agreed to a child. It was not long before a new babe was born into the royal family: a wrinkled, red-faced butterball named Hald, who, in spite of Lisha's fears, his mother loved very much.

But the emotional strain of the fears and the physical trauma of the birth were too much for Lisha. A few days after her son was born, she lapsed into a coma from which she would not recover. A scant twenty days after Hald's birth, his young mother slipped peacefully from her coma into that deeper sleep from which there is no return.

Lon grieved as no one had seen before in that land where death was an old and familiar enemy. He blamed himself for demanding a child and no amount of reasoning from his brother or their many friends consoled him.

Hald was taken in and raised by Jhor's woman, Arella, who loved him almost as much as she did her own daughters.

Hald grew in the overprotective shadow of Lon's mighty arms. His father tried to make up for the loss of his beloved Lisha by spoiling him rotten.

All attempts by Lon's family, however sincere, to warn him of his excesses with the boy were met with increasingly bitter responses. Finally, Lon took Hald and moved into the fort by the mines where he raised his son in his own way, wrong though it might have been.

The current queen of the Gwundi was M'bili, who some said was actually the reincarnation of the ancient Janga whose spirit lived on eternally in the bodies of successive queens. Most of her people looked on M'bili as more of a mother than a witch, and most men among the Gwundi would have given their lives for her.

The two greatest sorrows in her life were at the same time her most deeply loved treasures: her twin granddaughters, Gabela and Gisela. It had been M'bili's wish, as was the custom, to step down as queen and turn over the throne to her daughter, the twin's mother, Jarana, when she reached adulthood and was ready to take the role as high priestess and queen.

Both Gabela and Gisela had been large babies, and the strain of childbirth had been just too much for the young mother to bear. Jarana died two days after giving birth without ever seeing her daughters.

M'bili had no other daughters to succeed her, and she had long since passed the age when she wanted to consider the possibility of having another child, even if it were still physically possible.

So she'd chosen to reign until the girls grew to womanhood and wait until then to decide which of them would take her place as queen.

However, as the girls grew older, M'bili realized that both could reign: Gisela as high priestess and Gabela as queen. For Gisela seemed to have inherited all the combined magical powers of her ancestors and had developed an almost friendly relationship with the fearsome god thing that dwelt in the caves behind the temple. She spent the greater part of each day in meditation or practicing her magical skills, which were awesome.

Gabela had other ideas. Although she possessed an unnaturally strong natural talent for the witchery arts, her greatest desire was not to reign as monarch, but to lead the Gwundi warriors in battle or to explore the unknown lands beyond the jungle.

Each morning the queen would watch as her granddaughters were dressed in regal finery by their handmaidens. And almost daily, Gabela would make her way to the camps of the warriors and return to the palace at day's end with her fine clothes torn and dirty and, more often than not, with a black eye, a split lip, or a bloody nose gained in friendly combat with the younger warriors.

By the time she was eighteen, Gabela acted less feminine than many of the warriors and could best all but the strongest in less than playful combat. Many a warrior found himself flat on his back for days while he recovered from injuries received from Gabela's not too dainty hands.

Fortunately, while she was as tall and strong as fully half the men in the warrior's camps were, she was endowed with more than an average share of womanly charms. In the jungle around the temple city, her charms were discussed by the young men as much as her prowess as a warrior maiden.

Many young men dreamed longingly of her abundant charms and wished he had the nerve to take her in his arms and make a real woman out of her. But none of them interested Gabela enough for her to acknowledge their tentative advances, and she and her grandmother both were beginning to wonder if she were doomed to be an old maid.

Gisela, in contrast, had already become much more adept at communication with their god than any of her predecessors had, and she'd almost completely taken charge of the temple worship. She was fully as tall as her sister was but lacked her muscular definition. Gisela had a beauty that was far more ethereal and stately than her sister's.

As M'bili sat on her carved throne reflecting on what the future held in store for her granddaughters, the ill-fated settlers on the plains were just beginning to gather their remaining possessions in preparation for their return to their city.

It took the survivors three days to round up their scattered livestock, then three more days to load the remaining belongings into the wagons and make ready to leave for home. Part of the delay was because the priestesses had at first refused to help with what they considered to be menial labor. But when it became apparent that without their help absolutely nothing would get done, they doffed their ceremonial robes and pitched in with the rest.

Yoki's braves had taken all the weapons and most of the golden religious artifacts, leaving the settlers physically and magically helpless. Fifty mounted and heavily armed Yaq warriors watching them from the nearby hills spurred their eventual haste in preparing to leave. When all were finally ready, the downhearted settlers began the long trek back into the jungle to the city by the great waterfall where they guessed their reception would not be a happy one.

The priestesses at last stood, shame faced and somewhat the worse for wear, before the queen. M'bili's first impulse was to declare war and march against the plains tribes. However, when her granddaughters reminded the queen that she had originally opposed the attempt to settle the plains, and when the priestesses described the size and strength of the army the Yaq had been able to raise in just three days, she reconsidered.

M'bili also recalled that she had predicted failure for the venture and had only allowed the settlers to go because of the impassioned pleading of Gabela, who'd hoped to accompany, if not lead, the party.

M'bili strongly scolded the priestesses for allowing the destruction of the settlement and especially for surrendering the golden temple artifacts to the plains "savages." She then called a council of all the priestesses and generals to decide what, if anything, to do about the Yaq.

Queen M'bili was generally inclined to send emissaries to Yoki with peace offerings and a mild apology, along with a polite but strongly worded request for the return of their holy artifacts. Gisela, the priestesses and most of the generals agreed, for the settlers had, even if unknowingly, trespassed on Yaq territory and the Gwundi would probably have reacted in much the same fashion to a seeming invasion of the jungles.

One grizzled old warrior disagreed and was very vocal in his demands that the Yaq be slaughtered to the last man, woman, and child for this abomination committed against their awesome gods and their fair priestesses. He loudly argued that he be allowed to lead such a punitive expedition against the Yaq for defying their gods and defiling their priestesses.

When the queen disagreed with him and politely pointed out that his opinion was in the minority—in fact, he was the only one who felt as he did—the old general apparently forgot his relative position in society and started to vigorously argue his point.

M'bili glared down at him from the throne without comment, and everyone in the great hall wondered at her unusual restraint until the watchers realized that the argumentative general was visibly shrinking in stature. It appeared that the louder his arguments, the faster he shrank.

When his rapidly diminishing physical condition finally became apparent to the general, he quickly silenced his protests, threw himself face down on the floor in front of the throne, and begged for the queen's forgiveness and mercy. She easily forgave his trespass but, as a reminder to all present of her unquestionable authority and her frightening power, left him in his greatly shortened condition.

The dwarflike general excused himself from the royal presence and hurried from the hall, somewhat hampered by his clothes and armor, which had retained their original size and shape. The spectacle of an old man the size of a child dragging a sword as long as he was tall, his helmet down over his ears, and with his trousers and cloak tangling his feet as they dragged on the polished wooden floor, brought no chuckles from the assembly. They knew all too well that it could as easily have been the fate of any one of them and might still be at some future date; so all kept silent and avoided as much as a glance at the retreating figure.

After many tedious hours of debate on the relative merits and drawbacks of several suggestions, M'bili settled on her original idea to send a delegation of priestesses with a lightly armed escort on a mission of peace.

Recalling how vigorously Gabela had pleaded to go with the original expedition, M'bili placed her in charge of the peace delegation with explicit orders not to provoke the Yaq chieftain and to bring back as much information as she could about him and his people.

Gabela started to protest at what she thought was seemingly menial task for the heir to the throne, but just at that time, the diminutive general returned to retrieve some of the armor he'd not been able to carry when he left in haste. One look at him was enough to convince Gabela that she had best not overtax her grandmother's already short temper and she agreed to go.

M'bili then called the tiny general before her and ordered him to lead the escort, with the promise that if the mission returned successfully, he would be returned to his original stature. If he really distinguished himself in some manner, she added, she might be moved to give him a little extra stature and add a few years onto his already long life.

M'bili also had in mind that the general's appearance would serve as graphic warning to the Yaq of what she could do if provoked to anger.

Gabela, a score of priestesses, and the little general left the palace to prepare the caravan that would carry the young princess to a meeting that would greatly alter her life and ultimately affect the future of the world.

Chapter Thirteen

For six generations, M'gori had been building his kingdom on the high plateau above the cliffs. At first glance he appeared to be about thirty years old and only a hard look into his eyes gave any indication that he was in fact an old man. Generations of his followers had been born and died and M'gori still lived, growing more powerful each passing day.

Twice each year he repeated the sacrifice and grisly meal that kept him eternally young; and twice each year another ripple of fear swept through the jungles from above. Countless others had been sacrificed to the evil gods of M'gori and his priestess in revolting ceremonies that are best left undescribed.

Several generations of inbreeding among M'gori's followers had produced some horrible mutations. They kept many of those offspring alive, bred, and crossbred them to produce even more revolting monstrosities. M'gori kept those inhuman things under control almost as pets to enforce discipline on any who strayed from his will.

The still young priestess occasionally retreated to her private caves where she even forbid M'gori to enter, and conducted mysterious rites unknown to any of her followers. Most of those rites were simply conferences with the other Daemoz; but on many of those days, she practiced rituals unknown on earth and tried desperately to increase her personal power over the other Daemoz to eventually gain enough strength to rule over them all and possibly even to challenge the master.

M'gori was jealous of the priestess and fed up with her open contempt for him. He sought ways to rid himself of her so that he could deal directly with the gods she represented.

For years he pleaded to the gods to communicate directly with him; and for years he was frustrated, until one day during one of his more and more frequent arguments with the young priestess she inadvertently revealed her plans to him in a fit of rage.

M'gori seized upon the opportunity and that night, in the dark recesses of his caves, he brutally sacrificed ten young children in an attempt to gain the attention and questionable favor of the evil gods. To his eternal dismay, he gained the attention of the one being whom he should not have disturbed.

Chataan itself visited M'gori, not in the flesh, for it had no flesh and no restrictions of form and substance. The evil presence of Chataan suddenly filled M'gori's cave, and he quietly fainted from stark terror.

M'gori awoke in violent convulsions over the thought of what he'd done, and an unholy laugh seemed to rattle through the air of the cave.

A soft, mocking voice inside his head told him how he would be required to serve his new master, and even M'gori was revolted by what he heard. He tried to flee from the cave but felt himself rooted to the floor as if he were a tree. He listened in terror as the evil presence communicated its wishes to him. The most disgusting rituals M'gori had been able to imagine were child's play compared to what Chataan told him to do. He tried desperately to find a way out of his predicament, but when he begged the evil presence surrounding him to let him go and live as before, he felt his life drain out of him.

The unseen grip that held M'gori motionless released him, and M'gori collapsed in a heap. He suddenly began gyrating about the floor of the cave in awful convulsions, emptying his bowels and bladder involuntarily as he trashed about in the dirt. Blood spurted from every orifice in his body, and his mind contorted in agony from hallucinations of fearsome monsters.

For what seemed like hours, M'gori was subjected to the most awful punishment ever inflicted on any man. And when it finally subsided, he lay sobbing in his own filth until Chataan jerked him upright and softly inquired how he would like to spend eternity in that state.

M'gori fainted again at the mere thought of it.

When he awakened, the presence was gone, but the memory of that ordeal kept M'gori awake for many nights.

The young priestess had mysteriously vanished during the night and was never seen again on earth or spoken of by any of M'gori's followers. M'gori was no longer the strong leader of his people, but merely a frightened puppet whose invisible strings extended beyond the limits of space and time.

Yokagi had not yet been dead sixty days, but in that short time Yoki used all the abilities at his command, as well as those of his uncle, Kana, to keep the Yaq nation intact. The difficult task might well have been impossible if not for two extraordinary events: the young warrior's transformation on the hilltop, which was apparent to all, and the taking up of Yokagi's body by the gods of thunder, which more than two thousand amassed warriors from more than twenty Yaq villages witnessed.

Now another problem had come up to plague the young chief. His scouts reported that another party of Gwundi was approaching across the plain. But this time the band consisted of mostly female priestesses with an escort of just a few lightly armed warriors. Yoki began issuing orders to prepare a force to ride out and meet the Gwundi with a heavily armed band of warriors, but Kana persuaded Yoki to stay behind and receive the Gwundi in a manner befitting a Great War Chief.

Kana then proposed that Yoki let him lead a smaller party to meet the Gwundi on the open plain and determine what they wanted. Then, if their motives were peaceful, he would lead them into the Yaq village to meet Yoki. Kana reasoned that if they wanted to make trouble, they would have come with all the troops they could muster and that this may very well be a peaceful mission.

After putting up a feeble argument, Yoki admitted the logic and wisdom of his uncle's reasoning and relented.

Soon Kana left the sprawling city with a small band of but a dozen warriors, flanked by two larger groups riding just out of sight but within easy call, just in case of trickery.

Yoki spent the next nine days pacing in nervous frustration, and several times each day he started to form a war party to go see what was happening with his uncle and the Gwundi.

On the tenth morning, when he felt he could no longer stand the wait and was about to muster the entire city to go after Kana, a rider came with the word from Kana that the Yaq party would return before midday and for Yoki to prepare to receive a Gwundi peace mission.

Yoki's first impulse was to ride out to meet them with the entire Yaq army to impress them with a show of might, but the older and wiser warriors persuaded him to wait in the city and meet the Gwundi on his own ground. Yoki agreed with their advice and went to his tent where he dressed in his most splendid war regalia, complete with the scarred and worn bear helmet, which was all the gods had left him of his father's impressive cloak. He then reconsidered and stripped to a simple leather loincloth and breastplate, which impressively exhibited his muscular body.

When Kana and the Gwundi reached the Yaq city, Yoki stepped out into the midday sunlight and stood proudly in front of his tent, awaiting the arrival of the Gwundi.

Kana, in his wisdom, had made the Gwundi, especially the priestesses, dismount from their wagons and walk into the city to spare the Yaq people the indignity of having to look up to the Gwundi as they rode through the city. Besides, having to walk up the dusty central street of the city past the openly hostile eyes of the Yaq people would make the Gwundi uneasy and give Yoki a decided edge, as well as to put the haughty priestesses in their place.

Yoki's tent stood on a rise at the end of the street, which helped add to his already impressive appearance and left the priestesses and their followers slightly out of breath and at a great disadvantage for their first meeting with the Yaq war chief.

As he watched the Gwundi approach, the cat like grace and easy stride of the warrior leading the party impressed Yoki. While all the priestesses and most of the warrior escorts seemed almost to drag as they walked up the dusty street, this warrior strode with his feathered head high and proud at the head of the column actually forcing Kana to trot his horse to keep up. Then a ludicrous dwarf of a warrior almost running to stay apace of the rest drew Yoki's attention. But the dwarf was dressed as a leader rather than as a clown.

When he returned his gaze to the proud warrior, Yoki realized with a shock that this was not a man, but a woman. And such a woman! Nearly as tall as himself with rippling muscles sweating slightly in the midday heat, adding a sheen to an almost perfect body and with a beauty of face that momentarily took his breath away.

Unlike the other women, she wore no ceremonial dress, just a loincloth and bodice of soft leather that displayed her figure at its finest. She wore her long black hair pulled back and tied like the tail of a horse with white Eagle feathers tied in her hair like a halo. Around her neck she wore a necklace made of the claws of the jungle cats on a leather thong, but no other adornments.

Gabela had spent most of the long journey steeling herself to meet the Yaq chieftain and was now mentally rehearsing her formal speech of greeting. She had expected to find a grizzled old fool of a warrior surrounded by lesser chiefs and such. But as she walked up the street, she saw in front of what was obviously the tent of the chief a lone figure, not in elaborate war dress but a simple loincloth and breastplate with a striking great bear's head helmet.

As she approached, the figure seemed to grow taller and more massive with each step. And when finally she was close enough to see his features, Gabela completely forgot her speech and almost the whole purpose of the mission.

This was a man!

He was a man such as she had dreamed of as a young girl but had never been able to find as a woman and had almost given up hope of ever finding.

Gabela stopped a few paces away from this heroic figure of a chief, and for several minutes they simply stood staring into each other's faces. Yoki suddenly realized that he should say something impressive in greeting, but somehow he couldn't utter a sound. He cleared his throat noisily and blurted, "Uh, hello."

"Uh, hello," Gabela echoed, lacking the inspiration to say anything else at the time.

Hearing a strange noise at his side, Yoki turned to see Kana, who was almost choking with the effort to keep from laughing out loud. "Great War Chief of the Yaq," Kana proclaimed with a wide grin. "Son of the Great War Chief Yokagi and blessed of the thunder gods, I bring you Gabela, princess of the Gwundi, with offerings of peace and friendship."

Yoki and Gabela quickly snapped out of their stupor and made their speeches of greeting. Soon the Yaq elders and the Gwundi priestesses were deeply involved in peace and trade negotiations in the old village meeting house, which still served as the religious and political heart of the spreading city.

The negotiations dragged on well into the night with the Gwundi at first demanding, then requesting, and then finally pleading for the return of their golden temple artifacts. The Yaq bargainers held out and refused to return the golden trinkets, as they called them to the outrage of the priestesses, unless they received a large quantity of the strange weapons the Gwundi had used against them in their first unhappy encounter. Yoki had no use for the gold as such but dearly wanted to get his hands on more of those bows and arrows. The gold gave him a good bargaining tool.

Finally they worked out an agreement to the satisfaction of both groups, and the parlay broke long after dark. The Gwundi party lodged in a group of tents near the center of the city where posted guards could watch them, and then the city settled down for the night.

The negotiations continued for three more days. The parties discussed and finally rejected or approved many trade agreements. The details of those agreements are tedious and boring and of interest only to those who were required to implement them.

After the completion of the negotiations and the agreement to treaties by both leaders, Yoki declared a feast to celebrate the joining of two peoples in peace and friendship. This feast was required by Yaq tradition to last longer than the talks had taken, and the Gwundi were subsequently introduced to many new delights, including the fermented cactus drink, which when consumed in large quantities had the strange effect of completely removing one's memory and inhibitions before rendering one unconscious.

At one point during the festivities, Yoki and Gabela found themselves alone in his tent and they discovered that they had much more in common than most people might have thought.

As they parted, Gabela took off the claw necklace and handed it to Yoki as a remembrance of their meeting and a symbol of lasting friendship. Yoki then gave her a small ceremonial knife that his father had received from the head of a conquered tribe years before. It had a beautifully carved bone handle and a leather sheath decorated with beads and gems.

The following day when the Gwundi made ready to begin their journey back to the city in the jungle, Yoki stood in all his ceremonial finery in front of his tent as the Gwundi rode through the city. Gabela stood straight and tall in her ox drawn wagon, and as she passed Yoki's tent, she turned her head slightly in his direction and the corners of her mouth turned up in an irrepressible smile. Gabela stood tall only by her personal inner strength, for the cactus drink had taken its toll on all of the Gwundi, and they were experiencing the first hangovers in the long history of their people. A few of the men had overindulged and actually had to be carried to the wagons because they were unable to stand unaided. The slightest movement seemed to churn their insides in a most unpleasant fashion.

It was well for the Gwundi pride that they traveled in covered wagons, for they wouldn't have wanted anyone, much less the Yaq, to see them in their present condition.

Then all the Gwundi were gone and life in the Yaq city returned to near normal.

ᝈ᠀Chapter Fourteenᝈ᠀

A s soon as Gabela's wagon was out of sight of the city, she stepped down from the front platform and seated herself as comfortably as she could under the woven roof for the journey back home.

To the surprise of the Gwundi, none of them died from the after effects of the drinking. And by the time the caravan reached their home city, all had recovered sufficiently to swear never to do it again. All agreed not to mention that aspect of their journey to anyone, especially the queen, for even a few of the priestesses had been overcome by the drink and had cast aside their robes in the tents of young warriors.

While Yoki clearly displayed his impatience while waiting for Kana to return with the Gwundi party, M'bili did not show the slightest amount of concern for her granddaughter and appeared to have forgotten the expedition completely. But in her heart she had an unexplainable queasy feeling that something was dreadfully wrong, and by the time her granddaughter returned it was all she could do to remain externally calm.

M'bili and Gisela received the priestesses in the royal hall; and as Gabela strode toward the throne, she sensed that her life was already radically changed and would never be the same. For her occult senses told her that already a new life was beginning deep within her and that one day she would bear the child who would solidify the union of two great races.

Gabela's eyes met Gisela's, and she saw the questioning look of concern on her sister's face. That look was instantly replaced with one of surprise when Gisela dropped her gaze to Gabela's stomach, and then nodded slightly in approval. That action left no doubt in Gabela's mind that her twin was aware of the life within her and that she shared her sister's happiness.

None of this byplay was lost on M'bili, as she too was aware of the young girl's secret. For as soon as Gabela had appeared in the doorway to the throne room, M'bili had sensed a great change in her and sent a questing spirit undetected into her granddaughter's body. By the time Gabela had taken ten steps into the room, M'bili knew more about her condition than the young woman did.

M'bili decided that this would be a good opportunity to remind the girls that, while she may be old and somewhat tired of ruling the Gwundi, she was still the greatest power in the realm, and so she surprised both girls with her greeting.

"Greetings to you, granddaughter," she stated solemnly. "And greetings also to you great granddaughter," she added with a smirk. "I see; Gabela, that you have gained much by your encounter with the Yaq."

Gabela blushed furiously and dropped her head as her sister gasped at their grandmother's remark. M'bili smiled warmly and stretched out her arms to the red-faced girl. "Come, sit by my side and tell me of your adventures."

Gabela hesitated briefly, and then joined M'bili and Gisela on the dais.

M'bili dismissed the priestesses and escort, and then Gabela began to recount all that transpired since she'd left, even including the unfortunate encounters with the Yaq's fermented cactus drink.

The three women spent several more hours discussing the peace treaty and trade agreements negotiated with the Yaq. M'bili and Gisela both agreed that Gabela had made the most of a bad situation and achieved not only the return of the temple implements, but also a workable trade policy that could greatly benefit them during the coming years.

As M'bili listened to her granddaughters earnestly discussing the finer points of the treaties, she realized that the time had come for her to step down and relinquish the leadership of the people to the young women with no reservations about their abilities. She gradually withdrew from the conversation and, without their even realizing it, let the two young women completely take over.

While she sat in silence, M'bili searched Gabela's mind and heart and found to her pleasure that Gabela had gained compassion, the only thing she'd lacked to make her a good ruler. Her encounter with Yoki had been more than just a temporary, pleasant physical relationship, and Gabela had, for the first time in her young life, found what it meant to want to please someone else more than herself. While Gabela's romantic liaison with Yoki may not have been the best course of action, the resultant benefits far outweighed the drawbacks.

Motherhood was probably just what she needed to complete her education and give her the insight to be a good queen.

For many long days, M'bili prepared the two girls for their new roles: Gisela as high priestess and Gabela as queen. Both were completely satisfied with this arrangement, although Gabela had some reservations about taking the throne just as her condition was becoming apparent to all.

M'bili put off any further delays in her retirement when one morning she picked up her ancient yellow cat, who some jokingly suggested was the only thing in the city older than M'bili herself, and walked out of the temple, through the city, and into the jungle. She was last seen heading in the direction of Janga's caves, which merely added fuel to the rumored speculation that she actually was a reincarnation of that legendary queen.

When the time came for Gabela's child to be delivered, she was assisted in childbirth by the priestesses, but not by her sister. Gisela had gone deep into the caves behind the temple to plead with the gods for blessings upon the child.

Unknown to Gisela, M'bili was also entreating the gods on behalf of the baby, but in an entirely different manner. M'bili had been uneasy about the future for some time because of many dreams of death and destruction. She knew that only the old gods could prevent her dreams from coming true.

Deep within Janga's caves were secret shrines and altars unknown to any but a select few queens.

Here M'bili prepared grisly sacrifices of both man and beast, and other things not of this earth, to the ancient fearsome gods.

It is best to leave the details of those rites undescribed, for the mind of man can stand only so much without breaking when subjected to such horrors. Suffice it to say that what transpired that night even sickened M'bili, and she never fully recovered physically from the ordeal.

Before the child was born, both mother and aunt were frightfully aware that this was to be no ordinary child, even for a Gwundi witch. For, unknown to M'bili and hidden even from her awesome powers, Gisela and Gabela had discovered a supernatural link with the as yet unborn child while it was still developing in its mother's womb.

Finally, Gabela gave birth to a beautiful baby girl, proving that M'bili's vision had been accurate. Soon both Gabela and Gisela were holding strange mental conversations with the baby, which often awed and sometimes frightened them when they considered the stupendous power of the mind they encountered in the tiny body.

This was Mibara.

Rollo grew to be a fine young man with his father's size, strength, and leadership ability, and his mother's good looks and common sense to temper his intelligence. He also had some of the talents that had caused his ancestors to be driven from their homes.

Rollo had the ability, as his father had, to resist spells and curses cast at him by even the most powerful witch or sorcerer, and some unknown trait in his mother had actually strengthened this ability instead of weakening it, which usually happened when mutants bred with normal people. He also discovered that if he concentrated he could impress his will on some weaker-minded people. Not enough to control their minds, but enough to influence their ideas and decisions on occasion.

Animals were a different story altogether. With little effort he could control the actions of virtually all of the smaller animals and strongly influence the larger, more intelligent creatures. Although he rarely used most of his abilities, this talent came to be of great use for hunting and fishing. Later in his life, Rollo used this power in less pleasant circumstances.

As Rollo grew into manhood, it became apparent to all that he would take Rhon's place as leader of the people. And when Rhon stepped aside to join the elders, there was no opposition to Rollo assuming leadership.

The people traded meat, grains, and gold to the Ghorn for wood, and they built houses near the river. Soon a large permanent city grew where before there had been a scattering of tents. Life became pleasant and most forgot the old, hard days when they'd had been outcasts. The mutant traits that had been a part of their lives for so long soon all but disappeared, and only a few latent abilities, like Rollo's, remained.

Eventually Rollo took a mate from the people, and she gave him many sons and daughters. Most of them were unimportant, but their youngest daughter, Valesa, had a great impact on the society of the people and all of their neighbors.

Valesa grew to be a beauty, and she knew it and used it. She inherited from both her parents the ability to influence, even so lightly, other people's minds and emotions. Before she was fully grown, she was using her beauty to attract men to her, and then she used her not so visible talents to give them pleasures they never dreamed of before.

To the shame of her parents and all the women of the people's city, Valesa became a prostitute, selling her awesome favors for gold and other treasures. Soon she had a multiple room house of her own on the banks of the river at the edge of town and travelers passing through the city often stayed at Valesa's Inn.

Before long Valesa hired other young girls to keep up with the demands of the business, and she only bestowed her favors on special guests who could pay more for her special services.

Needless to say, her parents disclaimed all relationship to her, which didn't bother her a bit.

One fall day Rollo had walked far downstream from the city and sat lazily watching the clear blue water swirling over the rocky streambed.

Suddenly he sensed someone watching him and looked up to see a Yaq warrior seated on a horse directly across the river. This Yaq was even taller than his own great height, although not as heavy, and with the well-muscled body of a great athlete.

Though the warrior appeared to be several years younger than he was, Rollo sensed about him an air of strength of character not usually seen in younger men. But the thing that most caught Rollo's eye was a long scar that ran from the back of one of the warrior's hands, up the arm, across his bare chest, and down the other arm to the back of the other hand. There were also streaks of white in his jet-black hair.

As they measured each other across the river, the Yaq spoke.

"Who are you?" he demanded.

"I am Rollo, leader of the plains people," he replied as he stood erect. "Welcome to my land."

"Your land? Hah! Your bones will rot in 'your land,'" the Yaq snarled and reached behind him then brought forth a long, straight lance. As he drew back to throw it, Rollo looked about him futilely for something to hide behind while desperately trying to stretch his influence across the river to sway the Yaq from his deadly purpose.

Before either man could complete any action, a great bolt of lightning tore through the sky and crashed to earth in the center of the riverbed, filling the air with steam and rocks. A tremendous roar of thunder followed, shaking the earth and knocking both of them to the ground.

The panic-stricken horse galloped off into the distance as the two shaken men stared at each other across the steaming river.

In the middle of the river was a boiling whirlpool of steaming mud. Several dead fish floated to the surface and were carried away in the current.

"Who are you?" the Yaq repeated. This time incredulous awe replaced the contempt that was in his voice the first time he asked the question.

"I am Rollo," he replied. "What happened just now?"

"I don't know," answered the Yaq. "I am Yoki, son of Yokagi. My father and I have always been favored by the gods of thunder, but now I'm not too sure."

"I think your gods have just sent you a message." Rollo laughed as he carefully stood up and checked for injuries. At that Yoki laughed out loud and got to his feet, wiping the dust from his arms and legs. They stared across the riverbed at each other for a few minutes, each sizing up the other. Finally, Rollo waded across the creek and extended his open hand in a gesture of friendship. Yoki took the hand and grasped it firmly, not to hurt but to bond the two together in friendship

Again they exchanged greetings, and the two men sat under a tree talking for the rest of the day. Each was extolling the virtues of his people and way of life. As darkness approached, Rollo invited Yoki to come eat with him and spend the night in his city.

Although Yoki was eager to get better acquainted with his new friend and see the things he was telling him about, he was still reluctant to accept the invitation. His main concern was that his people would find his riderless horse and come searching for him and misinterpret what they found.

He was also not too sure how the plains people would receive the leader of the same Yaq nation that had treated them so harshly for many generations.

Finally, Yoki agreed to meet Rollo at the same place in two days, and then he would accompany him to his city. Both agreed that this was the better idea, as they would be able to prepare their own peoples for the meeting.

As they went their separate ways—Rollo upstream to his city and Yoki across the prairie to his home on the northern river—Rollo wondered idly whether Yoki had been affected more by the bolt of lightning or by Rollo's attempts to influence his mind.

It was a question that would never be answered.

They met as agreed and, although the nomad people were at first frightened of the giant warrior, they soon accepted Yoki's open warmth and friendship after Rhon reminded them how much they had prospered by his chance meeting with Hathor.

It was apparent to all that much was to be gained from a treaty of trade and friendship among their peoples. Yoki told of how the Gwundi and his people had reached just such an agreement many summers ago and of the wonders of the jungle he had seen.

After two days of talks, Yoki returned home with two horses loaded with tools and other goods to show his people. A few days later he returned with some of his elders and the old men of both groups easily worked out a treaty between their peoples.

While the talks were still in progress, a trade caravan arrived from the Ghorn and within days new treaties were in effect between all the peoples and peace reigned in the land.

∽

As might be expected, Hald grew up to be a total pain in the neck.

Almost from birth his father gave him everything he wanted. And by the time he was twenty, Hald had just about everyone in the army disliking him, if not hating him outright. His only redeeming quality was his above average intelligence and uncanny grasp of political and military intrigue, which made him a valuable man to have around in a country that was expanding more every day and might need his peculiar talents.

He had grown up in the army and rose quickly to a position that was second only to his father's in rank. But in actuality, Hald was the real leader of the army, for Lon had long since given up caring about anything but a skin full of ale to drown his sorrows.

Hald had seen the necessity of a strong inner core of faithful followers and had carefully selected his personal guards from those who thought as he did: that the easiest way to the top was to step on someone else, whether they liked it or not. He didn't trust any one of them but made it clear that the only way they could stay in favor was to protect him and serve him at all costs.

When he was firmly entrenched as the military leader, Hald began a campaign to build himself up in the eyes of the people by currying favor with the most influential citizens and quietly undermining the authority of King Jhor, who was now so busy with other problems he completely left the army in Lon's hands, or so he thought.

Jhor had, like so many others, been stricken with the congestive disease of the lungs that had almost claimed the life of Lon years before. While he was still mentally as sharp as ever, he was unable to endure much physical exertion and left much of the everyday routine to his councilors and other advisors.

This was the perfect environment in which a despicable person like Hald could flourish and he did.

The first thing he did was arrange his marriage to Jhor's oldest daughter, who, while very pretty, had all the brainpower of a gnat. Jhor was slightly pleased to get her married off so easily to the son of his half-brother and best friend, and he blessed the happy bride and groom. Lon actually stayed almost sober long enough to attend the wedding and not make a fool out of himself or embarrass his friends.

Hald then manufactured a distant problem and dispatched Hath and Thon with a contingent of Jhor's most faithful followers to look into an alleged incursion into Ghorn territory by Yaq warriors. As soon as they were well on their way, one of Hald's assassins slipped into Jhor's room in the deep of night and suffocated him, leaving no trace of foul play.

In the morning when the king's dead body was discovered, Hald was in the right place to take control of the kingdom with his personal corps of strong-arm men to back him up and no one in authority to question him.

Twenty-five days later when Hath and Thon returned, Hald was firmly entrenched as the new king and there was little they could do about it. They were told the simplest lies possible to convince them that Jhor's death had been natural and were given promotions and more duties to keep them busy and out of the way.

Shortly thereafter, Hald began an industrious building project that included a dam on the river, allegedly to improve the water supply for their crops, but really is was for controlling the flow of water to the plains people so he could charge them for the precious water they needed so much.

He also strengthened the existing forts and built new ones in strategic locations.

This gave many men new jobs and more pay on which Hald imposed something else new: taxes. He started taxing trade with the plains people and took a small share of everything that passed through the newly guarded gates of the city.

Within a year he was the richest and most powerful, the most feared, and the most hated man in the kingdom. And he loved it!

ᑦ᷍᷍Chapter Fifteen᷍᷍᷍

Rakh had the dubious distinction of being the first grandchild born to the emperor of Shanar. While this got him an abundant amount of attention from all present in the Palace of Light, it also got him enough attention so that he couldn't get away with anything.

It seems Rakh had inherited just about all the talent of all his combined male ancestors, some of whom were extremely powerful sorcerers and wizards.

By his twelfth year, there was very little he wasn't capable of doing in the way of wizardry and very little he was allowed to do. His father continually tried to get him to practice the simple routines of sorcery, but Rakh wanted to do great and wondrous things.

The old arcane rituals he found recorded in scrolls in the dusty library under the palace fascinated Rakh, and more than once he got in deep trouble with his father for trying one of them.

Like his aunt, Lisha, he sometimes called up things that were better left undisturbed, creating hard feelings among the palace guard and causing his father much consternation.

Shallim had long since given up the hope of Rakh someday taking his place as emperor. His more fervent hope now was that his grandson would live to be an adult and not be eaten in the basement library by something that didn't belong on this earth.

Much to his grandfather's delight, Rakh made it to manhood. Like his aunt before him, but for altogether different reasons, Rakh announced that he was going to the temple to study with the old priests and attempt to reestablish the "true religion" of the old gods.

So Rakh took the now much easier path up the mountain to the old temple, which had undergone a refurbishing since the new road passed so close to it, and began his studies. It didn't take long to discover that the older men had a much greater knowledge of the old gods than any of his father's contemporaries did.

They had a vast store of scrolls and books in their libraries, which Rakh had never heard of before. And he was in paradise with them.

The older priests had never seen one so young with so many piercing questions about the rituals of worship of the old gods. They delighted in bringing out scroll after scroll of ancient writings and exploring them with the young wizard.

He read at an amazing rate and had an astonishing capacity for memorizing the writings. And with almost total recall, Rakh could simply catalog the writings in his mind and call forth any passage at will.

Soon he left the priests far behind him in his quest for knowledge and some wondered where this store of knowledge could lead him. Rakh moved into the tower room with a pile of parchment and writing tools and soon was totally absorbed in creating what appeared to the priests to be new and more powerful spells and incantations.

After that, they avoided him as much as possible, which suited him just fine.

When his stomach grumbled, announcing its emptiness. Rakh would run down to the kitchen and grab a mouthful of whatever was handy, and then disappear into the tower for several more days until it was time for another raid on the larder.

His hair grew long and unkempt, and soon his clothes looked as if he slept in them and never changed. Finally, the older men could stand it no more and approached him, with some caution, about his personal habits.

He appeared amazed and looked down at his tunic, smelled it, and grinned ruefully. "I guess I have been preoccupied with my studies. Thank you, gentlemen, for reminding me. If you would be so kind as to supply me with clean clothes occasionally, I would be most happy to oblige you by wearing them."

With that he promptly disrobed and handed the filthy clothes to the nearest priest who immediately handed them over to the youngest and lowest ranking priest, telling him to dispose of them promptly.

Thereafter, the priests provided Rakh with clean clothes daily, and on occasion one of the men talked Rakh into washing his body and having his hair and beard trimmed. Even if he was the grandson of the emperor and was entitled to some privileges, the least he could do was to appear decently groomed and clothed while a guest in their temple.

So Rakh conformed, a little.

Valesa soon grew to be the richest woman, and probably the richest person, in the city of the plains people. Her inn by the river crossing was the largest and best-furnished house in the city and almost every man who came to visit the city stayed at the inn. The fact that it was a brothel only added savor to the good food and accommodations Valesa provided.

In the spring of each year, the river rose and made crossing difficult, so Valesa hired several of the local men and built a sturdy log bridge to carry the ever-increasing traffic above the cresting river.

This had the added effect of increasing the traffic past her business, because it was much easier to cross the bridge than to ford the river, even at low times. Wagons had a tendency to get stuck in the river mud and the bridge made the passage simple.

She then offered to pay for a new building for the elders to meet in, for they still held their meetings in an old tent, and it was difficult for all of them to crowd inside. After much debate about the merits of the offer and especially about whom the offer came from, the elders decided to accept the offer and Valesa had a new town meeting hall constructed, coincidentally, close to the inn.

Soon other new buildings were built close by and, despite the grumblings of the wives, Valesa's Inn came to be the informal town meeting place. There you could get a cool glass of ale and some good food for a reasonable price, served by an attractive lass who, for a little extra, would accompany you to one of the rooms for other delightful pleasures.

If all you wanted was a hearty hot meal and a place to rest from your travels, that was also provided with the assurance that your purse would not be lifted while you slept.

With the increased trade between all the different peoples of the land, the city of the plains people came to be the trading center of the known world. Traders of all the races came together there, usually at Valesa's, and bartered for their goods. And naturally Valesa profited richly from the trade and from the traders who passed through her doors.

Before long she added a large warehouse next to the inn for traders to store their goods while they traveled and traded, and again quite naturally, she took a fair profit from it all.

The traders never grumbled about that profit, for they all knew that while she was obviously in business to make money, Valesa was scrupulously honest and would deal harshly with any of her girls who cheated a customer. She didn't allow gambling or gamblers in the inn and had any who did make it past the door unceremoniously thrown back through it.

She hired a few of the larger, and more honest, young men of the town to serve as guards for the warehouse and to deal with any problems that might arise inside the inn, such as a man who thought he was too good to pay for the attentions of the girls, or the rare occasion when a customer had too much to drink and found himself transported to a bed and tucked in, not by an attractive wench, but by a hulking lump of a man who couldn't be dissuaded or defeated.

All in all, Valesa was a great benefit to the city and its people, even though many of the older women still turned their heads away when they passed her on the street.

This didn't bother Valesa, for she had all she wanted of life, except the one thing she could now probably never have, a good husband. Not too many men would be willing to take for a mate a woman who'd been in bed with unknown numbers of men.

Most still held to the idea that they would be the first and only man to bed their women, although any one of them would still jump at the chance to take a young woman to bed if given the chance. Men really irritated Valesa. She had watched their hypocrisy all her life and fought hard to keep from becoming bitter when all she really wanted down deep in her heart was to be tender to the right man with no witchcraft or artificial love to stimulate him, just herself alone.

"Not much chance of that ever happening," she thought as she sat watching the traders file past her doors.

Not much chance of Valesa ever being happy.

Within a scant year of Jhor's untimely death, Hald had destroyed the precarious peace that all his forbears had strived for so diligently.

Hald's dam was built across the narrow mouth of a wide valley and would eventually create a sizable lake, which would provide a great deal of food, fish, and much-needed water for irrigation, so the Ghorn people heartily approved the project.

However, completion of the dam reduced the flow of water to the city of the plains people by more than half, so Rollo sent a small delegation to Ghorn to investigate the shortage of water. When they discovered Hald's dam was the reason for the shortage, they vigorously protested the action and were summarily executed by Hald's guards.

Rollo knew that to attempt any action on his own would result in complete disaster for his people, so he appealed to Yoki for help. While the lack of water in the southern river did not directly affect the Yaq, who lived in the northern plains near the much larger of the two rivers, they had signed a treaty of peace and mutual aid with the plains people.

Besides, there hadn't been a good battle for several years now, and the Yaq warriors were beginning to feel they were becoming obsolete.

Yoki met with the clan councils, and they agreed that a threat against their allies could soon become a threat against all the peoples and it would be best to act now before the Ghorn moved against them.

Yoki formed a war party of a thousand men and moved them to the city of the plains people. Together with about six hundred of the plains men, they marched to the valley below the fort at the entrance to Hald's kingdom. They surrounded the fort and made many highly visible camps with huge fires and a great deal of activity.

The commander of the fort had dispatched runners to the capital city as soon as he'd sighted the war party. Now he nervously awaited word from the king.

After ten days of flexing their muscles in front of the Ghorn soldiers, a large mounted party in full war dress rode to the gate and demanded to see Hald.

The fort commander was a political lackey who'd never raised his weapon, or his voice, against any man and was now hiding in his quarters wishing they would all go away and let him alone. When the messengers returned from the king, Yoki told his warriors to let them pass, reasoning that two more men wouldn't make much difference in the outcome if it came down to a battle.

The message they brought to the fort, staffed only with two hundred men, created much consternation among the troops, and caused the commander to retreat further under his bed and cry aloud.

It said simply, "Drive that rabble off our land and leave no survivors."

The commander knew well that "that rabble" would surely survive any attempt to drive them away, and his garrison would last only a few days at most against that impressive army. He sent a lesser subordinate to the walls with a message for the Yaq to go away in peace and there would be no reprisals. The Yaq laughed in his face, screamed their contempt at the cowardice of the Ghorn, and made many uncomplimentary comments about their ancestry in general and their mother's sanitary habits in particular.

Unfortunately, one simpleminded hot head in the fort garrison took exception to this and launched an arrow at the war party.

It wasn't really a battle, being completely one sided as it was.

The war party suffered only a handful of casualties among their number, and when they rode away three days later, all that remained of the fort was a smoldering heap of ashes.

A grisly grove of tall slender trees now grew in front of what had been the rear gate. The heads of nearly a hundred Ghorn soldiers were planted on pikes, facing the Ghorn capitol in neat rows.

One survivor was barely alive, hamstrung, and blinded, with his nose, ears, fingers, and some other vital appendages hacked off, but his tongue left intact to tell the king of his poor judgment.

There could be no mistaking that message.

The victorious war party returned to the city, knowing full well that this was not the end of their problem.

Yoki left all but a few of his warriors in the city to fortify it against attack, and then returned to his own city to organize all his armies for battle.

Yoki sent riders to all the Yaq villages and into the jungle to the Gwundi city by the cliffs with a call to arms.

Gabela and Gisela responded to Yoki's call with more than a thousand fully armed warriors, eager for battle, and a hundred witch priestesses for spiritual support. Ten days after receiving Yoki's call, they set out for the Yaq city where they joined three thousand Yaq warriors to march against the Ghorn.

Hald hadn't been sitting by idly waiting to see what would happen.

As soon as he'd received the first word from the fort, he began to marshal his troops. And long before the combined armies of the Yaq and Gwundi were ready to march, his army had swept out of the hills to assault the nomad's city on the plains.

There hadn't been sufficient time to fortify the city against such an attack, and, while the defenders fought valiantly, the outcome was never in doubt. Women and children took arms against the invaders, and mutants who'd suppressed their talents for years came into the open and wreaked havoc among the Ghorn for a short time.

The battle ended as abruptly as it began.

A few of the mounted Yaq warriors, when they saw that the battle was lost, fled to take the word to Yoki of the disastrous end of the city on the plains.

The Ghorn herded the surviving defenders together into the town square where they separated the men from the women and children. They beheaded all of the men and left them lying in the dirt. Then the Ghorn soldiers took their time systematically raping the attractive women until they could no longer rise to the occasion.

Some of the soldiers took women for themselves as slaves, and they herded the rest of the women and children into Valesa's huge warehouse. They rounded up the remaining horses, and Hald chose a great red stallion for himself then sat haughtily watching as his soldiers drove the pitiful survivors into the warehouse.

A commotion from the inn caught Hald's attention, and he turned to see his soldiers bringing out a group of young children and a striking beauty with long red hair flowing down over a well-rounded figure.

"We found this one in the basement, hiding these children," a soldier told Hald. "We thought she might make a pleasant addition to your bed," the soldier laughed as he pushed Valesa toward Hald's horse.

Hald reached down, grabbed a handful of the silky hair, and laughed. "Pleasant, indeed. You will be well rewarded for this."

As he pulled Valesa's face closer to his, she raised her eyes and spat full in the leering face. "I'll die before I give you any pleasure," she snarled.

"No, my pretty thing; you will give me much pleasure before you die!" Hald yanked Valesa's hair and threw her to the soldiers. "See that no man takes her," he ordered. "I want the pleasure of breaking this wench myself."

The soldiers pushed the remaining children into the warehouse, and then barred the doors. Then the Ghorn soldiers piled all the combustible refuse they could find against the wooden walls and set the building afire.

As they rode off toward their capitol, they roared in laughter at the screams of agony coming from the pyre.

Soon all was still and the stink of burnt flesh mingled with the smell of fresh blood. Then the plains scavengers began to slink toward the unexpected feast that had been left for them.

When the surviving riders had come with the news that Hald was attacking the city, Yoki had been on the march to their aid for just two days.

The mounted Yaq rode on ahead in what they knew was a futile attempt to reach the city before it fell, with the foot soldiers following as close behind as possible.

It never entered Yoki's mind that Hald had really been Rollo's enemy and had as yet done nothing to harm the Yaq. The grisly sight that the massed armies of Yaq and Gwundi found among the remains of the nomad's city strengthened their resolve to scourge that madman from the face of the earth to meet whatever fate the gods saw fit for him.

The foot soldiers arrived in time to help, not to defend the city, but to bury the defenders. They carried the rotted bodies to a dry wash where the river had long ago changed its course, leaving a deep gully with steep banks. The soldiers piled the dead beneath the overhang, and then caved the bank in on the deceased, creating a simple but effective mass grave.

The warriors then washed themselves in the river to erase the smell of the burned and decayed flesh from their bodies. The smell eventually went away, but the image of the dead remained forever burned into the minds of each individual warrior.

It was a somber, deadly group that gathered around Yoki that evening as he made plans to rid the earth of Hald and all his people.

When they marched the next morning, it was without the usual good-natured chatter and songs of battle. Over three thousand warriors marched in almost total silence, with a single wish: to personally slay Hald.

Seven days later they reached the site of the burned out Ghorn fort and discovered that Hald had not wasted his time idly awaiting their arrival.

Yoki gained new respect for Hald when he saw what he'd done in such a short time. It had been just forty days since the Yaq had burned the Ghorn fort; but now in its place was an even more formidable obstacle. They'd built a wall of logs in the narrow pass behind the old fort with heavily fortified positions on the bluffs at either side.

The wall itself was not an impassable barrier, but it would slow the horses and foot soldiers enough to make them easy targets for the soldiers on the bluffs above them. The Ghorn had cut all the trees for more than a hundred paces below the new wall and used them used to build it. They'd even cleared the brush, leaving a clear field of fire with nothing to use for cover.

Yoki and his army drew back into the wide valley to make plans for the assault of Ghorn. He sent scouts to search out other ways around the wall, but Yoki feared that Hald had anticipated that possibility and fortified any other areas that might be used to attack him.

So began the long war.

There was water there from another small river and fields of grain and plenty of game, so Yoki sent for his people and they began to build a fortified encampment in the foothills below the Ghorn city. More Gwundi warriors came, and soon there were more than eight thousand soldiers with thousands more women and children in a new city.

The Gwundi priestesses set up a temple slightly removed from the city and started making magic against the Ghorn. The wise men of the Yaq also went aside to their own place and made supplication to the thunder gods to intervene on their behalf.

Though the Ghorn soldiers had a slight numerical advantage over the combined forces in the valley, they had none of the experience of the Yaq warriors and had not been hardened by jungle life as had the Gwundi. Even with his great physical strength, a single Ghorn soldier would be no match for the animal cunning of a Gwundi warrior or the agility and skill with weapons of the Yaq.

ℭ✍Chapter Sixteen✎℘

For three long years the battle was waged without either side gaining more than a momentary advantage. Both camps regularly sent raiding parties to harass the other. Although the raids had little lasting effect, they did keep everyone on the alert.

Hald was able to draw only a few of the closer cities to his aid, for most felt that it was his problem and that they would probably be better off with another king anyway.

Hald spent the first several days after returning from the destruction of the plains city giving instructions for fortifying his kingdom and seeing that everything was well under way. He was not mad enough to believe that this was the end of the conflict. He knew that the plains people had allies in the Yaq and fully expected an assault on his kingdom.

He was outraged when many of the Ghorn cities refused to come to his aid, most claiming that he started it all with the dam and the taxes and it was up to him to solve his own problems. He would have liked to send troops to punish them but couldn't spare them at that time.

After he wiped out the Yaq vermin and the war was over, Hald would take great delight in punishing those who refused to help him.

The thought that he might lose really never occurred to him. He was in an almost unassailable position with unlimited resources, whereas the Yaq were far from their homes and living off the land. It was just a matter of time until his army would overthrow them as easily as the city on the plains.

Hald had no idea of the size of the army facing him, or of the presence of the Gwundi warriors. And even if he had, it probably would have made no difference to his inflated ego.

With the preparations for defense well under way, Hald turned his attention to other, more pleasant pursuits and made his way to the rooms where Valesa was imprisoned.

In his delusions of grandeur, he thought he would simply brush aside her resistance with his abundant manly charms. And, if circumstances had been different, his ruggedly handsome face and great physique might have been enough for Valesa to revert to her earlier profession without much pause.

Hald had been accustomed to getting his own way all his life, and he'd never met a woman like Valesa, who fought off his advances with all her strength and will.

After several days of trying everything short of physical violence to have his way with her, Hald gave up all attempts at being nice and beat her almost unconscious then savagely raped her and left her half dead, crumpled in a corner of the cell like a cast off garment.

Valesa recovered from that beating and from successive beatings and violations of her body. Each incident of brutality only increased her desire to live and somehow repay this monster for his vile crimes against her and her people.

She used her unnatural abilities, even while Hald raped her. Although she couldn't stop him, Valesa was able to take most of the pleasure out of Hald's acts leaving him more frustrated and confused.

Soon his ego could take no more of her abuse. But rather than kill her and put her out of her misery, he sent Valesa to the slave quarters to live out her life with the rest of the dregs.

As the fates usually do, they added to her plight when, a short time later, she found she was with child.

Hald had no children from his other wives. When he learned that Valesa was carrying his child, Hald had her brought to his house and installed in relative comfort in a well-guarded suite of rooms with orders that she be cared for until the child was weaned.

When his son was born, Hald was away at the battlefront defending against a concerted attack by the Yaq.

He had left the defense of the city in the hands of two seemingly useless old soldiers who had been close friends of the former king and who were loyal to Ghorn, if not to him.

So Hath and Thon took the infant and his mother, and in the middle of the night stole out of Hald's city to make their way to the city of the strongest of those who'd opposed Hald. There they began a plot to overthrow Hald and restore Ghorn to its peaceful place in the society of man.

Hald had appealed to the Shanar for help, reasoning that his mother was of their people and they should be eager to come to his aid. They'd answered his request by simply refusing to become involved in any form of violence against any man and closed the mountain pass between their countries.

The war dragged on until, two years after the "traitors" had fled with his child, Hald found a giant of a man working in the mines in the hills. His wide shoulders were fully half a head above the head of even the tallest soldier in Hald's armies.

Completely unaware that there was a war going on, the dull-witted behemoth worked happily away, almost as a draft animal because of his tremendous strength and size. Hald immediately had him brought to the city and trained him to use a sword and spear.

Hald had a breastplate and helmet of hammered iron made for the behemoth and the finest armorers in Ghorn crafted a sword that required two ordinary men to carry it. Ordinary spears were as toothpicks to him and he easily carried a dozen in a quiver like arrows.

Soon the training was complete and the giant warrior was the most fearsome sight in all the land. He delighted in the attention he received.

After being wounded in an earlier skirmish, Hald was forced to stay behind in the capitol with the defending garrison. But with the giant at their head, the Ghorn army marched out of the pass toward the encampment in the valley, intending to sweep the opposing army into the plains and stamp it out of existence.

Naturally, the Yaq and Gwundi had other plans.

They had also built fortified positions around the valley, and the Yaq scouts reported the advancing army well in advance of its arrival.

The Ghorn marched on the city to find it only lightly defended and assumed that most of the Yaq had left and gone home, while actually they were in the hills rapidly moving around and behind to completely encircle the Ghorn.

The Ghorn soon found that every building and tent had been booby-trapped with some sort of lethal device.

Fire arrows rained down into the city from the woods, setting everything aflame. The order was given to fall back to the hills, but the Ghorn found themselves surrounded by the combined armies of the Gwundi and Yaq, and a methodical extermination began.

Soon most of the Ghorn soldiers were dead, wounded, or in flight. But in the open square, the giant in the iron armor sprayed Yaq and Gwundi blood around him like a fountain until all the warriors drew back and left him standing like a tree in the middle of a bloody meadow. He roared out a contemptuous challenge and waved the huge sword over his head, laughing at the cowardice of his foes.

Yoki ran into the bloody square and stopped short at the sight of the monster in iron.

He grabbed a bow from a nearby warrior and launched an arrow straight at the giant's huge chest to see it harmlessly bounce off the breastplate and fall to the ground. He knew the creature had to be killed; and as he looked around at his warriors, he realized he was the one who had to do it. His only chance was to get inside that mighty sword arm and seek a place for his knife to get past that iron plate; otherwise, his body would lie with the rest at the giant's feet.

Yoki circled carefully to his right, and then back to the left while making a few tentative feints with his knife, which just a few minutes ago had seemed a quite adequate weapon, to see which way the giant would react to his advances.

The giant's sword was his most feared weapon, and at the same time, it was his biggest handicap. As big as he was, the giant needed two hands to swing the sword, and he always swung it straight overhead and never level.

As he wondered how to get past that long sword, Yoki suddenly remembered the old tales of how his father had used the very knife he was holding to kill the great bear whose skull Yoki still wore as a helmet. He thought that if he could get past that blade, he might be able to get his knife up under the armor before the giant recovered and swung again. If not... well, that wasn't too pleasant a thought, and he pushed it quickly from his mind.

Tossing the knife from one hand to the other, Yoki danced in front of the giant, taunting him with all the vilest insults he could recall, thinking that if he could get the giant angry it might give him a much-needed advantage, however slight.

Suddenly, in the middle of a particularly offensive description of the giant's sanitary habits, Yoki quickly thrust his knife at the enraged face. And as the giant sword swung straight at Yoki's head, he lunged down and to the side, and then rolled against the giant's feet in the bloodied dirt.

When the sword struck the ground with a mighty thud less than a finger's width from Yoki's ribs, he turned, drove the long knife straight upward into the giant's exposed groin, and twisted the blade viciously. The giant screamed in agony as blood and foul smelling bile gushed from his torn entrails and poured down Yoki's extended arm.

Yoki jerked the knife free with another savage twist and rolled away from the giant's feet. As he started to rise, he lifted his eyes and, to his horror, saw the monstrous blade swinging once again at his exposed head. This time he was unable to dart out of the way; and as he tried to dodge the blade, he felt a tremendous blow, which seemed to explode inside his head, then nothing.

Yoki's life was spared only because the flat side of the blade struck his head instead of the edge. As the blade caromed off the bear skull helmet, the sharp edge ripped into his left shoulder, tearing through muscles and shattering bones like dry straw.

As the watching Yaq and Gwundi warriors cried out in dismay at the sight of the giant standing over what appeared to be Yoki's dead body, the giant released the sword still sticking out of Yoki's shoulder like a grotesque mutated arm and toppled slowly backward, hitting the ground with a crash. He lay in his own hot blood and filth, twitching as his life ran out onto the ground.

One Yaq warrior rushed forward and drove his sword under the edge of the helmet into the throat of the giant, then wrenched the blade sideways, nearly severing the great head. The giant gave one last convulsive shudder and died.

The warrior jumped in surprise as what he thought to be the dead body of his war chief groaned in unconscious pain behind him, and others soon rushed to the aid of their fallen leader.

The sword was carefully pulled clear and the ugly wound wrapped tightly to stop the awful flow of blood. Yoki's people quickly made a litter and tenderly carried him to the closest of the few houses still standing after the battle then laid Yoki on a makeshift bed. They dared not move him further because of the massive size of the wound and the fear that anymore movement might cause even greater injury.

Healers of both nations ministered to him, and the priestesses of the Gwundi joined with the wise men of the Yaq. By nightfall many powerful supplications had been made, both to the thunder gods and to the frightful gods of the Gwundi, on behalf of Yoki.

The next day a terrible fever wracked his body, forcing the healers to reopen the wound to cleanse it of dirt and bile. They wrapped the shoulder again in cloths soaked in strong potions and healing herbs, and then washed his tortured body with cool cloths wet with clean water from the river.

For six days the fever wracked Yoki's body as he lay unconscious.

Then, as suddenly as it had come, the fever left him. On the morning of the seventh day, Yoki began to moan and toss about, and he soaked the furs of his bed with torrents of sweat. The healers had to tie him down with wide bands of cloth to prevent him from opening the still unhealed wound, and they tenderly washed away the salty perspiration from his ravaged body.

It was many more days before Yoki completely regained consciousness, and even then he was confused and disoriented, with little memory of the battle and his fight with the giant.

Soon the healers nursed him back to the point where he could be moved back to the Yaq city and the homes of his people where he could regain his strength. But the healers and most of the warriors knew, though they kept it from Yoki for the time, that he would never regain the use of his left arm, and they wondered who would now be leader of the Yaq nation.

Chapter Seventeen

Mibara had the eeriest way of scaring everyone around her half to death.

Even as a five year old, she was able to move through space undetected, and she often appeared next to some unsuspecting priestess at the most opportune time to break something. She didn't actually disappear and reappear; mere mortals simply couldn't see her if she didn't want them to.

Fortunately, her mother and aunt were not mere mortals, and little Mibara got her cute little rear end paddled just the same as if she wasn't a very young, but very powerful witch. She put up with those indignities because she knew that her mother was not punishing her because she didn't like her, but only because she had been disobedient again and mommy thought she needed a lesson.

Besides, there was something inside her that her young mind couldn't quite pin down. It was almost as if she had another person in her head who told her what was right and wrong. She'd never told her mother or aunt about this "other person" because she thought they just wouldn't understand.

Once Mibara had a nice feeling of warmth and familiarity with her other person, and a funny word had popped into her head. When she asked her priestess attendant, "What's a Janga?" the young priestess had turned pale, and then turned away from her.

So she never again asked anyone about other persons inside her head, she just figured she was different from the rest of them, and let it go at that.

Mibara's aunt Gisela raised her while the girl's mother led the Gwundi people. That left Mibara a lot of time to herself while Gisela made magic in the caves.

When Gisela wasn't looking, it was kind of fun to go back into the caves and play with the people who lived there. It was disappointing that they would never let her see them, but as Mibara got older, she realized that they were not invisible people at all but were really supposed to be scary gods and other unearthly things.

They never scared her, and most of the time they were quite friendly, even if they were a little shy. Mibara was a throwback physically, for contrary to the large physiques of both her mother and father, whom her mother never stopped talking about, the girl was somewhat small. On her sixteenth birthday, Mibara was a full head shorter than her mother. This didn't seem to bother anyone, and she let it pass with a wistful thought that it would be nice to be tall and stately like her mother or her beautiful aunt Gisela.

At seventeen, Mibara traveled to the Yaq city on the plains to talk to their old men about the thunder gods. The old men's strange stories fascinated her, and she especially liked the legend of Yokagi's grandfather, who had climbed a high mountain to get closer to the thunder gods and seen the great white shining eye of one of the gods through the mists. They told of how the gods had taken the breath from his body and made him blind for his impertinence.

He had wandered for days and fallen down many times before his people found him, half crazy and raving about the great shining eye of the gods. Most of the younger men said the gods had made him crazy, but the old ones nodded wisely and remembered the story to tell the young children around the fires at night.

For many days she listened to the tales of the old men but in the end went away unhappy, for she still hadn't found what she was searching for. If she'd actually known what she was searching for it would have helped quite a bit. But she didn't quite know what it was and the other person in her head couldn't seem to help. She just kept hearing a funny word in her head that sounded like "Rak," and it just didn't make any sense.

For five more years, Mibara continued her search. Although she learned a vast amount about all the gods of all the peoples, she still couldn't find the one elusive thing that tormented her. That same dumb word, "Rak," kept going through her head and she was unable to make it go away or to figure it out. Finally, she went to her aunt Gisela and told her of the other person in her head and the strange sounds she heard. When she told Gisela of hearing Janga in her head as a child, her aunt grew very still and peered at her intently for several minutes.

"Don't you know what Janga means?" Gisela asked.

"No, I don't. I remember I just got a warm feeling and that word came into my head," she replied. "And lately another sound keeps coming back to me. A sound like Rak."

"Rak, I don't know," mused Gisela. "But Janga was the greatest, most powerful witch queen the Gwundi ever had. It was she who established the queen rule of the Gwundi and built this city. She began the worship of the gods in the caves that protect us and give us guidance. I think maybe she is trying to guide you to something and your power is so great that even she can't get through to you."

This revelation thoroughly shocked Mibara and sent her mind reeling. "You mean I'm more powerful than she? How can that be? I'm just a young woman and don't know anything at all about real witchcraft."

"There are some things that just cannot be taught," her aunt replied. "I believe you have more inborn ability than any other witch since, maybe including Janga herself. I have seen you do things that my grandmother, M'bili, could never dream of. And the way you talk to the gods as if they were your equals sends chills down my back. Let's go into the caves and try to contact Janga. Maybe if you let down your guards and try to listen, she will be able to contact you."

Together they went deep into the caves. While Gisela burned some strange things in the dark fire at the back of the cave, Mibara tried to relax and open her mind, as she had never done before.

Indeed, she had for years tried hard to close her mind to all the thoughts of other people that continually crowded into her head, and now it was difficult to let down the barriers.

Gisela came and stood behind her then began gently massaging her temples while chanting softly in some unfamiliar, but strangely soothing language. Soon her eyes were growing heavy with the smoke and the singsong rhythmic chanting.

"Now," her aunt said softly, "reach out with your mind and try to make contact."

Almost immediately a voice spoke softly in Mibara's mind, "Welcome great granddaughter." Mibara jumped halfway to her feet then relaxed as the voice continued. "I am Janga who speaks to you. Truly you have great powers, for I was unable to break through your barriers to talk to you. This has never happened before, and I am truly impressed, great granddaughter." She looked to her aunt and realized with a start that she also had heard the voice.

Gisela smiled at Mibara and spoke to Janga. "We are greatly blessed to hear from you great grandmother. This is a surprise to us, for no one has heard from you for many generations."

"Momentous things are about to happen," Janga replied. "And you, Mibara, are a part of those things. What you search for is a man of the Shanar from far across the stone mountains. His name is Rakh, and if you call he will come to you. Together you will make great magic to aid all the people in the time of their greatest need. The ancient prophecy is about to come to pass and even I cannot alter it. I will come to you again, but now I weaken. Being dead for many generations does tire one," Janga said with a chuckle as her voice faded away. "I will come again," they heard her say soft as a whisper in their minds, and then there was silence.

They sat in the utter silence of the cave for many minutes. Even the guttering fire had gone out, and their breathing sounded like a great wind in the stillness.

"We will call this Rakh," Mibara said. "He will come to us and we will make magic together." Her voice sounded strangely different to Gisela, and as they walked out into the light, she was shocked to her heart to see her young niece's hair had turned snow white and her skin seemed to shine with an unearthly light.

Mibara turned and smiled at Gisela then spoke with a voice no longer her own. "We are almost complete now. We feel the spirits of all the queens of the Gwundi within us, and we have their powers. In our ignorance, we had pushed it back, not understanding that all the voices in our head were the voices of our ancestors calling to us. When Rakh comes to us, we will be complete."

Gisela shuddered at the thought of what her niece had just become. Mibara was no longer a part of her family. In reality she was all of her family rolled into one awesome creature.

Mibara was, to all the rest of the world, no longer just alive, but more than alive.

As Mibara went back into the cave to call Rakh, Gisela sought out her sister to tell her the strange news.

Rakh had been studying in virtual solitude in the temple tower for fifteen years, and by then had the old men firmly convinced that he'd gone insane. Regularly, when they took food and clean clothing to the tower, they heard him talking excitedly to someone, or something. But when he opened the heavy door, they invariably found that he was alone.

They fervently hoped that he was slightly balmy and was talking to himself, occasionally changing his voice. That explanation was much preferred over any others they could think of at the time.

One pleasant afternoon, their worst fears were realized when, out of a relatively clear sky, thunder rumbled almost directly over their heads and the skies suddenly darkened menacingly. When one of the priests looked out of a window to see what was going on, he saw to his horror that the clouds were pouring from the tower windows and the thunder was, in actuality, over their heads, in the tower itself.

The priests ran up the stairs and saw what looked like steam seeping out from under the door. As they approached, they detected a nauseating odor of something long dead coming from the direction of the tower room. Muttering fervent prayers, they pounded on the door, hoping they would be heard over the rumbling thunder.

Then, as suddenly as it had begun, the thunder stopped. They continued pounding on the door, praying that what answered their knock would be Rakh and not something else.

But it was Rakh who unlocked and opened the door. And what a sight he was!

His clothes were black and singed with portions actually burned away. His hair was badly singed. The hair on his head and the ragged beard had burned half off and all that remained of his eyebrows was a charred stubble.

His eyes were slightly glazed and open wide, as if he'd just seen a great and wonderful sight and the image was still fresh in his mind. Looking behind him, the priests saw that dark smoke filled the room and was just beginning to drift out through the windows.

In the middle of the room, the scorched floor looked as if a huge fire had burned there, but there were no ashes or residue. But there were deep gouges in the blackened wood, as if some great taloned creature had pranced across the floor.

Rakh wandered from the room in a daze, and the priests, wanting to get him as far away from the room as possible, hurried him downstairs to the kitchen where he was washed, what remained of his hair was trimmed, and he was dressed in clean clothes.

During these ministrations, Rakh just sat on the wooden stool with the same dazed look of wide-eyed wonder on his face, which was starting to turn red from what appeared to be burns. Healing salve was applied to his face and hands, which were also burned, and only then did he respond to the handling.

"Oh my!" he whispered. "Oh my gods!"

He appeared about to collapse from exhaustion, so, even though the priests would have liked to question him about the strange activities in the tower, they took him to a small room off the kitchen and put him to bed. He curled into a ball and fell asleep almost as soon as his head touched the mattress and soon began snoring softly.

Unknown to Rakh, the vile thing he'd summoned from the depths of darkness was the physical manifestation of one of the evil Daemoz. And it had not been sent back into outer darkness, but was trapped in the nowhere/nowhen in between the dimensions of space and time until it was to be summoned again by its master to do its bidding.

Rakh slept for two full days. One morning, as the priests were preparing their morning meal, he wandered into the kitchen with a confused look on his now bright red face. "What happened?" he asked, scratching his head.

"We were hoping to ask you the same question," the elder priest replied. "You all but destroyed the tower and frightened most of us out of our wits. Whatever on earth did you have in there?"

"Nothing on earth, I'm afraid," Rakh mused. "I seem to have made a slight miscalculation in the strength of the spell. I'll have to do it better next time."

The prospect of a "next time" and what kind of thing might be called into the temple tower made the priests shudder in sudden fear. "I think there will be no next time in our temple. Your spells are just too much for our old building to stand. I'm afraid if there were a next time it might mean the end for our temple, as well as for all of us."

"Oh," Rakh mumbled. "I guess I'll have to find somewhere…." He suddenly jerked his head and seemed to snap out of his daze.

He looked around quickly. "Who called me?" he asked. Then he winced and blinked as if some unseen person had slapped his face sharply. "Who are you?" he demanded. "Why are you calling me?"

The priests stared at him in wonder as he continued to inquire of the thin air. Suddenly he clapped his hands tightly over his ears and almost cried. "Leave me alone. Please, leave me alone." He fell to his knees on the floor, and then curled into a ball like a baby with his arms wrapped tightly around his head, crying softly.

All of the priests were then certain that the strain of years of poring over the old scrolls and manuscripts had finally driven Rakh insane and that he was now hearing imaginary voices in his head.

What they didn't know, of course, was that he actually did hear voices in his head. Mibara, inexperienced with her powers, had broadcast a call to Rakh with all her awesome strength, and it had completely overpowered Rakh's tired mind, already strained nearly to its limit of endurance.

Realizing what she'd done, even over the vast distance between them, Mibara carefully withdrew her call and sent forth a soothing message, which quickly calmed Rakh and almost put him to sleep. Again, she sent out a call, softer and more friendly instead of demanding and curious. "Rakh, please listen to us. We are Mibara of the Gwundi and we must meet with you."

Rakh relaxed and sat up, listening curiously. "What do you want of me?" he asked cautiously.

"Come to us and we will be complete," the voice in his head which called itself Mibara answered him. It sounded very much like a female voice but there were traces of other voices blending into it which confused him.

"Are you one?" he queried.

"You are perceptive. We are the body of one, Mibara, with the spirits of many others within us. Join your powers with us and we will do great things," Mibara again told him.

"But how can I join with you? I don't know where you are or what you are."

By now the priests had realized that he really did hear voices and moved away from him in awe, thinking that it was the gods who were talking to him. Some fell to the floor prostrate and prayed while others simply stood by in silence.

"We will guide you to us," Mibara replied. "The journey will take many days and will not be easy, but we will protect you. Come to us and we will make you whole and you will be happy."

This last promise sounded too tempting to pass up for a wizard who was searching for truth and light, so Rakh told the priests he must be leaving and made ready for his journey.

As Rakh began his journey to Mibara, the war between the Ghorn and the Yaq had been going on for nearly ten years and travel in the plains was unwise, if not unhealthy.

He knew nothing of the wars, having been shut up in the tower for many years and paying absolutely no attention to what little news filtered in from the outside world.

Therefore it came as a great surprise to Rakh as he led his pack donkey through the high pass to find the road barricaded with a sturdy wall of logs and stone. He wasted the better part of a day finding a way around the barricade, and then was on his way again mumbling under his breath about the stupid lack of hospitality of the idiots who'd built such an obstacle.

Most of the few Ghorn he encountered on his way thought him a holy man and those who did speak to him soon thought him to be mad. They gave him food and avoided any further contact with him, for the Ghorn believed the gods protected the mad.

The gods may not have protected Rakh, but he was under the watchful care of someone almost as powerful as a god. The mind's eye of Mibara intently followed almost every step of his path across the eastern desert foothills, and more than once she directed his way by a subtle thought impressed upon his mind.

Once a Yaq war party passed within sight of him and sent a lone scout to investigate the traveler. After a brief conversation with Rakh, the scout returned to his party with word that it was but a harmless holy man on a pilgrimage to the daughter of their Great War Chief, Yoki.

The Yaq gave him more food and gifts and sent him on his way with their good wishes, which only confused Rakh more.

As he neared the jungles that were the home of the Gwundi, Rakh reached out with his mind and called to Mibara, more to see if he could do it than for any other reason. To their surprise, she heard the call as clear as if he were standing next to her in the palace. For the next several days, they carried on lengthy mental conversations as he walked through the jungle toward her home.

Many times he heard noises in the jungle undergrowth around him, but he never saw an animal or another human being. On one occasion he passed by some caves and felt such a deep depression and fear that he turned aside to investigate. As he approached the caves, the feeling became almost a physical presence pushing him back. He called out to Mibara and asked her about the caves. She quickly warned him to stay away from them, explaining that they were the home of the eternal queen Janga, whom he might be privileged to meet one day.

Finally, after forty days of travel, Rakh and Mibara met at the entrance to the great city by the waterfall. She chose to meet him there rather than in the temple residence to guide him through her city and show him the way personally.

As they walked through the city, oblivious to the curious stares of the people, they talked at great length about their respective homes and lifestyles. To their amazement, they found that, aside from their common interests in the old gods and ancient magic, they liked each other.

They were both extremely intelligent and realized that physical attraction had no place in their relationship, but the simple fact that both Rakh and Mibara were physically beautiful people made that relationship all the more pleasant. Soon they retired to the private rooms of the palace and became deeply engrossed in their studies of the ancient books and scrolls that Rakh's donkey had carried so far.

Chapter Eighteen

Rakh and Mibara found time for more than studies and before long Mibara discovered, to her amazement, that she was with child. The subject of children had never entered their conversations. Although they were not opposed to children, it did create a problem because Rakh and Mibara had reached a point in their studies where they wanted complete solitude and isolation from all outside influences.

They had planned to relocate their residence to the desolate swamplands to the northeast of the plains, and there commune with the old gods and the spirits rumored to dwell in the swamps. Now their plans were put in abeyance for a time while Mibara was pregnant with their child.

Soon after Mibara learned she was with child, she also learned from her mother, Gabela, and her aunt Gisela of the strange events that immediately preceded her own birth. They told her of their contacts with her while she was still developing in her mother's womb and the problems they had directing her undeveloped powers during the first few years of her life.

All the women concurred that extraordinary measures would have to be taken to raise the new child, whom they all agreed was to be a girl.

Finally they reached the conclusion that after the child was born, Gisela and Gabela would raise her, leaving Mibara and Rakh free to pursue their studies as they wished. With the help of the priestesses, they would be able to keep constant watch on the child and direct her as she grew to womanhood.

It appeared, however, that their fears were unfounded, for the yet unborn child showed none of the peculiar traits her mother had evidenced and appeared to be a completely normal baby. Even Mibara, with her stupendous power, was unable to communicate with the child's mind, and she expressed some degree of disappointment to Rakh about the child's strange normality.

Eventually, as always happens, the child was born and everyone was amazed by how beautiful she was. This was by far the loveliest child ever born to the Gwundi and, her grandmothers proclaimed, indeed in the entire world.

They named the baby girl Shallith. When her mother recovered from the childbirth, the baby was left in the care of two doting women who gave her all the loving care that grandmothers are known for.

When her parents were well on their way to the swamps and all the temple priestesses seemed adjusted to the new child, Shallith relaxed a portion of the barriers she'd constructed shortly after her conception and reached out across the land with an ease that would have surprised even her mother.

This tiny baby was the culmination of breeding many generations of magical powers directed unobtrusively by the old gods, who were not dead or disinterested in the ways of mankind. All the awesome talents of three races of people had been brought to focus in this small child, and her powers were beyond anything heretofore known to mankind.

Many generations of witches, sorcerers, and wise men would have been deeply disturbed to know that they were little more than pawns in a game so great they couldn't begin to understand it. The old gods and the four great spirits of this universe had for those many generations been manipulating mankind and giving him direction.

Even they lacked the absolute power to force every person alive on the earth to do their will, but they could influence and guide mankind through their plans. Now those plans were coming close to fulfillment.

So Shallith investigated her new world from her cradle.

While Rakh and Mibara dearly loved their new daughter, an almost uncontrollable passion drove them to continue their studies. When the child was a scant hundred days old, her parents left her with Gabela and Gisela and trekked deep into the swamps to set up the temple of their new, yet very old, religion.

They chose the swamp for two simple reasons: the complete isolation from the rest of the people, and the presence of bizarre spirits and demons, the familiars of the old gods, which were the only inhabitants of the eerie bogs and marshes.

They didn't desire or need human companionship in their new home, rather they greeted the unearthly denizens of the swamp as their neighbors, and soon they too were welcomed by the swamp as permanent residents.

Word of the defeat of Hald's army reached Valesa almost as soon as it did Hald himself. Many interested Ghorn from the other cities who had not sided with Hald had been watching the battle from a safe distance to see which way it would go.

While the ragged survivors of Hald's army were making their slow way back to his city with word of the resounding defeat, the observing Ghorn spread the message to their respective lords, most of whom were eager to step in as the new king of Ghorn.

When Hath brought the news to Valesa, she swept up her three-year-old son, Harl, in her arms and whirled him around in delight. She stumbled a little and Hath reached out his huge hand and gently took her arm to steady her.

Valesa's beauty was only slightly marred by the thin scar on her cheek that left her with an eternal half smile. Her legs had healed almost completely, leaving her with but a trace of a limp. But the scars inside would never heal.

Where before there had beaten a warm, compassionate heart, now burned an all-consuming fire of hatred for the man who had slaughtered her people and ravaged her body and mind.

Hath looked into her eyes and for a second his blood turned cold at what he saw there. There was no joy of celebration in those deep green eyes, only the look of unbridled abomination and the realization that now, possibly, Hald was accessible to her and she might realize her vengeance.

Feudal warfare tore through the forests of Ghorn for years and many homes were torn apart as thousands of fathers and sons died in the senseless wars.

Hald had concentrated his power and rebuilt his city more as a fortress than a place of residence. Hald's guards had foiled several assassination attempts and turned the would-be assassins into horrible examples of what awaited anyone else who tried.

Hald would have been very surprised to learn that most of the attempts on his life were backed by Valesa, who had risen to power as the only reigning queen of Ghorn. She was his principal challenger for the throne of all Ghorn.

With his personal guards and the remainder of his army, Hald was able to put down several attempts by the lords of other cities to wrest the throne from him, and he was once again able to assert himself as king. True, the kingdom had shrunk to less than half its former size and power, but even a small kingdom was enough for Hald's twisted ego. Soon he was making plans to invade the Yaq city on the plains to repay them for his embarrassing defeat.

Hald knew the Gwundi had long since retreated into the jungles to fend off another unknown threat from the north, and his archenemy, the war chief, Yoki, was now a helpless invalid.

He had heard rumors that the Yaq were divided by tribal conflicts, so Hald naturally felt this was the best time to avenge himself on the Yaq. But Kana and Yoki, partially invalid though he was, had rallied several of the Yaq clans around them under the leadership of some of the older chiefs who had served Yokagi and who still worshipped the thunder gods. They'd amassed an army of nearly two thousand mounted warriors who could hit and run and harass the vastly superior numbers of Ghorn foot soldiers who had no horses except for a few of their leaders.

The wars waged on for ten more years with neither side gaining a clear advantage until Hath and Thon, older but still mighty men, led Valesa's army in a surprise attack on Hald's city while his army was battling the Yaq on the great prairie. Riding with them was a young soldier of eighteen by the name of Harl. His mother had thoroughly indoctrinated him, and Harl hated Hald with all his heart and mind.

Valesa had unconsciously, with her mutant powers of suggestion, so ingrained that hatred into her son that she herself would have been shocked to realize how deep it went. Harl's entire being was absorbed with just two thoughts: love for his mother and hate for his father. Everything else in life was unimportant to him.

Harl had inherited the latent powers of his ancestor, Rhon, and no magic or spells could be used against him unless aided by a conscious effort on his part, except in the case of his mother.

His love for her was more like worship of a divine being than that of a son for his mother. Harl had absorbed her feelings and Valesa's powerful hatred had caused them to multiple many times over.

Hald's defending garrison fell swiftly to the attacking forces; and when he returned to his city several days later, his troops were exhausted from another frustrating battle and weary from the long march home.

They were not met by friendly families with refreshing food and drink, but by the rested and eager troops of Valesa who attacked without warning or mercy.

Most of Hald's soldiers, when confronted by the overwhelming superiority of Valesa's men, simply threw down their arms and surrendered. The attackers methodically cut down those who did resist. In a matter of minutes, less than a hundred survivors were herded into the square. Among them were several gravely wounded soldiers supported by the uninjured. Others seemed almost untouched by the battle.

Surrounded by a menacing ring of iron-tipped pikes, Hald's men waited with downcast eyes for the inevitable death at the hands of their conquerors. A few looked up as two people separated from the group of Valesa's officers and walked toward the prisoners.

One of the less injured prisoners turned toward the two and gasped as if he'd seen someone long dead return to life. He looked about nervously and tried to move closer to the center of the group, but when the others saw that everyone was now looking at him, they drew away from him as if he were the carrier of some terrible disease.

Valesa passed through the lines of her soldiers with Harl close behind and walked directly toward Hald, who was now quite visibly in a near panic and shaking violently. He turned and ran from them toward the encircling soldiers, lunging at one of the guards as if trying to impale himself on the pike.

"Don't hurt him!" Valesa commanded. "I want him alive!"

Hald tried to grab a pike from a soldier who simply twisted it away and turned the blunt end toward him. The others followed suit and prodded Hald toward Valesa and Harl, who were waiting patiently in the rapidly expanding opening in the center of the group of prisoners.

Hald fell to his knees in the dirt and buried his face in his hands, overcome by the growing despair of total defeat and now the prospect of death at the hands of Valesa. But before he was to die, she had another surprise for him.

"Hald," she ordered. "Look up and meet your executioner. Look into the face of your son." Hald's head came up almost as if lifted against his will by some invisible force, and he stared in surprise at the young man with Valesa. The surprise quickly turned to abject horror as he looked into those eyes and saw what awaited him there.

It took Hald fourteen days to die.

But long before he died his mind retreated from the pain into catatonic madness. His executioner seemed to grow angry with the now empty body, for the spirit leaving so soon, and inflicted more suffering on it until it no longer mattered, for the thing that was left had no likeness to humanity.

Valesa was absent from those proceedings, having to attend to affairs of state. She was fully confident that Hald would receive justice: his kind of justice.

Those of Hald's followers who had surrendered were questioned carefully, and some were allowed to stay on as subjects of the queen of Ghorn. Some others recognized as Hald's guard were executed, and many more were banished to the plains as new outcasts and nomads.

They sent messengers to the other Ghorn cities with the news that Valesa was queen, and those who wished to join her were welcome to come and pledge their allegiance. Those who did not could expect an unfriendly visit from the larger and better-equipped army of the queen.

Within two years, all of Ghorn was again united under one leader and peace began to be spoken of in the land.

A great change came over Harl now that one of his passions was gone. Where he had been a sullen, moody youth, he now became a devoted and loving son, always eager to please his mother and queen.

~

Shallith had no idea she was actually a finely honed weapon in the old gods war against evil and, even if she had known, there was nothing she could have done about it. She was, to all outward appearances, a normal, healthy young girl with extraordinary beauty but little or no magical talents.

Her mental makeup differed so vastly from her parents and other relatives that, in reality, she was not human at all, except in physical appearance. She was literally conceived as a cognizant entity and had made the decision before birth to conceal her true abilities from her relatives.

It was ridiculously easy for her to conceal her powers from everyone around her, though Gisela suspected there was much more behind that pretty face than was apparent to the casual observer. She tried many times to probe the mind of the child and each attempt met a solid wall just under the consciousness of the girl's mind. Everyday thoughts were exposed to both Gabela and Gisela but that ever-present and completely impenetrable barrier worried Gisela.

Shallith hid behind that mental shield until, as she began to blossom into womanhood, M'gori's raiders attacked a small village near the Gwundi home city while she and Gisela were visiting the village temple.

A mental wave of fear and confusion projected by M'gori's priests preceded the raid with the intention of reducing the residents of the village to little more than panic-stricken animals and make them easy prey.

At the first tenuous touch of that mighty blast, Shallith's own mental powers analyzed it, located its source, and turned it back against its senders with less effort than swatting an annoying insect.

The invaders, who were greatly outnumbered by the villagers, had expected to make easy work of the disorganized defenders of the village and take captives of the survivors at their leisure.

But the clear-headed Gwundi warriors attacked the disoriented raiders and cut them down like sheep. Shallith sent a gentle but irresistible mental command to the warriors to keep some of the priests alive and bring them to the temple for examination. In the haste of the moment, she was not able to conceal this from Gisela and she turned to her with a shy smile.

"I am truly sorry for not taking you into my confidence before this," she told the surprised Gisela. "I have long sensed that there was some great power directing my life from outside this world but I needed time to grow and there were many things I had to learn for myself. But I am now ready to fulfill whatever destiny awaits me."

Gisela suddenly felt a tremendous surge of power fill the room with a warmth and tenderness that almost made her want to cry, and she realized that Shallith had lowered the barrier that had shielded her mind from her family for all those years.

Shallith and Gisela then began probing the surprisingly weak minds of the invading priests.

It was obvious from the start that the priests were of little importance themselves and were controlled from a distance by some much greater force.

The Gwundi queens had long suspected that the frequent raids on the small villages were the work of one group, but they were never able to locate the source of those attacks. They had searched all the jungle lands and found nothing, but when they sent mental probes to the plateau above the cliffs, they invariably ran into an impenetrable area of darkness that defied all their attempts to look inside.

Shallith pushed forth a probe of such magnitude that many wild creatures caught in its path instantly died in their tracks, their simple minds stirred like broken eggs.

The probe struck the darkness and stopped, clung momentarily, and then rebounded with such violence that Shallith was barely able to ward it off in time to save herself and Gisela from sudden death.

As it was, Gisela was stricken unconscious by the blast and even Shallith was momentarily stunned by its force. But many of the unprotected villagers were either killed outright or rendered unconscious by the radiation of that superhuman force.

Shallith recovered almost immediately and constructed a barrier of force around the village to protect the survivors from the anticipated return attack.

But the defensive screens constructed by M'gori were designed simply to ward off the snooping probes of the Gwundi queens and the attack never materialized. M'gori was aware that something of unexpected power had struck his screens, but he had no way of knowing its nature or where it came from. He just assumed it was an unusually strong questing probe and gloated that his screens had so easily repulsed it.

Shallith revived Gisela from her semi-dazed condition, and they rapidly set about healing and repairing what damage they could among the villagers while they discussed the curious events that had just taken place.

What meager information the priests had was of little value to Shallith and Gisela, for they were almost mindless puppets driven by some unknown evil force inside that dark barrier. They picked the priest's minds clean and then turned them over to the warriors for execution.

The women returned to their city and, together with Gabela and the elder priestesses, began a careful and thorough investigation of the threat from the high country.

Chapter Nineteen

While Shallith had changed almost overnight from an apparently introverted young girl who had no noticeable talents other than the ability to melt even the hardest heart with her radiant smile, into a mature woman of spectacular magical powers, her parents had also changed, but into something quite different from their original appearances and personalities.

At the completion of their long journey into the swamps, Rakh and Mibara constructed a home for themselves, if it is permissible to call an invisible bubble of protective energy a home. They had gathered about them a following of swamp demons and other eerie creatures, most of whom human eyes had never seen before. The creatures themselves had never seen humans before Rakh and Mibara entered the swamps.

It had taken many long and arduous sessions invoking powerful spells and old incantations not heard on this earth since the earliest days of the ancient ones before the swamp dwellers could be coaxed from their hiding places to investigate the almost overpowering call that came from the newcomers to their home.

Even then it took the greater part of a year for Rakh and Mibara to gain the confidence of those unearthly appearing creatures, most of whom predated even the old ones by hundreds of years. But soon they had a following, of sorts, and reestablished the worship of the old gods among the denizens of the swamp who had not forgotten the old gods but had long ago strayed from their worship as had mankind.

Their "congregation" consisted of assorted misbegotten things, some denizens of the old world, part human and part animal, others were grotesque mutations of earthly swamp creatures, and a few were things not of this earth that lived partly in this universe and partly in a place so far beyond the comprehension of man as to be totally indescribable in human terms.

By this time Rakh and Mibara had commingled their minds so completely that they were actually one entity with two separate bodies. They no longer had need of food and literally nourished themselves on the primal energies of the swamp. They were bathed by the mists, dried by the wind, and clothed in the cold blue fires of the bogs.

Their bodies were almost neglected in the quest for the purest forms of worship, and soon the maintenance of their human forms was done almost unconsciously by means of their awesome magical powers. Indeed, those human bodies were more of an encumbrance than a necessity, and if it were possible, they would have done away with them entirely.

Instead they did the next best thing. Rakh and Mibara set aside the search for pure worship for a time and dealt with the distraction of having to accommodate the needs, such as they now were, of a living human body. For many long days they searched futilely through the old scrolls and manuscripts seeking a solution to their problem, and they were about to give up and resign themselves to accepting the limitations of their mortal bodies.

The appearance of a strange creature in the clearing next to their home interrupted their studies. There were many odd appearing things in the swamp, but this creature, which approached them in a manner indicating complete familiarity, was strange in that it was unfamiliar to them.

The most alarming aspect of the creature's appearance was that if you looked straight at it, it seemed to fade out of focus and waver like a reflection in a slightly disturbed pond. And when you looked away and caught a glimpse of the creature out of the corner of your eye, it seemed as if several semi-transparent beings were standing in a straight line and you could almost see all of them through each other.

Rakh was beginning to get a headache from staring at the thing as he tried to figure out what it was when Mibara, with her much greater perception, suddenly recognized the superimposed images as those of several of the familiar swamp dwellers.

When questioned about their condition, they simply explained that they occasionally joined themselves to communicate better and more fully share their experiences. They had never mentioned this talent because they thought Rakh and Mibara already knew of it.

Needless to say, Rakh and Mibara were astounded and overjoyed to discover this talent, and they wasted very little time learning to do it themselves.

Once Mibara had mastered the technique, it was a simple matter to fully join with Rakh. As they adjusted their spirits to this new situation, it became apparent to both of them that this was the way to the purest form of worship of the old gods. What more perfect unity in worship could be attained than through the perfect physical, mental, and spiritual unity of the worshippers?

Soon there was but one visible inhabitant of the swamps; one, yet more than one. Visible, yet not really visible, for if you looked directly at this creature, for lack of a better term, you would see a shimmering semi-transparent entity that flickered like the flame of a sputtering candle with many shapes but no discernible single shape.

This was a total fusion of all the creatures that followed Rakh and Mibara in the worship of the old gods. Unknown to the members of this strange union, the fearsome spirit of air sent by the old gods to guide the now completed congregation in their quest for true worship and adoration had quietly joined their coalition together.

Thus it was that Rakh and Mibara became one with the spirits and approached that final doorway leading to the ultimate fulfillment of the ancient prophecy so long ago given to the prophet Jirash Kin.

While the swamp dwellers were approaching a pure relationship with the old gods, others were also striving to attain a higher level of communion with their deities.

M'gori and his followers had accelerated the pace of their depravities and had now reached a state of such moral and spiritual degradation that even the most hardened warrior of the Gwundi trembled in terror at the mere thought of the evil beings of the high places.

Long ago, the last of the animals had fled the upper plateaus. Now M'gori was the supreme ruler of fully twenty thousand creatures that had once been human, but that could no longer qualify for that distinction.

They were the grotesque result of generations of inbreeding for the specific purpose of weeding out all traces of human intelligence and emotions and, coincidentally, most of the physical appearances of mankind.

These things were, in a limited sense, similar to the dwellers of the swamp in that many were part human and part something else. But the Daemoz spawned the "something else" that had been bred into M'gori's followers under the watchful direction of an entity that was totally evil.

Hatred was their only emotion. M'gori's followers hated every living thing in this universe, except M'gori himself, and often their hatred became so intense that it was beyond their control.

Then the raw hatred boiled over and great bloody riots broke out among M'gori's disciples. M'gori made no attempt to obstruct the bloodshed, for it gave them a release for their violent passions and also provided a ready source of fresh meat for their tables.

~

Shallith had no idea what she might find behind that awesome barrier, but she knew when she found the source of that power it would almost certainly be unpleasant. The possibility that she would not be able to defeat the barrier never occurred to her.

The only questions in her mind were, *"how much energy would it take and how soon would it happen?"* So it came as a disturbing surprise to her that, after several days of effort, she and Gisela were not able to penetrate the barrier. Shallith did get one quick glimpse through that screen by using all of their combined powers. What she felt, more than what she saw, frightened her and made her blood run cold.

It was a feeling she couldn't understand or explain, but it became clear to her that there were things inside that barrier that were beyond even her powers.

They returned to the Gwundi city and Shallith retired to the caves behind the temple where she went into an almost trance-like state, focusing all her abilities into a powerful instrument of pure energy, and then began the painstaking process of slowly and carefully probing the surface of the barrier. The barrier was perfectly round like a great globe of energy that rose high into the gray skies and even down into the earth. There, at the lowest part of the barrier, deep within the earth, was its weakest point. And there was where she began her work.

With a feather-like caress, Shallith touched the outer edge of the barrier; then slowly, a hair's thickness at a time, she eased the needle-sharp energy probe into the surface of the invisible wall. Days passed, and then weeks. Shallith had moved her probe a mere finger's breadth into the barrier. At first she met resistance, but as the probe continued ever slowly onward, the resistance gradually lessened. Shallith easily withstood the temptation to increase the pressure and move faster. Instead she kept up the steady pressure, and after many more weeks she began to get the first vague impressions of activity on the other side of the barrier.

There she stopped and waited, watching carefully to see if her intrusion had been noticed.

Finally satisfied that she'd been undetected, Shallith moved slowly upward. The solid earth itself was no hindrance to her senses. Once she'd completely passed through the barrier, Shallith stopped again far beneath the surface of the earth and patiently surveyed the gruesome spectacle of M'gori's world.

What she saw utterly sickened her and the urge to turn and flee was almost overwhelming, even to her superb emotional power. But she stayed and looked, and her revulsion grew into a terrible determination to destroy the evil spread before her.

As slowly as Shallith had entered, she withdrew from the awful scene and paused at the outer fringes of the barrier once again to be sure she had not been detected.

Shallith went to Gisela and Gabela and described what she'd seen and they spent much time in deliberation. Finally they decided they needed all the help they could get. So they sent messages to the swamps for the entity that had been Rakh/Mibara.

Shallith herself went to the cave in the jungle to confer with the spirits of M'bili and Janga. And together in union with the things that lived in the caves behind the palace, they appealed to the gods for wisdom and guidance.

The answer they received was simple: It was such a simple answer and so easily misunderstood. The enemy could only be defeated by the final union of all the peoples.

As many people do, they saw only the bigger picture and overlooked the simple truth. They saw the solution as a physical one; and in truth, their united armies would easily be able to defeat M'gori were he acting alone. But with all their combined intelligence, they simply made a mistake.

The answer did not refer to the combined armies of mankind. The union of all the peoples was to be the deliverer told of in the ancient prophecy of Jirash Kin. Only that deliverer would be able to defeat the evil forces behind M'gori.

So they began to make plans to unite all the peoples into one great race of humanity to defeat the unknown enemy with the combined physical might of their armies.

First to be contacted were the Yaq, for they were closest in distance and in spirit to the Gwundi. As the granddaughter of the Great War Chief, Yoki, Shallith traveled to their city on the plains, confident she could elicit their cooperation. Indeed, she had little trouble convincing Yoki to unite his people with the Gwundi to battle this blasphemous evil. He may have been an old man, partially crippled in the final battle with Hald's armies, but he was still the spiritual leader of the Yaq people and looked upon almost as a god for his nearly superhuman achievements.

The entity that had been Rakh/Mibara sent spirit messengers to Rashan, the current emperor of the Shanar, to beseech their assistance in the inevitable and unavoidable conflict. The Shanar had always been, and would always be, a peaceful people, totally opposed to any form of warfare or any other action that compelled one man to submit to another's dominance. But Rashan had seen in the smoke of the incense the terrible future that lay in store for mankind if this evil power was not defeated. So he reluctantly agreed not to join in physical battle, but to assist with all the mental powers of all the priests of Shanar and to guide and strengthen the armies of the nations.

With the peoples of the Gwundi, Yaq, and Shanar united against their common foe, Shallith turned to the Ghorn, not anticipating any resistance from Queen Valesa.

However, Valesa's mind had been warped and her heart hardened by years of abuse and betrayal.

She was not what we consider to be crazy, but her capacity for love and compassion had long since vanished.

She listened courteously to Shallith's messengers and just as courteously sent them away with a firm refusal of their request to join the other peoples against the common enemy. She was more than willing to carry on the trade that had become so indispensable, and profitable, to everyone. But she was still leery of the others after the long, bloody wars, and she trusted no one.

Valesa's response, or lack of one, puzzled Shallith. She blamed it on a simple misunderstanding of the request. So, to avoid any further confusion, she dispatched another delegation and accompanied the messengers so there could be no confusion or misinterpretation.

As soon as Shallith and Valesa met, they felt a strong affinity for each other. These were two women of tremendous vitality, who were, in effect, absolute rulers of their respective people. And yet, even though they were so different in nature, they were attracted like magnets.

Valesa was a fair and honest queen, who governed with the head and not the heart. She decided what was best for the people of Ghorn completely without emotion or compassion. She had as much love for her people as for the dirt under her feet.

Shallith, on the other hand, loved her people deeply. Even though Gisela and Gabela were the nominal rulers of the Gwundi, as queen and high priestess, they recognized that Shallith was in reality the one who had the ultimate power in the land and was the rightful leader.

Still, Shallith's in person request met with the same response as the first.

Even Shallith's impassioned pleas and vivid descriptions of the activities behind the barrier didn't soften Valesa's resolve. It seemed the more Shallith pleaded, the stronger Valesa's resistance became.

Shallith then added another element to her attempts to weaken Valesa's determination and gently tried to get inside her mind to thaw that frozen wall. However, Valesa had inherited from her father Rollo and her grandfather Rhon their ability to resist all forms of magical influence. So Shallith ran into a wall. She was mildly curious about that barrier, for it was unlike any she had ever encountered. With her extraordinary powers, it would have been fairly simple for her to break down that wall, but to do so would have destroyed Valesa's mind, and Shallith wanted her as a friend and ally, not a mindless puppet.

Shallith quickly sent a questing probe around the room and found that all the other Ghorn present were as she expected: most with a slight resistance to magic but no power at all.

Then she touched Harl's mind and found a shield like no other she'd ever encountered.

Unlike the evil barricade on the plateau, which was a seething barrier of sinister energy, or Valesa's solid block of passive resistance, this was like a boiling pool of quicksand dragging anything that came in contact with it down into a bottomless black pit. Shallith was caught off guard, and for a fraction of a second she started to slide into the abyss. But immediately she regained her composure and easily broke free from the pull.

She quickly looked at Harl, expecting some kind of recognition of the intrusion; but she was amazed to see no reaction at all on his face or on the surface of his consciousness. He was completely unaware of the barrier or its strength. The force came from deep within his subconscious without design or direction from his conscious mind.

She then carefully sent another gentle probe to scan the surface of the barrier in an attempt to find out just what it was, but she could do no more than touch the surface without being drawn toward the depths of oblivion. She slowly backed off and looked again with amazement at Harl who had absolutely no idea what was going on around him.

It would be no problem for Shallith to gain control of the people of the Ghorn but obviously she would have to use some other means to get close to Valesa and Harl.

With Hald now dead, the blinding hatred that had dominated Harl's life now had no outlet and had quickly turned into an almost obsessive love for his mother Valesa.

Shallith was not able to change that emotion, so she decided to use her substantial powers to transform herself into the most desirable woman in the world to influence Harl and take Valesa's place as the object of his love.

Unfortunately, every other man in the kingdom except Harl fell madly in love with her, and she was forced to alter her plans before the suitors mobbed her to death. Harl was moderately impressed by her beauty, but there was no one like his mother.

Magic still wouldn't work on him unless he wanted it to, and he didn't want it to. So Shallith continued to apply gentle pressure against the shield. Harl felt something but couldn't tell what was irritating him. He felt like there was a pressure on his mind, almost like a nagging headache, but he was unsure of what it was. He began to think it was some kind of spell and tried to find the source but couldn't pinpoint it. But he did get the impression that it was coming from a woman somewhere in the Ghorn city.

ᴄ⁄Chapter Twenty᷾

With the nomads gone from the plain, Valesa
and Harl began to rebuild from the
devastation left by the wars and set up a
trade empire with the capital city where
Valesa's old town had been.

Trade flourished for a while but soon began to drop off
as fewer travelers dared to venture across the plains anywhere
near the plateau. Attacks on lone travelers, and even caravans,
by abominable creatures from the plateau had increased, and
there were even occasional attacks made on Yaq villages near
the edge of the jungle.

In the dead of night, screams were heard from the
outlying areas of the villages. By the time the warriors roused
and ran to help, all that remained were scattered bloodstains
and barely identifiable pieces of bodies. Small villages were
deserted, and the Yaq people moved into larger fortified
encampments and posted warriors during the hours of
darkness to sound the alarm if attacked. The people lived an
uneasy peace for a time.

The Shanar sent wise men with their mysterious
powers across the mountains to assist the people of the
Gwundi and the Yaq; but the power of the evil from the
plateau continued to spread like a festering wound, and soon
no one left the cities and villages except with a large
contingent of armed men.

In the city on the plains, Harl was now a fully grown man and beginning to feel lonely. His love for his mother couldn't fill the emptiness in his heart, and he longed for a woman who was like Valesa. He was becoming more and more miserable and night after night he asked the gods why he couldn't find a woman like his mother and implored them to send him someone to share his life.

From her home in the jungle city, Shallith sent a questing spirit and listened to Harl pleading with the gods and realized this was the only way to get to Valesa: through Harl's unrequited love. She then began to make her personality as much like Valesa's as possible. She couldn't change her body any more than she'd already done; there was too much risk in more physical alterations.

Even transforming her personality could possibly cause her great harm, but even death wouldn't be too great a price to pay to defeat the evil forces of M'gori. Gisela and Gabela tried to dissuade her from this course, but her resolve was firm. She had to get through to Valesa and forge a union of their peoples or the prophecy couldn't be fulfilled, and they would all be doomed to extinction.

Shallith went into a deep self-induced trance and began the slow process of completely altering the outward appearance of her personality. She maintained her inner being but suppressed some of her own personality so Harl's mind would see the image of Valesa.

When the transformation was complete, Shallith and Gisela gathered warriors and servants around them for protection and traveled to the plains city to meet with Valesa and Harl, allegedly to discuss the menace threatening all their peoples and provide for their mutual protection. But the trip was a ruse to get near Harl, the real key to the power of his people.

They used all of their considerable power to set subtle traps on the surface of Harl's subconscious; and when he momentarily let down his subconscious guard while talking with his mother, Harl received the full force of all the awesome abilities of the collected Gwundi witches and fell out of his mind in love. He literally fell crazy in love with Shallith.

This created another more serious predicament that Shallith and Gisela had not anticipated. Harl still loved his mother, but that love paled in comparison to his new love for Shallith, which amounted to total worship. Harl's sole purpose in life was now to be with Shallith and to make her happy. The once mighty warrior of the plains people became, for all intents and purposes, a love-sick puppy!

In Harl's almost insatiable desire to please Shallith, he unconsciously relaxed and let down his barriers. She was able to influence him enough to moderate his almost overpowering longing to be with her all the time.

This allowed her enough freedom to travel back to her home long enough to make arrangements for their marriage and return with the rest of her family to the city on the plains.

Word of the impending marriage was sent out to the four peoples; in some cases by bands of messengers, and in others simply by communicating mentally with those who had the ability.

Vast caravans formed in the widely separated cities of the mountains, plains, and jungles to carry the military and spiritual leaders of all the nations and peoples to the ceremony. There was a strange lack of elation; and there were no gifts for the bride and groom, even though this was to be a royal wedding and should have been cause for lengthy festivities, for this union was not a cause for celebration. It was the beginning of planning and preparation for what all thought was to be a battle of the united peoples against the evil forces of M'gori.

The details of the wedding ceremony are unimportant. The only cheerful person in attendance was the groom, as he had no idea what was going on other than believing he was the happiest man in the world. Shallith would let him enjoy his newfound bliss for a while before she had to let him down slowly and once again make him into the warrior he once was.

The union of all the peoples was now complete. Or so they thought.

While the leaders of the nations began their plans to forge an army of all the people, only Rakh and Mibara, or more accurately, the entity that had been Rakh and Mibara were uneasy with the proceedings. They had unexplainable fears that the physical union of the peoples was not what was needed and returned to the swamps to commune with the spirits that resided. They wanted to discover the nature and extent of the power of the evil that threatened from the high plateau.

It soon became obvious to Rakh and Mibara that human armies wouldn't be able to conquer M'gori and that they would need a great deal of assistance from the old gods and their spirits.

They feared that the end times of the ancient prophecy of Jirash Kin were coming, and they gathered together with all the spirits of the swamps. Then Rakh and Mibara called Janga and M'Bili from their deep sleep in the cave, and assembled the prophets and sorcerers of the Shanar and united mentally as one massive powerful entity to communicate with the old gods and plead for their help. The gods informed them that their only salvation would come at the hands of the deliverer promised in the prophecy of Jirash Kin and that he would need all the help he could get from all of them.

So they sent messengers to the Yaq city and retrieved the knife of Yokagi and the sword of the Ghorn giant warrior Yoki killed, and they cast potent spells on them so they couldn't be used for evil, only for good. Then they sent the sword and the knife to a long abandoned crypt in the mountains above the old Shanar temple. Potent spells were set to hide the knife and sword until the time came when they would be needed.

After a time, the army was beginning to take shape. But while most of the people looked to Harl as the natural leader, Harl couldn't seem to concentrate on anything but Shallith. And his natural resistance to magic made getting him to change his mind all the harder. The spells cast on him earlier by Shallith and Gisela proved to be just too good. Instead of a strong warrior king, they had a love-struck man whose only desire was to be with his new mate. Shallith used all her powers to counteract the spells and was eventually successful in getting Harl to take charge of the army, but he still had trouble concentrating on war when he just wanted to make love.

Nature took its course and soon Shallith was with child.

At first everything was fine, and there were no signs of the trouble to come.

Shallith was not a small woman, but the baby was enormous and many complications arose. She was afraid to try and use more magic on her body to ease the childbirth for fear of harming the baby, and she stubbornly resisted all attempts of Gisela to help.

Soon the time came for the child to enter the world, and the High Priest Jathan and several priestesses assisted at the birth. But the baby was huge. The child was born; a beautiful man-child with fair skin and reddish fuzz all over his head. But the strain of delivering him was too much for Shallith, and she slipped into a deep coma, barely alive.

But this child didn't just inherit the abilities of his mother and father. He inherited all the breathtaking powers of all his ancestors from all the races. This small child embodied the physical strength and ability to resist magic of the kings of Ghorn, the courage and stamina of the warriors of the Yaq, the formidable magic of the queens of Gwundi, and the awesome mental powers of the priests of Shanar.

Completely unknown to all, a power outside of their world, from another time and space, guided and guarded the child from the moment of conception to shield him from harm. This unknown force constructed a barrier in the child's mind unlike any other known to confine his powers to the as yet undeveloped dark recesses of his mind. For unlike his grandmother, Mibara, he had no control over those powers. It would be many years before he would learn to utilize them or to understand even the smallest part of what he held within his brain.

Harl would not leave Shallith's bedside for several days while she was in the coma, refusing food or rest and lying beside her on her bed sobbing.

Then a completely unexplainable thing happened. As Shallith's body lay in a coma, her mind still barely alive, a voice came to her unlike anything she'd ever sensed before. In spite of her natural barriers, this powerful yet gentle voice quietly reassured her that she had borne a son and that her son would be J'Osha, the promised deliverer and that she could rest in peace. Shallith then slowly relaxed, smiled a soft smile, and then quietly slipped from this life into whatever lies beyond.

Harl went into an insane rage. He called Jathan and screamed at him. "That baby did this to her. Get that cursed thing and take it out and kill it!" Jathan was afraid not to obey his king and went to get the baby from the priestesses.

The women were in the ladies chambers caring for the child when suddenly a giant figure of a man with golden hair dressed in shimmering golden clothes appeared before them and said Harl wanted to have the baby killed.

The terrified women thought it was a god and those who didn't faint on the spot fell down on their faces in fear and awe. The golden giant then told the stunned women that he would take the baby to a place where it would be safe from Harl. He picked up baby and was gone as silently and quickly as he'd come. Jathan then came in and found the women crying and praying. And when the women told him of the visitor, he didn't know what to tell Harl and was afraid to offend the "Golden One" if he really was a god.

Finally, Jathan killed a goat and splashed blood on his clothes. Then he went to tell Harl that the baby was dead.

In the old stone tower in the stone mountains, the wizards and prophets were diligently studying their scrolls, trying to determine the course of action to take against the forces of M'gori when the shining golden giant appeared among them with the baby in his arms. Their initial reaction was about the same as the priestesses had been.

As they began to regain their composure, the giant told them to care for the infant as if the existence of the entire universe depended on the child's well-being. He placed the child in the hands of a prophet and quietly faded from their sight. They were all awestricken by what they thought was the god who gave the prophecy to Jirash Kin, and, naturally, they complied with his demands.

They told no one of the strange visit and kept the baby away from the sight of any of the rare visitors to the tower.

The monks of Shanar raised the child for nearly two years and he grew to be a large, healthy child with fair, almost golden-colored skin and reddish-blond hair, completely unlike his parents.

Just about everyone in the tower loved him. It was almost as if they couldn't help it. A few felt uneasy about their attraction for the baby; but for the most part, their love overcame the feeling.

To be extra cautious, the sorcerers placed protective spells around the baby so no human could find him. But the one old prophet, whom the rest thought was slightly crazy, was afraid of the baby, and felt that bad things were coming because of him; he got cold chills like death touching him whenever he was near the child.

He said nothing to the others, but spent much time in contemplation of the scrolls of history and praying to the old gods about the child. Eventually he went to the old crypt, apologized to his ancestor for disturbing his sleep, and took out the golden plates. Once again a prophet began recording the events of history on the plates of gold.

After two years, Harl had almost gotten over his sorrow and begun to make plans for war with M'gori when Rakh/Mibara came to the city on the plains and asked to see their grandson. Harl's fury stirred again, and he angrily told them the child died at birth with his mother; but they answered that they knew the child was alive because they could feel his spirit, but his location was somehow hidden from them. They couldn't understand how they could feel his presence but still be unable to find him, even with all their powers. When Harl insisted that the baby was dead, they disagreed more strongly and told him they would search for the child.

Harl went berserk and confronted Jathan, but he obviously didn't know where the baby was. Harl cruelly tortured Jathan to try and pry the secret from him, but Jathan died before he could tell Harl about the golden giant who took the child. Harl then questioned the priestesses, and they told him of the golden giant but they too had no idea where the child had been taken. Their strange tale was too much for Harl to believe, and he flew into a rage and beat them unmercifully until he was finally convinced they were telling the truth and had no knowledge of the whereabouts of the child.

Harl then completely forgot about the preparations for war and set out to find and kill the child with the same consuming determination that had driven his hatred for Hald. He sent messengers to the Yaq and the Gwundi, but they quite honestly replied that they hadn't any idea where the child was and that they thought he was dead, as Harl had been told. Harl refused to believe them and attacked their cities to search for his hated offspring. Naturally, they resisted and much blood was shed on all sides.

Unfortunately, now it seemed that many years of sacrifice and planning by generations of the peoples would be wasted by Harl's insane anger. Wars between them raged on for a year with no sign of the child, so Harl turned his attention to Shanar. The strong magic of the Shanar turned him back by at the mountain pass. His failure to get through the high mountains just convinced him more that the child was there. So he went back to his city and put together a larger army and attacked again, this time breaking through the pass by the sheer weight of numbers and marching down toward the cities of the Shanar.

Meanwhile M'gori sat in comfort in his stronghold on the high plateau and reveled in the tribulations of the people.

After much searching, Rakh/Mibara were finally able to locate the child in the old stone tower and sent a spell by the swamp things to the sorcerers and prophets in the tower to send the child where Harl could not get to him. They were not exactly sure where the child would be going, but they assumed it would be with the old gods, as they had received the spell from them.

The chief sorcerer studied the spell, unsure of its outcome, but placed his confidence in Rakh and Mibara and the old gods and began to recite the spell.

As Harl's army approached the tower, the chief sorcerer spoke the incantation, and the child disappeared with a small clap of thunder as time and space were torn.

The body of the child was transported instantaneously through space and time, but the essence of that child took an entirely different route through the otherness of elsewhere/elsewhen and nowhere/nowhen, and wandered aimlessly in utter darkness.

He was, but there was no feeling of being, no sense of place or time. All that existed in his mind was the awareness that he was, and the terrible feeling of being completely alone.

He felt the filmy touch of another presence and cried out in despair and loneliness in a desperate appeal for companionship, but then it was gone and he again withdrew within himself where there was only consciousness, that's all. Nothing else, except the awareness of consciousness.

No memory, no identity, no anxieties—nothing.

It was enough just to be.

ᑳᔈFirst Interludeᔈᑊ

S ilent as a ghost came the great shining comet. Out of the vast darkness of interstellar space it rushed onward, past the orbit of Pluto, toward the hub of the solar system.

Almost seven thousand miles in diameter at its core, the comet made its way past Jupiter, it's path arcing slightly as it was tugged from its course by the massive gravitational field of that monster planet.

It was only a minor variation in the path of the comet, a little bend in a line which would have sent it safely past the sun on its journey through space.

But now the comet was enroute to a collision with the sun except for the interceding path of a blue, green, brown, and white mottled ball called earth.

The comet wouldn't actually collide with the earth, but it would pass close enough to create utter havoc on the outer surfaces of both bodies. The comet wouldn't suffer greatly from the passing, being nothing but boiling gasses and clouds of vapor surrounding a semi-solid core.

The effect on the earth would be an entirely different story, for it was covered with vast oceans of deep blue water and wide green continents of land with high mountains and rolling prairies.

There were also living creatures on the earth, most of whom wouldn't survive the catastrophic upheavals when the great comet passed within just a few thousand miles of the earth's surface.

Many of those doomed creatures were human beings; men, women and children who went about their business in blissful ignorance of their fate. Of the very few who noticed the new bright star in the heavens, most were inclined to worship it as a new deity and hope vaguely that it was not an unfriendly god.

The very few who recognized the object for a "stellar wanderer" were part of a highly advanced civilization who lived on a large island in the warm seas between two of the larger continents.

An island called Atlantis.

The comet grew in the western sky, rising just before the sun each morning, fading in the noonday light and becoming visible again in the evening as it was setting in the east. Soon it was visible even in the light of day, and the astronomers of Atlantis became excited about the new star and peered at it through their simple telescopes as long as it was visible, never dreaming what was in store for them.

Even at its tremendous speed, it was many days before the comet began to fill the sky with its presence and the minds of all who watched with fear.

When the seas began to rise out of their beds and the winds rose to a howling fury and the very earth under their feet began to rumble and shake, mankind realized their inevitable fate and went stark raving mad.

As the comet approached the earth, mighty Atlantis shuddered in agony, sank quietly beneath the raging seas, and was gone, forever hidden from the eyes of man—an end somehow not befitting her glory.

Earth tumbled in its orbit, spun crazily backward by the gravitational pull of the passing comet. The land heaved and split, creating new mountain ranges and seas and refiguring the face of the land.

Then the comet passed as quietly as it had come, rushing on into a wildly elliptical orbit around the sun.

It would pass again into the outer reaches of the solar system before it returned to visit earth with destruction almost three thousand years later. It would then be many more hundreds of years before the comet settled into a stable orbit, ironically as the closest neighbor of the planet it had so recently ravaged.

For several years, violent earthquakes wracked the earth and volcanoes spewed forth great fountains of lava that flowed and cooled and became part of the land. The seas heaved and washed over the earth, carving new coastlines as they receded and creating new beaches and bays where none had been before.

Finally, the earth was still and the pitiful few humans who survived huddled in their caves a third of the way around the globe from the sunken ruins of Atlantis, reduced to a state of almost mindless savagery by the events of the past years.

The sun now rose in a completely different direction, the earth having been turned halfway over on its once upright axis. Now there were seasons of winter cold and summer heat where once there had been mild weather all the year long.

There were many other changes in the earth, but they mattered little to the survivors who were forced to battle for a meager existence on a strange, hostile planet with little or no tools to work with and the unexpected awaiting them with each sunrise.

In the new mountains of what would someday be northern Iraq, the upheavals from within the earth had exposed rock and earth that had not seen the light of day for many thousands of years.

High on the side of a rocky gorge, strangely smooth square stones protruded from the earth. If anyone had been there to inspect those stones, he would have marveled at the way they were joined together, almost as if they had been carefully carved and fitted by human hands to make a wall.

Behind that wall, which couldn't rationally be a wall, there was a small room-size cave deep in the rock that contained many peculiarly shaped lumps of rust; lumps that might easily have been mistaken for manmade artifacts except for the simple fact that, other than the inhabitants of Atlantis, man had not yet learned the art of ironworking. And the iron tools of Atlantis were at the bottom of a sea still simmering with the heat of boiling volcanoes.

Mixed among the rusted non-tools were several heavy plates of golden metal that were covered with peculiar markings and carvings and what appeared to be the decaying skeletal remains of a man like creature.

With an almost infinite patience, the elements began to weather the faces of those strange smooth stones, blending them slowly into the surrounding terrain until only the minutest inspection could have detected any difference from the rocks around them.

Man survived.

For many generations, mankind scratched and clawed his way back from barbarism. Long forgotten were the former ways of life, and most men completely disregarded the half-remembered tales of a greater glory long ago.

Still, some remembered and they passed those tales on to their children and to their children's children; and the tales became legends that were slightly distorted with each telling until only a part of the truth remained.

Man spread from the valley into the hills and built more cities, and he built temples in which to worship the gods and sometimes to worship himself. And men were evil and sinned against each other and worshipped vile gods with obscene rites. They made living sacrifices of their children to those gods and fought long bloody wars with each other over nothing.

Then it began to rain.

Man, in his ignorance, thought the gods were punishing him for some wrongdoing, for no man had ever seen rain like this before. Frightened, mankind made even more offerings and sacrifices to his gods in a feeble attempt to stop the ever-increasing downpour.

And it continued to rain.

The rivers overflowed their banks and flooded the cities, and man fled to the hills to escape the rapidly rising torrents. Still the waters rose and covered the hills and countless thousands were swept away and perished in the flood. The waters continued to rise and covered all the plains and the hills and even the mountains, until only a handful of people survived in a great boat they had built in the northern mountains.

The rain continued for many weeks. And when it finally ceased, all mankind, except for the few who escaped in the boat, had perished beneath the muddy waters. Months later, the waters began to recede, and the survivors landed their boat on the high mountains of the north far from the plains where man had once flourished.

And man survived.

In a rocky gorge not far from where the survivors landed their boat, the receding waters washed away the accumulated dirt of centuries and once again those strange smooth blocks of stone were exposed to the light of day.

Once again mankind began to spread across the land.

From the northern hills, man moved into the valleys below, now somewhat changed by the floods, but still fertile and livable. In the plains by the rivers, he rebuilt his cities and villages and there he tilled the fields and grew crops to feed his families. Mankind increased in number and spread across the mountains and plains in all directions and built cities wherever he settled and man prospered.

He moved across the mountains to the west and found a fertile plain next to a vast sea and a clear blue river that flowed the length of the land into an inland sea that had no outlet. And he settled there and built cities on the river and in the plain south of the inland sea.

Eventually man built cities on the fertile plains where two great rivers flowed. Erech and Akkad and Ur and many other great cities rose in the land between the rivers.

The greatest of these cities was Babel where man built himself a tower to reach to the skies.

A mighty tower with a base as wide as some small cities and with many levels like giant steps made of bricks of clay and with stairways and ladders with which man could climb into the heavens.

And men began to think of themselves as gods.

Near the ruins of Babel, on the plains by the rivers, rose another great city with magnificent wide boulevards, airy plazas with fountains and trees, and beautiful gardens atop the buildings where the wealthy relaxed among the flowers.

This new city rapidly became the center of earth's civilization. It was the richest, most beautiful city of all mankind and, as its influence spread throughout the land, it became the most powerful. Soon the city grew to be a nation and this nation, as well as the city, was known as Babylon. And all the people of the land between the rivers paid homage to Babylon.

In the rocky hills far to the north of the city, a lowly goat herder wandered through the rocky defiles, searching for a part of his flock that had bolted during the night when the ground trembled and shook. Earthquakes were common in this land, and they usually caused more inconvenience to the herdsmen than damage to their possessions.

There isn't too much harm an earthquake can do to a simple tent, but they always frightened the herds and much time was wasted rounding up the strays.

As usual, one of the stupid goats had climbed halfway up the side of a steep gorge and no amount of coaxing could entice it to climb back down. So the goatherd tied up his skirts and began to climb after the goat, all the while crooning softly to soothe it so that it wouldn't climb higher out of reach or bolt and fall.

A few feet below the level of the wayward goat the goatherd stepped up onto a large smooth stone that, as he put all his weight on it, shifted slightly, causing him to slip and scrape his bare shins on the hard rock. That didn't improve his already bad temper.

But as he started to describe to the goat in very ungentlemanly language exactly what he was going to do to just what tender parts of the goat's anatomy, he saw a glint of bright yellow in a narrow cleft behind the shifted rock.

Without thinking, he thrust his hand into the cleft and brought forth a heavy yellow plate of what looked very much to his uneducated eyes like pure gold.

The goat, now completely forgotten, climbed down off the rocks and headed back to the camp where he joined the rest of the herd and took a nap. The goatherd sat dead still for a few minutes staring in rapture at the great wealth lying on the rock before him: a golden key to wealth and happiness. He then pulled off his cloak and wrapped the beautiful golden plate almost reverently in the rough cloth.

He made his way carefully back to his camp cradling the bundle in his arms more carefully than he would a newborn baby. He crawled into his tent, first looking all about to make sure no one else was around, then rolled out his precious find on the dirt floor of his small tent. Even in the semi-darkness the gold was mesmerizing in its beauty.

Only once in his life had he held a gold coin in his hands. That was the day a traveler had bought two young goats and paid him with a tiny wafer of gold. Now he possessed more gold than he ever dreamed existed and thought he was the richest man in the world. For three days he did little else but sit and fondle the golden plate. It was flat and roughly square, about two hands width across, and had neat rows of peculiar curly marks on its entire surface, as if someone had scratched them with a hard stone or metal tool.

His biggest problem, he finally decided, was how to convert the plate into spendable coinage without being robbed or cheated out of his treasure. In the end he decided to seek the advice of his cousin who, although not a merchant, was somewhat rich and thought of by most as a wise and honest man. He didn't have much respect for the cousin who, in his opinion, wasted most of his time making funny looking marks on flat pieces of gray clay with a sharp stick, but he knew no one else he could turn to. He wrapped the plate in goatskin and made his way out of the hills to the city where his cousin lived.

The scholarly cousin, who was not particularly fond of his overly aromatic relative, was at first inclined to have him chased away from his house; but when the story unfolded, he hurriedly sent his servants away instead.

He carefully unwrapped the package, and then gasped in wonder at what lay before him. For what he saw was not a plate of gold, but something he and several other scholars had been trying to develop for many years.

A written language!

Not one he recognized, for there was, to his knowledge, no written language yet in existence among the peoples of the earth.

But there was no doubt in his mind that this was writing, not just a design or decorative pictures, and not like the crude symbols used by his people to record their histories; they were groups of symbols formed into words and thoughts.

Unfortunately, the goatherd was completely wrong about the honesty of his scholarly cousin. It took but a little time for the scholar to convince his naïve cousin to lead him to the place where he had found the golden plate.

The hole in the rocks was not large enough for a man to pass through, so they both pried at the loose stone until it was pushed aside enough to make room for them to crawl inside. The scholar prudently let the goatherd go first in case a serpent or other unfriendly creature awaited them.

When the goatherd cried out that he had found more of the plates, the scholar cast caution aside and almost dove into the opening. There he found a space large enough to stand and six more of the plates in a depression in the rock wall. Had he not been so fascinated by the gold, he would have wondered about the nature of the space, for it looked more like a room than a cave; but gold has a way of clouding men's minds and all he saw was gold.

Once they were sure there were no more than six of the plates, there was no more need for the continued existence of the poor goatherd. While the goatherd was staring in near rapture at the plates, the scholar bashed his head in with a large rock.

Unfortunately, nature chose that exact moment to shake the earth again, and the opening in the rock closed with a rumble. The unlucky scholar beat on the rocks until his hands were bloodied and broken, but the hard stone didn't move, and eventually he collapsed in exhaustion. From time to time he arose again and beat at the unyielding stone, but he soon he gave up and not long after he quietly departed the land of the living, rich beyond measure but unable to spend any of his ill-gotten wealth.

The golden plate which he had left in his residence was soon found and melted down for jewelry and ornaments for the wealthy, completely disregarding the markings on the surface.

Part Two

◦◦Chapter Twenty-One◦◦

M ohamed hated Iraq. He longed for the familiar neighborhoods of his native Iran and the lush shores of the Caspian Sea where his family patiently awaited his return. But the American archaeologists paid good money for an English-speaking man with a knowledge of archaeology and jobs were hard to find in 1948. He and his American boss, George Shaw, had agreed to disagree about religion. Mohamed no longer tried to convince George that Allah was the one true god and that Mohamed was his prophet, and George had agreed not to try and convert Mohamed to Christianity. They'd grown to be close friends in spite of their vastly different backgrounds.

Their friendship had grown closer a few months ago when George and his wife, Nancy, lost their eighteen-month-old son to dysentery, and George had turned to Mohamed to help console Nancy. Mohamed and his wife had lost a baby daughter a few years earlier, and he was able to empathize with their pain.

George and Nancy were part of a team exploring in the area of the recently discovered ancient habitation site at Karim Shahir in northeastern Iraq looking for more evidence of early civilizations. The team had been exploring in the area for more than a year when the baby died, and they had seriously considered going home to the United States but eventually decided to stay on and continue working as a sort of therapy.

One spring morning, Mohamed awoke early from a restless night and decided to go and dig around at the latest excavation site before the others team members awoke and crawled out of their tents. As he worked, he heard a strange sound in the distance like a baby crying. At first he thought it was one of the worker's children, but the crying sound came from the opposite direction from the camp, so he decided to check it out.

As he followed the sound, he rounded a small knoll and was stopped dead in his tracks by what he saw. There among the rocks was a small white boy child, completely naked and looking as if it had been taken right out of a bath and dropped on the sand. He quickly rushed to the child, took off his coat, and wrapped the baby against the morning chill. He looked like an American baby, about two years old, with reddish-blond hair and blue eyes. The child appeared healthy and well fed with no sign of exposure, as if it had just been put there.

Instinctively he looked around for a parent; but there was no one in sight, so he took the child to the camp and woke George. His first reaction was of utter disbelief, but Mohamed finally convinced him he was telling the truth, so George woke Nancy and told her about the baby. She naturally wanted to keep the child and raise him as her own, but George was hesitant and said they should at least check and see if they could find the rightful parents.

George and Nancy decided they should do the right thing, but after several weeks of searching they could find no word of a missing baby. There were no other white people that they knew of anywhere in the area, and they could find no word of a missing child of any race. So, after much discussion and prayer, they decided to keep the child and raise him in place of their dead son. They named him Joseph Alan Shaw.

There were a few questions about the boy, but only a small number of their closest friends knew of their first son's death, and they kept their silence and asked no more questions.

Over the next several years, the family occasionally moved back to the United States to take a break from the rigors of the excavating and digging and to raise more money to enable them to continue their exploration. Young Joe became fluent in both English and Arabic and seemed to enjoy conversations in Arabic with the local Iraqis more than speaking English with family and what few English-speaking friends the family had.

During this time, his parents regularly took him to church whenever possible. And when there was no church nearby, they taught him Bible stories and read to him from the Bible, and he practically learned to read with the Bible as his primer. They were pleased and surprised by his ability to memorize and quote entire passages of Scripture with ease.

He dutifully attended church and Sunday school with his parents whenever they were able to go and did his best to please them by listening to the stories and reciting passages of Scripture.

Over the years, his parents frequently tried to get Joe to accept their religious beliefs, but somehow he just didn't feel what they felt. What they believed seemed reasonable to him, and the Bible stories had a ring of truth to them, but he couldn't find a place inside himself that accepted their beliefs. They continued to regularly expose him to their Christian behavior and practices but tried not to force it on him and prayed regularly that he soon would accept their way of life.

As a boy, Joe very often had strange dreams, almost nightmares, and he frequently woke up in the middle of the night mumbling in a strange language, not English or Arabic or any other language his parents recognized. Being devout Christians, George and Nancy were concerned and confused, and they prayed about him continually.

Along with the dreams was a recurring feeling that someone was watching him. Often he felt a "presence" and turned quickly to see who was there. But there was never anyone to be seen. Eventually he got used to the strange feeling and learned to ignore it; but it never went completely away. He sometimes thought he was "possessed by demons" as some of the characters in the Bible stories he remembered, so he never told his parents of the dreams and voices.

When he was about ten, Joe secretly started keeping a journal of the things he saw in his dreams, relating them as well as he could because some of the scenes were almost indescribable and often even beyond his comprehension. He kept the journal a secret from his parents, because he was reluctant to tell them of the strange dreams, and they worried enough about him as it was. Somehow it seemed important that he not forget the dreams; and as time passed, he compared his notes on newer dreams with the older ones. The one recurring theme seemed to be one of strong magic and much fighting with swords and spears and people speaking in a language Joe had never heard but that had a strangely familiar ring to it. However, soon the dreams seemed to become less frequent, and the dreams and the journal were shortly forgotten.

About this time Nancy became ill and was tentatively diagnosed with pancreatic cancer. The family cut all their ties in Iraq and moved permanently to the United States, settling in western Los Angeles close to the Pacific Ocean. They had been in the arid deserts for so long that the smell of the water and the sounds of the surf were a refreshing change, and Nancy made a small improvement.

George took a staff position as a lecturer in archaeology at a big university in Los Angeles that had a large and well-equipped hospital where Nancy received the best care possible, and the family easily settled into the urban lifestyle.

With the permanent move into the frenzy of life in Los Angeles, Joe again began hearing voices. Not distinct words or conversation, but a murmur of countless subdued voices seemingly coming at him from all directions. As a small child he'd often heard occasional murmurings in his head but ignored them because he simply thought everyone heard them.

But with the move into an area where there were tens of thousands of people concentrated closely together there came an increase in the voices. At first it frightened him, mostly because, with his religious upbringing, he was afraid the devil was inside his head. But he soon learned to block out the voices, and they ceased to be a distraction.

He continually got excellent grades in school but rarely studied hard and seemed to have a knack for remembering everything he read and had the uncanny ability to recall it at will.

While Joe was in the eighth grade, his almost perfect grades made other students jealous of him and occasionally the teachers became suspicious of how he always did so well. One day his history teacher asked Joe to stay after class for a few minutes. When they were alone, the teacher told him, "Joe, I know you're not cheating because I watch you carefully. But I can't understand how your answers to test questions are almost verbatim out of the text books." Joe told her that for him the tests were simply a matter of reading the book then visualizing the textbooks and writing down what he "saw." She seemed doubtful, so Joe picked up a book from her desk, opened it to a page at random, glanced at it for a minute, and then set it face down on the desk. He walked to the blackboard and wrote down the entire page word for word exactly as it was in the book. He then asked her not to tell the other students, as it might make him more of an outcast than he already was and she agreed.

He generally tried to avoid crowds and social activities but seemed to be drawn into them by his almost unwanted popularity. Students and faculty alike were drawn to him as if by a kind of invisible magnetic field, which to a great extent irritated Joe and caused him to withdraw even more into a shell.

Joe was popular in school, mostly because of his size and rugged good looks, and he was liked by just about everyone, but he was basically a loner and made few, if any, really close friends. Girls were not an essential part of his life, and even though some girls openly expressed an interest in him, he just didn't care. It was not that he completely neglected girls, but his liaisons were strictly for physical gratification with no emotion involved, and most of the girls went away feeling used rather than satisfied.

When he entered high school at fifteen, Joe was 6'1" and 180 pounds and heavily recruited by the coaches to go out for football. He watched the team work out, and the physical side of the game appealed to him; so he finally gave in and in his freshman year he was put on the "B" team where he stood out like a sore thumb among the smaller players, who were really just learning to play football.

In his sophomore year he moved up to the varsity and was assigned to play on defense, first at linebacker, then at defensive end as he grew even bigger and stronger.

At first he was extremely aggressive and often seemed to lack feelings for those he accidently hurt. He didn't actually try to injure the opposing players; he just didn't try not to hurt them. This caused some ill feelings among the other players, but everyone still seemed to like him and couldn't really explain why; they just did, when his attitude would and should have made enemies, not friends.

He soon learned to moderate his aggressiveness so as not to hurt his teammates, draw penalties for unnecessary roughness, or injure the opposing players. After a short time he became the backbone of the team's defense.

Joe had an uncanny awareness of the plays the opposition would call and always seemed to be in the right place to make a tackle or, at least, to change the direction of a play.

One Friday night during a game, Joe was concentrating on the quarterback, trying to "read the offense," when he suddenly got a clear picture of the play that was in the quarterback's mind and almost straightened up and backed away from the line.

He quickly regained his composure and called out the play; a sweep to the left, which would bring the ball carrier right into his area. He easily fended off the blocker and flattened the runner for a loss.

It didn't take long for Joe to realize that, although he couldn't actually read minds, when he concentrated on the quarterback he could basically see the play in the quarterback's head. With practice it became relatively easy for him to see into the mind of the opposing players and know what play they would execute before it was consciously called.

The morality of this didn't bother Joe at all, and he used all the abilities he could muster to be a better player. But he kept this "talent" to himself, mostly because he thought it was a little weird and didn't want to be labeled as any stranger than some already saw him.

When Joe was seventeen and a senior in high school, his mother's pancreatic cancer suddenly grew aggressive, and her physical condition deteriorated rapidly. After a very painful and blessedly short illness, she died.

George was devastated; but Joe seemed curiously unmoved by her death, almost uncaring. He did his best to hide his lack of feelings from his father because he knew it would hurt him if he made his absence of feelings known.

Joe was a little saddened but not really hurt by her death, and he wondered what was wrong with him. Why didn't he care? He spent a good deal of time thinking about how different he was from others his age, but it was more of a curiosity than a concern.

He was voted "Most Likely to Succeed" by his high school senior class and chosen as the "Most Valuable Player" on the football team. At graduation he was 6'5" and 230 pounds and was selected to the high school All American second team. Joe was heavily recruited by several universities and colleges. He eventually settled on the same university where his father worked, mostly because he wanted to please his father, and it was close to home.

At the university he majored in history with an emphasis on Ancient Eastern history. He couldn't explain his fascination with the subject, but he just couldn't seem to get enough of it and spent a good deal of his leisure time in the school library reading all he could find on eastern history.

Naturally he played football and was outstanding as a defensive lineman, partly due to his size and strength, but mostly due to his ability to know the oppositions' plays as soon as they were called.

Whereas in high school the coaches called all the plays, in college the defensive players were encouraged to use their minds as much as their bodies and to try and recognize the play the offense called and react to it. This suited Joe just fine, and he began to try harder to see what was in the mind of the quarterback. Before long the coaches recognized that Joe had some kind of an edge, so they moved him to middle linebacker and had him running the defense.

In his sophomore year, Joe made the starting varsity and was touted as a sure thing for the All-America team; and he would possibly be considered for the award of best college linebacker in the country.

But eventually Joe began to alienate even the people who liked him, because he appeared to have a complete lack of feelings and his episodes of overt aggression. It didn't seem to bother Joe because he felt he didn't really need friends anyway.

He spent much of his free time in the school weight room away from the social life of the other students and resisted all attempts to enlist him in one of the fraternities on campus. When he wasn't pumping iron, Joe could usually be found running alone in the hills near the university.

In 1967 during his senior year, the majority of the student body was very antiwar. Joe continually got into arguments with the very prevalent campus liberals about the Vietnam War and America's involvement. He couldn't understand their aversion to war. War seemed fine, almost agreeable to Joe. The politics of it didn't matter to him; war and fighting just seemed natural and almost enjoyable to think of.

As graduation time approached, Joe was set to graduate near the top of his class in academics and with a reasonable certainty of being a high choice in the pro football draft.

Then just a month before graduation, his father was killed by a drunk driver who ran a red light and broadsided George's car. Joe was somewhat depressed but had no real emotion and even began to get angry at himself for not feeling what seemed to be the right thing.

He went into deep self-introspection and lost all desire for school and football and just about everything else. Only his photographic memory and natural intelligence got him through the last two final exams and graduation.

He cut all social ties, packed up all his parent's belongings in a storage locker, rented out his parent's house, and enlisted in the army, as fighting seemed the natural thing to do to clear his head.

Basic training was a snap, and after the first few days he proved himself to be a natural soldier and extremely efficient fighter. At first the cadre singled him out and picked on him because of his size; but soon he was left alone, partly because of his great physical strength but mostly because he just didn't respond to the harassment.

When basic training was completed, Joe was sent to Vietnam with the rest of his company and assigned to a front line infantry unit.

He soon found that he enjoyed combat. In practice it was almost the same as football, but now it seemed to be easier because Joe didn't have to take it easy to avoid hurting or killing his opponent.

Joe spent much of what leisure time he had on refining his ability to see into the minds of those around him and soon was able to reach across distances and feel what the enemy was planning and avoid their traps.

He was almost too good a killer, and quite often he frightened the brass because of his callous attitude toward death; he didn't fear it and didn't seem to enjoy it, it was just a part of the business of war. His favorite weapon was the large Commando knife that he used with deadly efficiency.

Only the memory of the religious training from his parents kept Joe from becoming an altogether cold blooded killer, but still his attitude sometimes frightened him because he knew people weren't supposed to behave the way he did.

Joe was a natural leader, and even though he tried to avoid responsibility, other soldiers were constantly looking to him for direction. His superiors took note of this, and Joe was rapidly promoted up through the ranks until he made sergeant.

In spite of his size and simply because of his abilities, Joe was assigned to a special operations squad whose sole function was to search out and kill Viet Cong leaders. This suited him just fine, because he no longer was under the close supervision of higher-ranking officers who didn't actually do any fighting. Now he and his squad were on their own, and there was nothing to hold him back. Joe's ability to know the thoughts of the enemy helped him and his men to become the most effective team in the area.

He and his men worked quietly and efficiently and made an immediate impact on hostilities in their region, causing the Vietcong to put a price on their heads, dead or alive, preferably the former.

Then in 1970, Joe was badly wounded on a mission. He and his squad had just started a reconnaissance patrol when the man in front of Joe triggered a Vietcong booby trap. The man was killed, and Joe suffered severe shrapnel injuries to both legs. Joe missed "seeing" the booby trap because it didn't have a mind; it was just there.

The mission was aborted and both men were carried back to camp.

After triage treatment, Joe was flown to Hawaii. Following a lengthy convalescence, he found himself out of the army with nowhere to go. He no longer had any ties in Los Angeles or, for that matter, anywhere else.

While going through his parent's personal effects, Joe found his mother's diary detailing how he was found in the desert of Iraq and decided to go to Iraq and try to trace his origin.

While sorting through his few belongings to decide which things he would take and which he would leave behind, Joe came across the old journal recounting his childhood dreams and spent several hours deeply engrossed in the book.

Soon the strange dreams started coming back with vague, confusing scenes of ancient combat; strange magic; and very weird, bewildering pictures. At times he felt as if someone was making his mind do things he didn't want it to do and didn't understand.

Joe brushed up on his Arabic; and after some effort in acquiring a student visa, he enrolled as a graduate student in a small school north of Baghdad that emphasized the study of ancient languages because somehow they seemed very important.

Much unrest began to develop between Iran and Iraq, and it was starting to look like he was in the wrong country at the wrong time. He was about to leave Iraq for some other place when an ancient settlement site was found near some ruins far north of Baghdad, near the Turkish border.

The new site was at a level of excavation that predated even early Sumerian settlements. But what got everyone's attention was another nearby discovery: a cave deep within the side of a rocky hill above the ruins that looked like it had a manmade rock wall several feet back from the cave entrance.

What they found in this small space created a great deal of confusion and spawned many heated arguments among the archaeologists and scholars.

Behind this wall were the remains of two ancient decaying skeletons and six flat plates of gold that were covered with what appeared to be writings in a completely unknown language. But scattered among the bones were shards of pottery and other artifacts that predated all history from a period between 9000 and 12000 B.C. The bones themselves dated from early Sumerian times, about 4000 BC, causing even more confusion.

After much discussion and study, the plates were loaned to the language school where Joe was studying to see if the scholars there could make some sense out of the writings.

Everyone else in the school was completely baffled, but the scribbling on the golden plates seemed somehow strangely familiar to Joe. He worked with the local students and instructors for several months trying to decipher the writings as tensions rose in Iran. Joe stayed on despite the political turmoil. The Iraqis tolerated him because of his zeal and apparent ability to grasp concepts of the unknown language.

Late one night, Joe was working with another graduate student when suddenly the scribbling on the golden plates began to make sense and the whole language seemed to pop into his head. He started translating out loud almost unconsciously while the other student wrote, and when he came to the critical spot and spoke the ancient incantation of the priests of Shanar out loud, he disappeared with a small clap of thunder. Seconds later, the golden plates also disappeared with a soft "pop!"

The student who remained quietly fainted. When he regained consciousness, he considered what would happen to him when he tried to explain the truth of what had occurred to the school staff. So he quickly packed a small bag and headed for the border.

Part Three

Chapter Twenty-Two

In the stone tower in the mountains of Shanar the sorcerers and the old prophet were just starting to recover from the shock of the disappearance of the baby, which, truthfully, was quite unexpected, when they were knocked flat on the floor by a bigger and louder disturbance as the floor shook, and a peal of thunder quietly rumbled through the room.

As they began to recover their senses, they saw a naked blond giant of a man sitting on the floor looking just as dazed as they were. He was the biggest, most heavily muscled man they'd ever seen. The man had golden blond hair, shining blue eyes, and skin like burnished gold.

He spoke in what to them was a completely unknown language "Holy shit! What was that?" Then as he looked around, the man said, "Where am I and who are you guys?"

Naturally the old prophet and sorcerers almost had heart attacks; then they all started asking questions of the blond man, with everyone talking at once and no one understanding anyone.

Suddenly the crazy old prophet stopped and just stared at the newcomer for a few seconds. Then he began to jump around, almost dancing, and pointed at the newcomer shouting, "It's him! It's him!"

The others stopped talking and asking questions of the man and turned to the prophet. "What are you screaming about, you old derelict? It's who?"

"It's the promised one! J'Osha, the Golden One. The deliverer," he cackled.

Then the rest of them joined in with the same chant. "It's him! It's J'Osha, the deliverer!" And they fell on their faces on the floor in an almost worshipful manner.

Joe had the distinct feeling that somehow he'd been transported into an insane asylum and was surprised to hear what sounded like his name included in the gibberish of the language the men were speaking.

He was still asking questions when suddenly the noise seemed to fade and everything got dim, as if the sun had gone behind a cloud. And then it got really spooky as the thing that was Rakh/Mibara and their followers appeared in the air in the middle of the room; not quite touching the floor. Everyone got really quiet, and Joe heard a voice as if in his mind. *"Welcome, Grandchild! We have sensed a disturbance in the ether and traced its origin to this place."* Now there was total silence as the spooky thing continued. *"We know not yet from whence you have come, but your presence here at this time is indeed welcome."*

Everyone else stood in stunned silence for a few seconds, and then the very air itself seemed to creak and groan, and strange, foul odors, as if something long dead had been unearthed, filled the room. An unbelievably old person, wrinkled past determination of sex or age, faded into view and appeared sitting cross-legged in midair. It was Janga, still alive after almost two hundred years. Her horrible cackle scared everybody except Rakh/Mibara, who greeted her amiably. "Welcome also, honored great grandmother. We hoped you were awake but couldn't locate your presence."

Then there was what appeared to be a big family reunion, with Janga and Rakh/Mibara apparently talking over old times. The prophet and priest sorcerers were huddled together in a corner in reverent rapture, while Joe continued to ask what was going on; but no one was paying any attention to him.

Joe finally got fed up and picked up the robe dropped by sorcerer, wrapped it around him, and just sat on the stone bench scratching his head. When he got tired of waiting, Joe stood up, dropped the robe, tried to pick it up, and then bumped his head, which only aggravated him more. He got madder, dropped the robe, picked it up again, wrapped it around him and yelled, "QUIET!"

Dead silence.

Rakh/Mibara then broke the silence and spoke to Joe directly into his mind, which at the time was the only way anyone could communicate with him.

Joe realized they were speaking inside his mind and asked, "How can you talk inside my head? And how do they know my name?"

"What is your name?" they asked him.

"Joe Shaw," he responded.

"Then you are truly the promised deliverer," Rakh/Mibara answered.

They explained the reason for the excitement and told him of the ancient prophecy of Jirash Kin. Joe said, "No way! I'm nobody's deliverer!"

This brought about more explanations with Rakh/Mibara bringing Joe up to date on the events of recent years and explaining to him that Harl and his army were at that moment storming the high passes to Valley of the Moon with the intent of destroying everything and everyone.

As the conversation continued, Rakh/Mibara and Janga began to realize that the union of all the peoples described to Shallith was embodied in this man, not in people and armies.

Meanwhile, the entire world known to mankind was at war, and Harl was coming closer.

Those in the old temple would be safe for a time only because of the spells surrounding it, but eventually Harl would see through those spells and kill all the people he found. Rakh/Mibara and Janga would survive simply by going somewhere else.

Suddenly Joe realized that they were speaking in his mind in the language of the ancient golden plates and almost reluctantly he started to believe them. Rakh/Mibara then linked all their minds, and Joe was scared half out of his wits but couldn't help but listen. They put Joe into a shallow trance-like sleep and taught him all the history of all the peoples and crammed his mind with the facts and fables of hundreds of years of their civilization.

They found a closed area in his mind that they were unable to penetrate, even with their massive powers, which just made them more curious and more convinced that this truly was J'Osha, the deliverer. They found that they couldn't give Joe magical abilities; they could only protect him somewhat from magical harm using their own supernatural powers.

Rakh/Mibara sent messengers to get the sword and the knife from the crypt where they'd been hidden and tried to give them to Joe, but he resisted saying it wasn't his fight. They continued to steadfastly urge him, telling him that it was his destiny and again recited to him the old prophecy. Joe tried to resist but felt strangely drawn to the sword.

He mechanically reached out for the sword as if his hand was directed by some power outside of his body. When he took the hilt in his hand, Joe felt a power flow from the sword into him and fill his body. In a near panic, he dropped the sword and the power faded. Rakh/Mibara saw this reaction and quickly picked up the sword and gave it back to Joe. He reluctantly took the sword in his hand again, and all the power from the old gods of thunder filled him. He felt like he was growing inside with a strange sensation of being thousands of years old and very wise, yet unable to recall that wisdom as if in a half-remembered dream; and it scared Joe half to death.

Rakh/Mibara and Janga told him that he was truly J'Osha, the promised deliverer, and that only he could use the sword. While he wielded the sword, it could only be used for good.

Joe reluctantly gave in and the education really got under way.

Joe's complete instruction took but a short time; and with the knowledge of several hundred years of history safely tucked in his mind, he had no choice but to believe that somehow he really was this promised deliverer.

So Joe reluctantly went out to battle Harl. It felt strange fighting a man who, if what Rakh/Mibara and Janga told him was true, was his natural father but appeared to be about his same age. Naturally he had never seen any father that he could remember, other than the one who raised him; but when Joe saw Harl, he did look somewhat familiar. He saw the resemblance to himself. Harl had the same features, although he wasn't as tall or heavy as Joe. And Harl had the same coloring as Joe, except Harl had lots of freckles.

Harl had no idea who he was about to fight; he only knew that this was apparently the champion chosen by his enemy to oppose him, and soon the battle was under way.

The troops of the opposing armies sensed something special in the battle between Harl and the big stranger. Most of them unconsciously stopped to watch.

Joe was bigger and faster and in better condition than Harl, but Harl was much more experienced with a sword. Joe had never used one, but he'd seen lots of movies and had a vague idea of what to do; but he was no Errol Flynn.

Joe was protected by all the spirits but was still no match for Harl. That was partly because deep in his mind he didn't really believe all this was happening. He thought it was probably just a bizarre dream. And besides, everybody knows there's no such thing as magic.

Joe was beginning to get worried. Even if this was only a dream, he was slowly being beaten down by Harl and was close to being severely injured or killed. It was starting to get desperate when something or somebody "entered" his head, like another person moving into his brain with him. This entity took over all control of Joe's body, and he heard a strangely familiar voice in his mind say, *"Don't bother me; I'm kind of busy now!"* This thing in his head almost pushed Joe's mind aside and suddenly the tide of battle turned 180 degrees.

Joe felt like a spectator watching from inside his own head as his body started doing things with the sword that he simply didn't know how to do. The thing/person inside him felt almost like a friend, and somehow Joe was not afraid of it/him.

It was not a completely one-sided battle. Joe was obviously winning, but he was wounded and weakened. However, now he was fighting with greater skill and cunning experience. Then Joe struck a mighty blow to Harl's shield, staggering him and knocking him off his feet. Then Joe swung the heavy sword with all the strength he had and struck another tremendous blow to Harl's side, mortally wounding him. Joe watched dispassionately as he died. It was a weird feeling to watch the father he'd never known die. Joe tried to tell Harl he was sorry, but Harl cursed him with his dying breath and Joe thought, *"Well, crap on you anyway,"* and felt no pity for him.

As Joe was close to passing out from his injuries and exhaustion, he turned his concentration inside his mind to ask what/who was there. The answer he got was not really an answer. *"Don't trouble yourself about who I am and what's going on. You know me, we've met before, although you can't remember it. We'll meet again when I have more time to explain. Now rest and get well. I can promise that you'll live a very long life. I can't stay any longer. We'll meet again."*

The presence in his head seemed to fade out, and Joe was not sure if he was passing out or if it just went away. Then he fainted, still wondering.

Joe woke up in bed in the stone temple covered with bandages and in a great deal of pain. Muscles and joints all over his body that he hadn't used in that manner before, ached from the unaccustomed strain. While he was recuperating, he thought it over and decided not to tell anyone about the presence in his head. They might have thought he was as crazy as he almost thought he was.

When Harl died, the Ghorn army abruptly quit, as they really didn't want to fight anyway. They had just been afraid of their king.

And the war was over.

As things began to settle down, Joe realized that the life he was now living was the life of the dreams he'd had as a child, and he became even more confused. Things that had been totally alien to him just a few days ago were now a familiar reality. The foreign language the people around him were speaking became increasingly more familiar and soon he was speaking it with ease.

The priests, leaders, and sorcerers of all the peoples had a meeting and determined to make Joe leader of the united peoples. Joe immediately tried to quash the proposal; but when they told him that he was the rightful leader because he was the son of Harl and Shallith, the grandson of Yoki and Gabela, the grandson of both Rakh and Lisha, and so on, Joe finally gave in when it became obvious he couldn't turn it down. Because, where could he go?

A few people resisted the idea of this stranger from nowhere becoming their leader, but the priests and elders convinced them with reason rather than with force.

During his first few years as leader of the peoples, the "friend" in his mind visited him regularly, making suggestions, and teaching him how to do things that he needed to know. Eventually Joe accepted this friend and respected, even sought, his advice.

Joe built up the nomad city on plains as his capital, figuring it was the best place; right in the middle of everything and not of any one people. He taught them how to irrigate the plains to raise crops for all, trying to remember his high school and college classes that could help make life better.

It took some time for Joe to get used to his new role as leader of the world, and he steadfastly resisted all efforts of the people to treat him as such.

He just wanted to be treated like everyone else and refused to answer when called any of the kingly titles. Eventually the people got used to it, and his popularity grew as they accepted him as one of their own.

Much progress was made in all areas. Joe reestablished trade between all the peoples, which gave all of them new goods and increased everyone's quality of life. He "invented" nails and other tools that were common in his early life but unknown to the people he led. After much trial and error, and a lot of help from the local blacksmiths, he finally made a crude saw. He then had them build a saw mill on the river driven by a waterwheel with wooden pulleys and ropes to cut the trees of the forests into lumber for houses. Then they sent the wood to the cities and new towns. Where it had taken dozens of logs to build a crude building before, now the same number of logs were cut into rough planks to make many more and better homes.

People who were raised in huts and tents now had solid houses with wooden floors to resist the changes in the weather. All of this elevated Joe to almost godlike status in the eyes of the people, and he gained more popularity each day.

Soon Joe sent for the leaders of all the tribes and clans and representatives from the common people. He set up a democratic government with all members having an equal voice in the affairs of the people. By so doing, Joe was unwittingly following the old prophecy of Jirash Kin.

For a time, everything was rosy. Janga was happy and went back to caves to do whatever it was that she did deep in those caves, Rakh/Mibara returned to the swamp to commune with the spirits there, and the old prophet died happy. Joe's grandmother, Valesa, was still alive and well and was treated like the queen mother. She had no hard feelings about the death of Harl. As Joe's only real living relative (you can't count Rakh/Mibara or Janga as living), Valesa became a great teacher to the young leader. Joe tried to establish one religion based on what he remembered of his parents Christianity and some of all the current religions, but it didn't sit well with the people who hung on to their worship of the old gods, so he dropped it. But everything else ran smoothly for many years and much progress was made.

For about fifteen years all went well and life was good. Everyone forgot about M'gori and the vile things on the plateau.

Everyone was happy, except Chataan.

Chapter Twenty-Three

There was just too much good and too many happy people to suit Chataan. Evil was suffering. So he began to make plans to take a hand and change things to suit his purposes, and he got M'gori involved. M'gori and his followers got together with the spirits sent by Chataan and began to make trouble. Things started to go wrong.

The dry seasons lasted longer and crops failed, forest fires destroyed the trees and the lumber supply vanished, the mines were getting worked out, and previously tame animals began attacking people. Everything that could possibly go wrong seemed to go wrong, and the people began to grumble.

This continued for about five years, and soon the government of the people was losing control as many people went back to "the old ways" and worshipped the false gods, which was just exactly what Chataan wanted.

Rakh/Mibara came back out of the swamp, and they warned Joe that outside forces were at work, upsetting things. The swamp creatures were restless; they were not following orders and were causing trouble. Rakh/Mibara called on Janga, and she grudgingly came out of her solitude. Then they merged with Joe's mind. He didn't really try to stop them this time but could control them to a limited extent, and they cooperated.

They sent a mental probe to the high plateau to try and find the cause of the trouble, because they suspected that their difficulties originated there. They found M'gori's barrier and, like Shallith before them, were able to quietly probe beneath the barrier and discover what drove him. They realized that they couldn't cope with that much power yet and fell back to regroup. Simply stated, they need more muscle.

Janga brought the spirit of air from the deep recesses of the caves beneath the earth; the spirit of earth was already in the sword; the spirits of fire and water came with Rakh/Mibara, and all merged in the mind and body of Joe, along with others he didn't recognize.

He felt kind of like a spectator watching what was going on inside him and remembered the feeling when the thing/person joined with him when he battled with Harl. It was almost the same but different; these things felt uncomfortable to him.

The realization finally set in that all of it was real and what was happening was simply good versus evil; and Joe was caught right in the middle of it without knowledge of which side was which. Joe traveled to the old stone tower to consult with the priests and sorcerers there and saw one of the old prophets scratching on the gold plates and realized that they originated in this time. The archaeologists had dated the plates at between 9,000 and 12,000 BC.

These people had no legends or folk tales even slightly resembling Adam and Eve and the Garden of Eden, or Noah and the ark and the great flood, or the Tower of Babel, or any of the other events that were more or less common knowledge to everyone he had associated with.

Joe tried to remember all the things he hadn't paid enough attention to as a child in Sunday school about God and the Bible, and he suddenly realized that if the dating was even close then those times are before Adam and Eve and those people were the pre-Adamic man he heard discussed only as an improbability; if that was the case, then none of those people had souls, and he was one of them!

Shock and then deep depression set in, and Joe fell into a deep melancholy for several days as he tried to figure out what to do. Should he accept the help from the strange spirits out there and fight what appeared to be evil or just give up? After all, if what his parents or whoever those people were who raised him, taught him was all true, then he couldn't get to Heaven no matter what he did. So what was the difference?

Finally, Joe went off in private to a place on a high hill and tried to pray to the God of the only parents he knew. Joe spent many hours in anguished supplication and finally fell asleep. Strange dreams came back to him, and the familiar but strange person/thing came to him again in his dreams and told him there really was a God and all would be well with him as long as he followed what he felt was right in his heart. As he began to wake up, Joe tried to remember the dream. He didn't think it was an angel that spoke to him; it seemed more like the person who came to him when he fought Harl but somehow older and wiser.

Joe decided to go along with the locals and their spirits and fight whatever evil that was out there. If he helped them win, then he will have done something good; if not, well, he'd just have to see what would happen.

Joe rejoined Rakh/Mibara and completely let down what barriers he could. Then Janga, Rakh/Mibara, and many others, much more than the first time, joined inside Joe's mind. Then he was connected again by another presence, much different than the rest, and Joe recognized it as the person who was with him at the battle. But now it was definitely a person and not a thing; a person who was somehow very familiar and Joe asked him, "Don't I know you?" The person laughed and answered, *"Sure you do! You may not recognize me yet, but you know me as well as you know yourself!"* Joe was hit with a tremendous emotional shock as he really recognized the "visitor" as himself, in some way completely different but still the same.

"Me? How can another me be in my head?" Joe asked. "He" answered, *"It's a long story, and you'll understand it completely later; but now there's a job to do, and it'll take all we've got to handle it! Let's get to work. Take a deep breath, kid; this is going to be a bumpy ride!"* And with that statement, all the barriers that had been set up in Young Joe's mind many years before were released. All the suppressed abilities of all the generations of all the peoples came flooding into his conscious mind.

He actually staggered under the weight of what suddenly possessed him but recovered almost immediately as "Old Joe" merged with him completely and what had been two became totally one. They became J'Osha!

With the barriers down, there was no longer anything keeping the others from merging with J'Osha and all that was Rakh/Mibara and Janga and countless others unnamed and unnamable flowed effortlessly into his being and became an entity with powers unlike any seen or even dreamed of since the beginning of time.

All the combined entities that now made up what had been Joe Shaw traveled instantaneously to the barrier on the plateau and, with their now unheard of powers, easily breached that which before was impenetrable and confronted the evil forces of M'gori. The battle began.

But as Joe had changed into J'Osha, M'gori had also changed into something as inhumanly evil as Joe was fundamentally good. Chataan well knew that to defeat the powerful forces arrayed against it, things had to change; and it changed into something not of this universe. What had been M'gori ceased to exist, and his place was taken by Chataan itself, joined with all the remaining Daemoz.

Strangely, the battle was not all physical and not all supernatural, but some of both and some of something else completely different.

J'Osha (strangely, now he felt that the name fit) felt like he was moving randomly through space and time and other through indescribable dimensions, sometimes like blinding beams of light and other times like crawly dark wormholes, and others in a manner totally beyond human comprehension. The conflict waged on for many seconds/eons/light years, and J'Osha again felt himself growing, as if joined by other forces from other places, but he had no way to describe how he felt.

In time the battle turned in favor of the forces of good, and Chataan was being beaten back into another space/time continuum. In desperation, Chataan pulled out all the stops, risking total self-destruction. It unleashed all the primal forces of the other universe at J'Osha and earth in one gigantic blast of energy, even by galactic proportions.

Earth was decimated, washed clean of all life. The seas boiled and the mountains crashed down and earth rocked and reeled in her orbit around the sun.

Everything was dead; there was no life left on earth, no life except Joe. And what he had couldn't really be called life in any form we recognize. Space itself was ripped in two, and Joe was instantaneously blasted through a hole in the space/time into another elsewhere/elsewhen, nowhere/nowhen.

ℰ𝒟Second Interlude𝒞𝒩

C onsciousness, that's all. Nothing else, except the awareness of consciousness.

No memory, no identity, no anxieties; nothing. There was no sensation of feeling in his body, because he didn't have a body; and there was no sense of loss, because he had no remembrance of ever having a body.

He was; but there was no feeling of being, no sense of place or time. There was not even a spark of curiosity in what there was of his mind and that didn't bother him in the least, for all that existed in his mind was the awareness that he was.

No past, no present, no future; nothing but consciousness.

Slowly he became vaguely aware of another presence and attempted to reach out to it, but he was met with an almost overwhelming wave of desperation and loneliness and quickly withdrew, and then just as quickly forgot about it.

There was a momentary shadowy stirring at the extreme edge of that consciousness, the merest wisp of a feeling that something very important should be happening; but before he was able to bring what little attention he had into focus, the thought passed.

It was enough just to be.

Sometime later, how much later really didn't matter because there was no awareness of the passage of time, the vaguest beginnings of discomfort stealthily scratched at the outer edges of his consciousness. It wormed it's way quietly inside, toward his mind's hiding place, and then slowly grew like a nebulous cancer in his id, multiplying in intensity until it burst upon his awareness with a shock of intense pain.

Pain that his barely awakening consciousness couldn't yet comprehend steadily increased until he thought it would tear him apart.

He felt as if he were expanding in many directions at once; outward toward the far edges of awareness, and inward to the very core of his being.

Then it did tear him apart, and he actually felt himself explode!

Softly, like a giant soap bubble in slow motion, he burst into countless filmy shards, but somehow he remained intact.

He was intact! He had a body!

He was alive!

But in that split second of realization that he was alive, there also came the realization that there was nothing to breathe and that he was dying.

Part Four

⮑Chapter Twenty-Four⮐

Mankind was at war with "them" and had been for many generations. Thousands of years ago man had expanded throughout his home galaxy and into intergalactic space. The old planet earth had long since been deserted because all her natural resources had been used up. What once was a beautiful green and blue planet had been left as a dirty gray-brown wasteland stripped clean of vegetation with most of the seas polluted before mankind realized what they had been doing, altered their lifestyle, and moved on.

The war was not going well and mankind was slowly being pushed back into the center of their own galaxy by "them" aliens from somewhere across the universe. They were not quite organic, not quite humanoid, not quite machine, but something entirely different and beyond human understanding. They were as far beyond man's comprehension as a computer would be to a slug crawling in the dirt.

Countless generations ago, man had outgrown the need for war as everyone had everything they needed and no one desired more. The occasional nonconformist who did want more than his neighbor was "reeducated" by what the ancients would have called brainwashing, and then placed back into society.

Weapons were no longer needed by the enlightened masses, and the means for making them had been all but forgotten. So the war went badly until man once again learned the ways of killing.

The aliens were a collective hive intelligence directed by a central intellect entity/unit on their home planet. The aliens had an insatiable thirst for knowledge and spread across space in all directions collecting specimens from all the beings they encountered, and then "sampled" their intelligence by draining their brains (or whatever else passed for the seat of intelligence) of information and storing all the data in semi-organic computers in their ships, eventually transferring all the data to a central unit at their home.

Once the contents of the mind were gone, the aliens dissected the remains and studied the anatomy of the being. They preserved specimens in their ships for eventual transfer to their home. They were always looking for more information; and if a race resisted, they were simply exterminated. There was no emotion in it, for the aliens had none, simply a thirst for knowledge.

The major difference between these aliens and man was that the aliens collected and stored the knowledge and never went back to it—like filling a vast library with books and never reading them—whereas mankind was always looking for ways to use the knowledge they gained.

Countless millennia ago, a long forgotten race of super beings, who were almost entirely intellect with virtually no discernible bodies, created this race of things to collect information for them and sent them out across the galaxies. Then they simply died out, for reasons known only to the old gods. And their creations went on collecting knowledge wherever they found life.

Mankind had been unable to capture any of the aliens or their ships because they always destroyed their ships when there was a possibility of capture. Man had no idea what they were, where they came from, or even what they looked like. There was never much left after a nuclear implosion.

Mankind was finally able to establish a base in a small solar system near the aliens' home base, hidden from their view behind a massive black hole. It was by nature very dangerous, but it was their only chance to spy on the aliens with reasonable safety.

Eventually the aliens detected the messages sent back to mankind's bases and searched out and attacked the base, destroying the entire planet with a newly developed negative-matter-type weapon. The weapon was designed with information gleaned from another of the races scanned by the aliens and had never been used or even tested before. Everything in that area of space was flooded with enormous amounts of negative energy that tore a gaping hole in the space/time continuum.

~

And what there was left of Joe Shaw burst through that hole from elsewhere/elsewhen, nowhere/nowhen.

The aliens were watching and studying from a distance in a remote ship, because even they were not sure of the power of the new weapon. When their instruments detected a human-type creature suddenly appearing in space, they instantaneously englobed the creature with a force field and pulled it into their ship. What they found would be confusing to most beings, but only aroused more interest in the aliens, as they'd never seen such a creature before. It resembled a human but was in comparison almost a giant, very different from their usual catch. They thought this may have been a new human being genetically engineered to combat them. They took Joe to their mother ship to examine him painstakingly before putting him on the "machine" that would drain his brain into the memory banks.

Most human males were then about 5'5" and 120 pounds, lean and muscular with slightly larger brain cases. They were basically computer types. The being the aliens had caught was about 6'5'' and 270 pounds with huge muscles and entirely different internal organs.

He was completely unconscious with only the slightest discernable trace of life; but he was alive. After examining the body, the aliens put him on the machine and examined his brain. They found no memory, only the slimmest awareness of existence; they tried to stimulate the memory centers, but totally shorted out the whole nervous system, sending him into convulsions. So they sedated him completely and vacuumed his mind and pumped everything into their data banks with all the rest of the information gathered over several millennia of exploration.

At that instant, a human warship was returning to the now destroyed base and came out of ether drive almost on top of the alien mother ship and attacked without hesitation. Mankind too had a new weapon but, unlike the aliens' weapon, it had been tested and perfected. They stunned the alien ship with a stasis freeze ray that shut down all activity of all kinds on the alien ship and zapped everything in the ship into a deep-freeze-like condition.

Cautiously, they approached the ship. When a crew boarded, they found what also appeared to them to be a giant in the examining room. Naturally they thought it was a trick or a booby trap. None of them had ever seen or even heard of a man that big since prehistoric times, so they kept the giant frozen and took him to their base along with the alien specimens.

The crew of the alien ship was made up of just four beings (for lack of better terminology) that were all different in appearance. One was vaguely humanoid in shape with appendages similar to arms and hands, another was an amoeba like mass about the size of a couch, the third was more machine than anything else, and the last appeared to have melted into a sticky goo.

All were completely devoid of any lifelike functions, and it appeared that the stasis freeze beam had "killed" them.

The alien ship was towed to a base on the small moon that orbited mankind's new home planet where it could be examined in relative safety. For a long time they kept the alien ship frozen, because they were afraid that if it were unfrozen it might implode and destroy all or part of their base.

Finally, they decided to unfreeze the ship and moved it into space far enough from all their outposts that, if it did implode, it would cause no harm. Then they unfroze the ship and waited. Nothing happened. So they towed it back to the moon base and left it for future examination.

Joe was taken to the base hospital for examination. And after much debate they decided he was a human but definitely a throwback to some earlier age. What they did find was completely different from a normal man. Unlike them he had an appendix, tonsils, and other organs that hadn't been seen in man for more than 5000 years.

In the hospital they scanned the giant for brain waves and just didn't find any, only a complete blank, except for the simplest motor functions. Medical science had advanced much over almost 14,000 years of human history, and they were able to unfreeze him very carefully. They restored all of his basic bodily functions, but there were still no thought processes.

The aliens attempt to stimulate his memory had shorted out all of his nerve synapses and made his reaction time virtually instantaneous. The ancient magic in his head had left a black area in his brain that even the aliens' machine had been unable to crack.

After much study and discussion, the doctors decided he really was human but theorized that somehow he was from some other time. His brain and mind were intact, just empty, like a newborn baby with no instincts. So they set out to reeducate him to possibly find out where and when he came from.

The education began. The doctors tried to teach him using many standard methods, but Joe had no mind to use to learn. Finally they tried a "dream machine," which was most commonly used to re-stabilize insane people, to reach Joe's mind, and eventually they made contact.

Joe learned exceptionally fast, much too fast for comfort. In two months he learned simple speech and was reading in four months. By eight months of study he'd reached what was equal to what would be high school level, which made his teachers uneasy; then he seemed to slow down to normal and everyone relaxed.

After about three weeks of training, Joe's mind awoke; and while he still had no memory, he had a desire to learn. At about three months Joe became aware that he could hear the thoughts of his teachers. At first this was of no concern to him, but eventually, as he progressed, he realized he was going too fast and was causing suspicions among the teachers. So he slowed down, on the surface.

At seven months, Joe tried a new tack and began to influence their direction of teaching without their awareness. They just felt happier that he was learning so fast and wanted to help. So Joe hid his talents from his instructors and continued to learn.

The alien mind probe had made Joe's brain work incredibly fast. His body was already almost superhuman and now his reflexes were practically instantaneous, virtually zero reaction time. The thought became the deed. The doctors continued to test during Joe's education, completely unaware that Joe had been dictating the direction of their teachings; and they were ecstatic over what they believed correctly was a "superman." Joe was unable to hide all of his physical abilities in the manner that he could hide his mental powers.

Some vague recall came back with his advanced education, but only hazy pictures like partly forgotten dreams. Most of his brain remained hidden behind the barrier, but he had small pictures that leaked in during off-guard moments. He remembered being in combat, but fighting in Vietnam was all mixed up with swords and sorcery, and he couldn't sort it out. Joe went to the libraries of ancient history and studied the wars of old earth and found a history of the Vietnam War and things started to come back. No specific memories, but an uneasy feeling of déjà vu.

He came across image discs of ancient magazines from the past. While reading an article from 1970 on the Vietnam War, he came upon a picture of an army recon team. There in the middle of the group was Joe Shaw, himself. There was absolutely no doubt in his mind! What was now an old scar on his jaw was a new cut in the old photo.

The current date was 12,376 by the old standard earth calendar, which made Joe over 10,000 years old! But the doctors said his age was about 40 to 45. And he still couldn't remember.

So Joe completed his reeducation as far as it was possible for them to teach him. Try as they might, they just didn't have any more information for him to learn. Joe still had no memory, only disconnected images.

Physically he was a superman; mentally Joe was a borderline super genius, and he was almost frightened by all the "stuff" he had, even though somehow it seemed right that he had it. It was a good thing he couldn't remember yet; it would have been too much to grasp at that stage of his development. He still had a feeling that there was so much more to learn and that he had so much more room to put it in. He felt incomplete because he still had no memory. And after two years he felt like a very big, very smart baby.

Finally Joe was told what had happened to him, and he became obsessed with going back to the alien ship, which was still being studied at the top secret space navy yard on the moon orbiting the home planet.

He wanted passionately to go back on the machine that had vacuumed his mind and try to get his memory back. He used all his mental powers to influence higher ups and finally got permission to help study the alien ship. The scientists were still baffled by the controls and were willing to take whatever help they could get, figuring that since Joe was on the machine when they found him, maybe he could help. He worked with the scientists on the ship and on the mind machine while the war continued.

It was not going well for mankind, and the aliens were getting closer all the time.

At last the scientists thought they had solved the mind machine's controls and figured out a way to reverse the process. It was simple for Joe to convince them he was the one to be the guinea pig, and he was connected to the machine. The scientists turned the machine to what they thought was the lowest setting and turned it on.

Wrong!

All the data banks of the entire ship began to download their data into Joe's brain. The first blast would have killed him, but his brain cut off all outside stimulus and shut down everything but minimal body functions before the data banks emptied. His body went into a deep coma while his super brain shunted most of the data into unused areas of the brain and filled up all the nooks and crannies.

He acquired information on the aliens as well as much of the collective intellect of all the races the aliens had captured and intellect vacuumed. Joe now had the knowledge of how to defeat the aliens. He kept his body in a coma-like state while his brain sorted through the information he'd gained, then rested and built up strength.

◌ᔕ Chapter Twenty-Five ᔕ◌

Three days later, Joe awoke and summoned the top scientists and engineers. He explained to them some of what he had learned from the information in the data banks of the alien ship. Because of the fatal effects the stasis freeze beam had on the aliens, the scientists quickly began to direct the building of ships and more powerful weapons to defeat the alien invaders.

With the knowledge Joe had gained from the alien machine, mankind now had the capability to build ships that could travel between galaxies instantaneously by warping space upon itself and simply "stepping" across the gap. The scientists had long since stopped being amazed at Joe's abilities and eagerly went along with whatever he wanted.

Man's existing fleet fought a delaying action against the aliens while all their energies were poured into building ships equipped with the new drive and the improved weapons systems.

Joe now knew the exact location of the alien's home base and the strength of their fleet. Soon a mighty armada of ships equipped with a much more deadly variation of the stasis weapon appeared as if out of nowhere and attacked the alien's home base. Whereas the older weapon had merely frozen whatever it touched, the new version sent out a ball of energy that killed everything it touched—animal, plant, and machine.

Everything would simply stop functioning.

The aliens fought back with all they could muster, but the complete surprise of the attack had destroyed much of their fleet and what was left was quickly dispatched into slightly radioactive dust.

A rear guard was left behind to mop up any alien stragglers that might return to their home cluster unaware of the massacre.

And the war was essentially over.

Once again Joe turned his attention to his roots.

He went into seclusion and started digging into his newly regained memories. He sorted his own memories from the memories of almost countless other beings whose memories had been stored in the alien data banks. He hadn't taken the time to really reach back into his own past because of the urgency of the war, but now he had nothing else to do.

As his memories slowly began to return, Joe remembered his early life in Iraq, growing up in Los Angeles, the dreams of his youth and the almost constant feeling of being watched, football and Vietnam, and, most confusing of all, living many years in the strange land of his dreams; a land of odd people and magic and the battle with Harl and being king of those strange people.

As his memory completely returned, Joe remembered how that life had ended.

That memory caused him to spend a great deal of time in serious deliberation. For several days he just sat and thought about the clear memories of his past and what it meant about his future.

He couldn't understand the reasons for what he knew had happened; but now he knew his destiny and there appeared to be nothing he could do about it.

He also realized that somehow he must have traveled back in time to his earlier life, because he now remembered having been contacted as a young man and being taught by what or who he now realized was himself. Then he had to figure out how to go back to his childhood and teach himself the many things he remembered being taught. This task gave him many sleepless nights.

Several times he went back to the alien machine and with his newfound abilities, searched the data banks for information that might be useful.

In the ancient memory of an unknown alien race, Joe found that they possessed the ability to project their minds through space and time and he began to dig deeper until he found what he was looking for.

At first he was reluctant to sending his mind back in time because he wasn't sure what would happen to his body while he was "gone." He set up a recording device to record what happened while he projected his mind and tried a short trip back in time. But nothing happened; he didn't go anywhere.

Curious, Joe tried again to go to times and places in the recent past but was also unsuccessful in all of those attempts. Frustrated, he tried sending a gentle probe back to his early youth and was able to make contact with himself. At first he just touched the surface of his mind without letting his younger self become aware of the contact.

Joe withdrew and checked the recording device. He found, to his amazement, that no time had transpired. He tried sending a probe back in time to just watch his younger self without making mental contact and was also able to do that without much effort. Again his visits to the past took up no time in his present.

After trying several times to visit other times in history, Joe realized that he couldn't go to any place or time where he hadn't actually been in his earlier life and apparently couldn't "touch" any mind but his own.

After much testing, and some almost deadly mistakes, he sent his intellect back to the time of his birth and watched himself being born, which at first caused him a good deal of emotional trauma; but he soon became engrossed in watching his own birth.

As he watched the priestesses clean up after the child was born, Joe was suddenly startled by the appearance of what looked like a shining golden giant of a man in the middle of the room. Then the man turned, and with great surprise Joe recognized the man as himself.

This golden man then told the priestesses that the king intended to kill the baby and that he would take the child to a safe place. The golden man quickly took the child from the shaken women and disappeared.

Joe spent a great deal of time considering what he'd witnessed, because it simply meant that he had not only projected his mind across space and time, but he'd actually sent his physical body.

As Joe toiled with this new problem, he refined the process of projecting his mind through tedious experimentation and made many trips to his mind as a baby. The thought of being inside his own mind as a child caused some disturbing conflicts at first, but they were resolved with practice and patience.

At first he couldn't get into the child's mind because of subconscious barriers, so he backed out and moved very slowly with gentle steady pressure. He still couldn't get through, so he went back in the child's mind to the early stages of development inside Shallith's womb and found no barriers there. So, after much deliberation, he carefully built the very barriers that had caused him so much trouble earlier.

As an experiment, and to satisfy his curiosity, Joe tried to go back farther in the child's mind; but as he approached conception, he ran into a gray area that began to suck him in like a seething whirlpool. It was like a really bad nightmare you can't quite remember and aren't sure you want to. It was very frightening and caused a tremendous pressure inside the brain. Joe struggled, using all the massed power of all the collective minds and barely got out. He never tried that again!

As the child grew, Joe made several trips back and gently touched the child's mind. Eventually the child recognized him as a friend, and Joe got into the young mind and began to teach. *"Relax, little guy. There is much you need to learn, and we have all the time in the world."*

He made several attempts to travel to the time of his growing up in Los Angeles, but for some reason he couldn't make contact with his younger self. He could visit the correct time and space, but he could only observe, as it were, from a mental distance as Young Joe grew from a child to manhood.

Eventually he realized that the barriers he built in the unborn child were not complete, and the younger Joe had inherited from his Ghorn ancestors the ability to block invasions into his mind. His desire to be alone and not be bothered by outside peer pressure effectively sealed his mind from intrusion. It was not until much later when he relaxed his resistance so that Janga and Rakh/Mibara could communicate with him that, Old Joe would be able to communicate with him.

Joe knew he needed to physically travel back to the "old world" and searched his new memories for the information he needed. From time to time he went back on the alien machine to search for information he needed. There was a machine used by one of the races conquered by the aliens that allowed them to travel through time, and Joe could easily build a copy of that machine; but he needed a superconductor metallic cloth to make a full bodysuit to create the electrical field necessary to make the trip.

An alloy of gold and the alien metal would work fine, but gold was no longer of value and there was not enough on the new home planet of man to make the suit. It was just not a natural ore on the new home planet.

All he had to do was to go back to old earth and get the golden plates.

But how?

Once again he went to the alien ship and searched the data banks for something he could use, and finally he found what he needed. He was able to build a machine somewhat resembling a large ancient microwave, send back to old earth, and retrieve the gold plates with the ancient inscriptions from the university lab in Iraq. He then used gold from the plates to make the suit he needed to transport his body.

He refined the ability until he was certain he was able to send his entire body without danger. After much practice with short hops and some mistakes, it became possible for Joe to move back in time; but each trip was physically and emotionally exhausting. He realized that one complete trip was all he would be able to handle, so he planned it carefully.

He made one partial trip to the time of his birth but did not completely materialize, staying just outside the border of visibility and appearing to the attendants as a shining golden glow. They simply thought it was a sign from the gods.

Finally, Joe overcame the psychological discomfort and went back again to the time of his birth; he took the child from the priestesses and carried himself to the temple of Shanar.

He made many experimental trips back in time and polished the process of joining with Young Joe's mind with just a gentle touch, keeping outside the feeling of his consciousness.

He often wondered what would happen if he didn't make contact with the younger Joe on one of the times he remembered contact having been made but was afraid not to do it because he thought the consequences might change history as he knew it and really mess things up. So he studiously watched Young Joe grow and recorded each time contact was made to be sure he didn't miss one.

As he made more contact with the mind of Young Joe over the years of his life, he realized that he'd greatly assisted him physically in the battle with Harl but he'd had no knowledge of, or the ability to use, the heavy sword like those used in Young Joe's time.

The use of swords had ceased thousands of years ago and the few that still existed were in ancient museums seldom seen by contemporary men.

Finally, after trying to no avail to find books or videos on ancient sword fighting, Joe tried to send a probe back to medieval England to watch knights in battle, but he couldn't do it.

He dug back into his memory and watched Harl in battle to observe the art of fighting with a sword. After watching and studying for a time, the thought came to him that because Harl was his natural father he might be able to contact him. He reached out and gently sent a probe into Harl's mind and found that his premise was correct.

Joe felt his own muscles stretch and strain as Harl swung the heavy sword and stored all that knowledge in his own powerful brain. He could not influence Harl's actions, but he did gain insight into his style of fighting and eventually used it against him.

Joe then sent all his intellect back to the time of the battle with Harl and joined his younger self. Young Joe realized something had taken over control of his body, and he heard a strangely familiar voice in his mind say, *"Don't bother me; I'm kind of busy now!"* Old Joe then used all his abilities to defeat, Harl but not before his younger self had sustained some injuries.

Young Joe had almost passed out from his injuries when he turned his attention inside his mind to ask what or who was there. The answer he got was not really an answer. *"Don't trouble yourself about who I am and what's going on. You know me, we've met before, although you can't remember it, and we'll meet again when I'll have more time to explain. Now rest and get well. I can promise that you'll live a very long life. I can't stay any longer. We'll meet again."*

As Young Joe was actually passing out from his injuries, Old Joe blocked the pain nerves and gently put him to sleep, then softly withdrew.

He then made another mental trip to the ancient past to the time immediately after his birth and made contact with his natural mother, Shallith. Even in her comatose condition, it took several days for him to gently push aside her mental barriers. When he finally made contact with what consciousness she had left, he told her that her son was to be the promised deliverer. Joe reassured her that all would be well with her son and she could rest in peace.

What remained of that once powerful mind was barely able to form the question, *"Who are you?"* Joe paused a moment, and then answered, *"I am your son! I am J'Osha!"*

That was the most emotional and heartrending thing he had experienced in his life. As he watched, his mother seemed to relax both physically and mentally. She smiled a soft smile, and then left the land of the living.

Finally, and with some reluctance, Joe traveled a last time back to the past and again joined with the younger Joe. But now the Young Joe felt it was definitely a person and not a thing; a person who was somehow very familiar. Joe asked him, "Don't I know you?"

The person laughed and answered, *"Sure you do! You may not recognize me yet, but you know me as well as you know yourself!"* Young Joe was hit with a tremendous emotional shock as he really recognized himself, in some way completely different but still the same.

"Me? How can another me be in me?" he asked. "He" answered, *"It's a long story, and you'll understand it completely later; but now there's a job to do, and it'll take all we've got to handle it! Let's get to work. Take a deep breath, kid; this is going to be a bumpy ride!"*

And with that statement, he released all the barriers he'd set up in Young Joe's mind many years before. All the suppressed abilities of all the generations of all the peoples came flooding into his conscious mind.

He actually staggered under the weight of what hit him, but recovered almost immediately as Old Joe merged completely with his mind and what had been two became totally one.

They became J'Osha.

With the barriers down, there was no longer anything keeping the others from merging with J'Osha and all that was Rakh/Mibara and Janga and countless others unnamed and unnamable flowed effortlessly into his being and became an entity with powers unlike any seen or even dreamed of since the beginning of time.

All the combined personalities that now made up what had been J'Osha traveled instantaneously to the barrier on the plateau and with their now virtually unlimited powers easily breached that which before had been impenetrable and confronted the evil forces of M'gori and Chataan; and the battle began.

In time the battle turned in favor of J'Osha and the forces of good and Chataan was being beaten back into another space/time continuum. In desperation, Chataan pulled out all the stops, risking total self-destruction and unleashed all the primal forces of the other universe at J'Osha and earth in one gigantic blast of energy, even by galactic proportions.

Earth and the solar system were decimated, washed clean of all life. The seas boiled and the mountains crashed down and earth rocked and reeled in her orbit around the sun.

Everything was dead; there was no life left on earth, no life except Joe, and what he had could not really be called life in any form we recognize. Space itself was ripped in two and he was instantaneously blasted through a hole in this space/time into another elsewhere/elsewhen, nowhere/nowhen.

Twenty-three thousand, four hundred and eighty-seven years later, in a small room somewhere within the planet-wide city that was the home of mankind, the body that had been Joe Shaw quietly stopped breathing, and what was left of his consciousness all but faded away. Then the physical body simply ceased to exist.

Final Interlude

The battle was done! In one cataclysmic blast of energy, all the forces available to Chataan and the Daemoz had been directed against J'Osha and the planet of man.

The planet was toppled in its path around the sun, and it was shaken to the core by great quakes. Mountains crumbled and fell, and new mountains were raised in their places.

Oceans leapt from their beds and swept across the land, cleansing the earth before they settled into the new valleys and low places to make oceans where none had been before. Where man had lived on the earth was now only a blasted waste, washed clean of life by the primal fires of this universe that had been loosed in the final moments of that terrible conflict.

The evil Daemoz had perished in the first instant of that awesome conflagration, consumed in one last suicidal sacrifice to their master. The four great spirits and the good Daemoz lasted only slightly longer, and then flamed into nonexistence.

The old gods fought valiantly against the raging energies turned upon them by Chataan. Energies that, once loosed, could not be controlled by the old gods or Chataan and which threatened the very existence of this universe. The old gods united and became one, lasting only a little longer through the pooling of all their strength, and then passed silently into utter nothingness.

Chataan alone survived, although nearly drained of its own powers by the raging primal energies it had turned loose on this universe. That horrendous conflagration finally subsided and diffused into space leaving behind a vastly altered starscape.

J'Osha was gone, ripped from this universe, and catapulted past time and space by the stupendous blast that desolated the planet he had once called home. The essence of that which had been Joe Shaw was no longer among the living, for there were no living. Life had ceased to be. He had not died, but neither did he live. He just was.

◦❧◦

Consciousness, that's all. Nothing else, except the awareness of consciousness.

No memory, no identity, no anxieties; nothing. There was no sensation of feeling in his body, because he didn't have a body; and there was no sense of loss, because he had no remembrance of ever having a body.

He was; but there was no feeling of being, no sense of place or time. There was not even a spark of curiosity in what there was of his mind and that didn't bother him in the least, for all that existed in his mind was the awareness that he was.

No past, no present, no future; nothing but consciousness.

Slowly he became vaguely aware of another presence and attempted to reach out to it, but he was met with an almost overwhelming wave of desperation and loneliness and quickly withdrew, and then just as quickly forgot about it.

There was a momentary shadowy stirring at the extreme edge of that consciousness, the merest wisp of a feeling that something very important should be happening; but before he was able to bring what little attention he had into focus, the thought passed.

It was enough just to be.

The body of the child who was eventually to become Joe Shaw was transported instantaneously through space and time, but the essence of that child took an entirely different route through the otherness of elsewhere/elsewhen and nowhere/nowhen, and wandered aimlessly in utter darkness.

He was; but there was no feeling of being, no sense of place or time. All that existed in his mind was the awareness that he was and the terrible feeling of being completely alone.

He felt the filmy touch of another presence and cried out in despair and loneliness in a desperate appeal for companionship, but then it was gone and he again withdrew within himself where there was only consciousness, that's all. Nothing else, except the awareness of consciousness.

No memory, no identity, no anxieties—nothing.

It was enough just to be.

Epilogue

All the world was dark. The sun and stars were blotted out, and the earth was void of life. The cities were washed away as sand, and the fields were bare. Nothing grew or lived on the face of the earth or under the seas. The mountains were broken down to dust and the seas were dried up in their beds. Everywhere was desolation, darkness, and stillness.

"AND GOD LOOKED UPON THE EARTH AND SAW THAT ALL WAS DARKNESS AND DESOLATION."

"AND THE EARTH WAS WITHOUT FORM AND VOID. AND GOD SAID, 'LET THERE BE LIGHT!'"

~GENESIS

About the Author

I was born in Los Angeles into a happy middle class family, with two older sisters and a younger brother. We all learned to read at early an age because our mother was an elementary school teacher before she married and we were introduced to the "Wonderful World of Words." I was an avid reader and spent much of my free time on the bench in front of the bookcases in our front hallway. By the time I finished grammar school I had read most of "The Complete Works of William Shakespeare," most of Edgar Allen Poe's works, "The Bounty Trilogy," "The Three Musketeers," and many others; including all 16 volumes of "The New Students Encyclopedia" which was my mother's in school.

As a young boy I mostly read westerns and dreamed of being a cowboy, but at about thirteen I came across a worn paperback copy of a collection of Science Fiction/Fantasy stories, and I was hooked! Hoppy, the Lone Ranger and Red Ryder "bit the dust" and were replaced by Kim Kinnison, Lazarus Long and Conan the Barbarian. I grew up on Asimov, Bradbury, Heinlein, Smith, Clarke and the rest and was fascinated by L. Sprague De Camp's Harold Shea series where men traveled into parallel universes where magic was possible. Later I was greatly influenced by the way Asimov took three separate stories; "I Robot," "Foundation" and "The Caves of Steel" and wound them into the fabulous "Foundation" series.

I worked after high school at the family radio/TV business until the draft caught me and I spent 2 years in the U.S. Army just after the Korean Conflict. Shortly after I got home from Korea I met and married the most beautiful girl in the world; Bonnie Jean, who has stuck by me all these years and who gave me three gorgeous, intelligent daughters.

When the family business fell on hard times I joined the Culver City Police Department and retired after twenty years of service. For the next twelve years I worked at various security jobs; from driving an armored truck part time to managing three Southern California counties for a contract security company, and finished my working career with five years as Security Manager for the Los Angeles Mission on "skid row" in downtown L.A. until I retired completely from work in June of 1995.

From the mid '60's until 2013 Bonnie and I travelled extensively with a series of trucks and trailers and covered just about every state west of the Mississippi and a few on the east side. We particularly loved camping in the Rockies and spent most of the time wandering back and forth from New Mexico to Canada, stopping at just about every National and State Park campground along the way.

In between all these things I worked part time as a marshal at a golf course in Simi Valley, CA, where I lived, which gave me free golf and contact with a lot of interesting people.

I started writing poems at about 13 or 14 when I discovered that young girls were "turned on" by having poems written for and/or about them and continued writing poems and short stories, mostly just for the fun of it, until I was drafted into the Army and sent to Korea. With no shooting going on I spent a lot of leisure time writing poems and short adventure stories and passing them around to the other G.I.'s to read.

Somewhere around 1960 I came up with an idea for a Science Fiction short story in which a future space soldier is captured by the "Aliens" and his memory drained from his brain. He is then turned loose in his spaceship with the emergency beacon on at full power with the aliens waiting around to pick off anyone who came to rescue him. He is eventually rescued and the main part of the story is his re-education by doctors and scientists. The working title at that time was "Man-101." The main thrust of this story became the outline for part four of Exogenesis, with necessary changes to fit the current story.

One of the books I read the most, being raised in a Christian family, was The Bible and I was fascinated by Old Testament history; primarily the first chapters of the book of Genesis. I had many questions which my parents and teachers were unable to answer to my satisfaction so I began a study of ancient Biblical and secular history in an attempt to resolve these questions.

Some of the ideas which particularly intrigued me were the possibilities of "Pre-Adamic Man" and the alleged "gap" between Genesis 1:1 and 1:2. Out of these studies came the idea for part one of Exogenesis and all I had to do was fill in the middle.

Real work on the book didn't start until after I retired from the Police Department and it was set aside many times for many reasons; mostly work, school and raising a family, and was only taken up again seriously after we moved to Prescott, Arizona, in 2005. Several medical setbacks gave me a lot of spare time while recuperating and the book was finally completed in 2014.

1% where